KV-636-162

LOOK OUT FOR LUCIFER!

Radium is not a substance that can be quietly stolen and no questions asked. Inspector Faithfull and his sergeant, Somers, have the task of catching the thieves. But they have to contend with the unexpected appearance of the glamorous Miss Georgia Nash. Then Wister Hale, a newspaper reporter, begins accurately forecasting the movements of police and crook alike. The Inspector is baffled, but the answer comes with a suddenness which surprises everyone — except Wister Hale!

Books by Ernest Dudley
in the Linford Mystery Library:

ALIBI AND DR. MORELLE
THE HARASSED HERO
CONFESS TO DR. MORELLE
THE MIND OF DR. MORELLE
DR. MORELLE AND DESTINY
CALLERS FOR DR. MORELLE

ERNEST DUDLEY

LOOK OUT FOR LUCIFER!

Complete and Unabridged

LINFORD
Leicester

First published in Great Britain

First Linford Edition
published 2006

British Library CIP Data

Dudley, Ernest
Look out for Lucifer!.—Large print ed.—
Linford mystery library
1. Detective and mystery stories
2. Large type books
I. Title
823.9′14 [F]

ISBN 1–84617–457–0

Published by
Thorpe (Publishing)
Anstey, Leicestershire

Set by Words & Graphics Ltd.
Anstey, Leicestershire
Printed and bound in Great Britain by
T. J. International Ltd., Padstow, Cornwall

This book is printed on acid-free paper

1

The Assistant Commissioner walked over to the large window of his office and stood looking out at the busy river. A train rattled over Charing Cross bridge, and two tugs ploughed their way upstream with a string of barges behind them. It was a pleasant spring morning. He reflected a trifle wistfully that if he had been five years older he would probably be spending this morning on his favourite golf course. A police boat of the river patrol swished importantly towards the pier and reminded him of his morning's work. He returned to the small heap of folders neatly stacked upon his desk.

He opened the first folder and browsed through its contents for some minutes, then pressed the key of his dictograph.

'Ask Superintendent Russell to come in.'

While he was waiting he made a few

pencilled notes on the pad beside him.

Russell was an alert man in the early forties, who had a reputation for reliability allied to a certain amount of imagination which had secured for him comparatively rapid promotion. He came in quickly and closed the door quietly behind him.

'Come and sit down, Russell,' murmured the Assistant Commissioner, nodding in the direction of a vacant chair. 'Can you spare ten minutes?'

The Assistant Commissioner was always scrupulously polite to his lieutenants.

'Yes, sir, of course.'

Russell replied in his clipped accents which gave the impression of extreme efficiency. 'I suppose you want to see me about the radium robberies, sir,' he went on. He had already noted the file which lay open on the desk.

The other rested his arms on his swivel chair and swung it gently through an arc of thirty degrees.

'We've got to move pretty quickly,' he announced. 'I've just come from the

Home Office, and they're getting in quite a state there. Last night's was the fifth robbery this month — that makes nearly four grammes of radium gone.'

The Superintendent pursed his lips thoughtfully.

'Four grammes,' he repeated, 'that's about a seventh of an ounce. It doesn't seem much, does it, sir?'

The Assistant Commissioner toyed with his silver pencil and smiled somewhat ruefully.

'I agree it doesn't sound much. But even before the war it was worth twenty thousand pounds a gramme.'

Russell looked surprised.

'I'd no idea it was as precious as that.'

'Since the atomic experiments its price has no limit. That's why the Home Secretary is inclined to panic. He's afraid the stuff may be falling into the wrong hands, possibly an agent of some foreign power that's experimenting with atomic bombs to no good purpose.'

'I can see he's been reading the *Daily World*,' Superintendent Russell commented shrewdly. 'That fellow Wister

Hale has been making a lot of fuss about it. Says that if a small nation — one of the Balkan States for instance — got hold of the atomic bomb secrets they might become world dictators overnight.'

'It is rather a grim thought. By the way, who is this Wister Hale?'

Russell smiled rather uneasily.

'Search me, sir. I have tried to find out once or twice, but the *Daily World* editor's inclined to be awkward. I even put the Press Bureau on to him, but we're no wiser, I'm afraid.'

The Assistant Commissioner frowned.

'I don't like this undercover work from the Press,' he muttered. 'There are times when it puts us in an awkward position — makes us look damned fools. Whoever this man Hale is, he seems to know a damn sight more than he should.'

A thought struck him.

'You don't think it could be anybody at the Yard?' he queried suspiciously.

Russell shook his head.

'I don't know what to think, sir. All I know is that their editor is going round Fleet Street boasting that their circulation has gone up a hundred thousand since Hale started writing those articles. So it doesn't seem very likely that he'll let the cat out of the bag just yet.'

'I don't see why they should make such a confounded mystery of this business,' snapped the Assistant Commissioner. 'The man might be useful to us, and he owes it to the country to work with us.'

'There's always the chance that he may not be British,' suggested Russell. 'But I'll have another go at the editor, sir, and see if I can get anything.'

'Good,' the other nodded approvingly. 'In the meantime, what are we going to do about tackling this radium racket?'

Russell looked worried.

'I can't see that we can do much more, sir,' he replied. 'I've got five of our best men on it, and they're working night and day.'

'I see,' mused the Assistant Commissioner. 'Is there anyone else likely to be free soon?'

The Superintendent pulled a small blue notebook from a side pocket.

'There's Detective-Sergeant Somers

— he's just finished that job at Grimsby.'

'Oh yes, bright lad, Somers, We might as well have him in on this radium business. Very young, of course, but I've noticed he seems to have more luck than most of the lads, and we can do with any luck that's going on this job.'

Russell made a note in his book, wondering what the newspapers would say if they could hear a Scotland Yard Chief putting his trust in the goddess Fortune. But he offered no comment.

'Anyone else?'

'Nobody else of any consequence, sir, unless Inspector Faithfull.' The Superintendent hesitated.

'Faithfull!' echoed the Assistant Commissioner with a chuckle. 'Is he still alive? Well, well, good Old Faithfull! What's he been up to lately?'

Inspector Faithfull was obviously the subject of some private joke among the Yard personnel.

'What's he been up to lately?' repeated the Assistant Commissioner with some interest.

'He's been on loan to the county forces

quite a lot, sir. He was after the Westwood jewels — that took him over six months, but he did recover them when we'd given them up for lost. Then there were the fire-raising cases at Glasgow, the dope-smuggling at Cardiff, and just now he's giving evidence in the Oxford murder.'

'You mean the college scout? Good Lord, that happened about a year ago, didn't it?'

'I'm afraid Faithfull insists on taking his own time, sir, but we have to admit that he's got some results in most of his cases. He seems to be able to wear the criminal down in a style of his own. Lord knows exactly how he goes about it, and it certainly takes time.'

The Assistant Commissioner smiled.

Secretly he had a soft spot for this middle-aged member of his staff who had graduated from some remote west country village, and who had the courage to go his own gain in the face of all the bustle and turmoil of the modern criminal world.

'All the same, I doubt if he's quite the

man for this radium job,' he mused, thoughtfully stroking his chin. 'We want results and we want 'em quickly, or the Home Secretary's liable to blow up and call in one of these confounded amateurs who get under everybody's feet and make a damned nuisance of themselves. No, I don't think we can use Old Faithfull.'

'Unless — ' began Russell suddenly, his face lighting up.

'Well?'

'I was wondering if it might not be an idea to team him up with Somers. Faithfull would be a restraining influence, which is what that young man needs at times — '

'And you think Somers might speed up Faithfull?' The Assistant Commissioner was not a little amused at the idea. 'I wonder if we dare risk it.'

'I could keep an eye on them, sir. And if it doesn't pan out, we can soon switch one of them on to another job. Faithfull's always been pretty hot on robberies in the past — '

'That's just the snag, Russell. Maybe it's too far in the past. The men in this radium set-up are using all the latest tricks and playing for some of the biggest stakes in the history of crime. I'm afraid Faithfull will be simply swept off his feet.'

'I wouldn't like to bet on that. He has a knack of catching up with things when you least expect it. The last time I was in his office I found him reading a book called *The Use of Barbiturates in Modern Crime Solution*.'

'Good heavens!' ejaculated the Assistant Commissioner with a comic gesture. 'There must have been a mistake somewhere!'

'Oh no,' Russell assured him, 'Faithfull said he often got hold of American books on the latest developments in crime detection. They saved them for him at his library. He told me they made nice light reading!'

'Well, better hold him in reserve for this radium business, unless something turns up that's more in his line.'

'Very good, sir.'

Russell made another note, then said with some diffidence:

'I can't help feeling that the brain

behind these radium robberies is something we haven't come up against before. It may be some foreign crook of course.'

'Always that chance,' the other agreed. 'That's one of the unpleasant aspects of the affair. We're dealing with unknown quantities, maybe some of the finest international brains.'

'Nobody's ever been unscrupulous enough to break into hospitals before,' murmured the Superintendent, biting his pencil.

'Nobody's ever had such an inducement. Radium is at an enormous premium, and we can't keep our eye on all of it. The stuff's scattered all over the place in tiny portions. Some at hospitals, clinics, research laboratories belonging to all sorts of people. We can't possibly check on it. What we've got to do is go to the root of the trouble and discover this master-mind.'

'A pretty contemptible mind,' sniffed Russell, 'to deprive hundreds of hospital patients of stuff that cures them, all for the sake of some sort of political jugglery.'

The Assistant Commissioner pulled at his lower lip.

'I should say hard cash was the prime consideration. However, that's a secondary matter as far as we're concerned unless it leads us to the head of this organization.'

The door opened and a sergeant came in with a buff envelope which he handed to the Assistant Commissioner.

'The messenger said it was urgent, sir,' he announced.

The Assistant Commissioner frowned, resenting the interruption, and tore open the envelope. He looked up quickly at the sergeant.

'Who brought this?' he snapped.

'Just a messenger boy, sir.'

'All right, you can go.'

The Assistant Commissioner read the letter again, then passed it over to the Superintendent.

'Damned impudence!' he snorted.

Russell read the note through and allowed at last:

'He has got a cheek, sir.'

The letter said:

Dear Assistant Commissioner,

Re the radium robberies. May I suggest Inspector Faithfull has his points?

WISTER HALE.

With a muttered imprecation, the Assistant Commissioner screwed it into a ball and flung it into his wastepaper basket. Russell stooped and retrieved it, smoothing out the creases carefully.

'I make a hobby of saving little things like this,' he said. 'You never know when they might come in useful.'

2

Detective-Sergeant Somers balanced precariously on the back legs of his chair while conducting a jerky telephone conversation with his immediate chief.

Somers was a dark, intelligent young man, with slightly aquiline features and a mobile mouth. He had a habit of running his words together, particularly when he was excited. At the moment, his face wore a somewhat petulant expression and his voice was tinged with a faint note of protest.

'I just wanted to know if this is true about my sharing an office with Faithfull, sir,' he said. 'No, sir, I've nothing against him really, but I have had an office of my own up till now. Yes, I know we're pushed for room.'

There was a long pause as he listened to a lengthy explanation, during which his expression changed electrically.

'Yes, sir,' he said at last, 'I agree it's

quite a break for me to be put on the radium job. But to work with Faithfull! I mean — well, he's a bit of a stick-in-the-mud, isn't he, sir? . . . Well, I suppose if it's the Chief's idea he must have some reason at the back of his mind. All right, Super, if you'll send down the file I'll get on with it.'

He slammed down the receiver and heaved a sigh.

Imagine expecting him to work with Old Faithfull! What would they think of next? He told himself that there must be a bit of a panic on among the high-ups.

One of the star pupils of the police college at Hendon, Somers had made the most of all his opportunities since joining the staff of the Yard. Furthermore, he had been favoured by luck most generously on some of his cases, though he was not always ready to admit this. In fact, Detective-Sergeant Somers had a good conceit of himself, which is no bad thing to have if one is out for material success. And Somers never entered the Assistant Commissioner's well-appointed office without indulging in the luxury of imagining how he would change things round when it was *his* room.

His present poky sanctum he was now sharing with Inspector Faithfull, and into which he had just moved, was just large enough to contain a couple of desks, two filing cupboards and two extra chairs for visitors.

As the first arrival, Somers promptly chose the desk by the small window, which opened on to an uninspiring view of the grey-stone building on the other side of the road.

He was half-way through the radium file when the telephone rang.

It was his current girl friend.

'I thought I asked you not to telephone me at the Yard,' he began, none too pleased. He took himself very seriously, and firmly believed that business and pleasure should be kept in water-tight compartments. Whereas Carol, who was a show girl in non-stop revue, had always found business and pleasure inextricably entangled in her life, and had no intention of making the least effort to separate them.

'But listen, darling,' she protested in reply to his admonition, 'Eddie's just given me two tickets for a film trade-show at the Palace this afternoon. It's one of those crime pictures — I thought you'd be crazy to see it.'

Somers suppressed a snort.

'My dear girl, how often do I have to tell you I've a job of work on hand? I can't take time off to go to the pictures whenever I feel like it.'

'But, darling, everyone says what a marvellous film it is, and I'm sure you'd learn an awful lot from it. And if you don't come, I'll have to ask Jimmy.'

Fortunately, Somers was not deeply smitten where Carol was concerned, and he was able to see the funny side of the situation.

'All right, dear, you go with Jimmy, and you can tell me all about it. I'm always ready to learn!'

He was engaged in further interchange of pleasantries with Carol, who it seemed was not up yet and was telephoning from her bed, when the door opened quietly and a stockily built, middle-aged man walked in, looked round, and went to the desk behind the door, which he carefully closed after him.

Somers placed a hand over the mouthpiece.

'Hallo, Inspector,' he murmured, 'shan't be a minute.'

Inspector Faithfull nodded, sat down and began to look through some papers.

He had something of the appearance of a country game-keeper; his suit bulged in unexpected places and was very well worn. His face was plump and he had a red complexion which somehow discounted the gimlet grey eyes, and a slightly turned-up nose added to its disarming quality. Dismissed so often as being of little account had put Faithfull on his mettle and accounted for many of his triumphs, which had been gained by sheer tenacity. He had joined the police force on his demobilization in 1919 because it was the only job he could get. Never for a minute had he considered himself a born detective, and he regarded his job of running criminals to earth as prosaically as if it were grafting fruit trees or making biscuits.

He lived in a small villa at Mitcham and much to his wife's disgust steadfastly refused to dig the garden or even cut the lawn. He had been brought up in a little Somerset village, had been compelled to spend most of his spare time in weeding the family half-acre, and declared that he had had enough gardening to last his lifetime. His interests were wide and varied, for he had a curious mind, but his only regular hobby was newspaper crossword competitions, whose glittering prizes of fabulous sums never failed to lure him. It was a pursuit which had proved singularly unremunerative, despite the hours and pounds he had expended upon it.

But his weekly crosswords had become a part of his life, and it was said that Faithfull had only been seen to lose his temper once, on the occasion when a rumour ran round Scotland Yard to the effect that legislation was to be set in motion to suppress the crossword competitions. Whereupon Faithfull had expounded in no uncertain manner on the subject of the rights of a citizen in a free country!

When Somers finally put down the telephone, Faithfull seemed to be quite absorbed in a file of photographs that he was studying carefully.

'Good afternoon, Inspector,' began Somers politely.

'Afternoon. I see you've pinched the best desk,' was the blunt reply.

Somers blushed.

'I — er — well, if you'd like to change, sir,' he offered.

Inspector Faithfull grunted.

'No, I'd just as soon stay here behind the door,' he growled perversely. 'That's where a lot of people in this building think I ought to be, so they won't be disappointed.'

Somers managed to keep a straight face and said very seriously:

'Oh, well, if you're quite sure you don't mind, Inspector.'

Faithfull looked across at him suspiciously for a moment, then returned to his file.

'I haven't lived to my age without

learning to accommodate myself to most situations. There are some things worth making a fuss about, and a sight more that aren't. This is one of them. When you get to my age, you'll learn the secret of a happy life is to save your energy for things that are worth while.'

Somers frowned slightly.

'I don't know that I've ever particularly wanted to be happy,' he confessed.

'Oh?' said Faithfull, rather surprised. 'Then what do you want?'

'Just to be busy — doing fresh things — seeing people — tackling problems — '

Old Faithfull sighed.

'You youngsters are all the same. Why don't you say you want promotion and have done with it?'

'Weren't you the same at my age?'

Faithfull rubbed his right hand through his rapidly thinning sandy hair.

'We weren't waited on hand and foot, and sent to police colleges in my young days,' he replied. 'If you didn't fight tooth and nail you spent all your life as a village copper at thirty-five bob a week.'

There was a far-away look in the grey

eyes for a moment, then he returned to his file.

Somers shifted rather uncomfortably in his chair and wondered if he should broach the subject of the radium robberies. Faithfull certainly gave no sign of being anxious to discuss the matter, but went on steadily ploughing through his file, occasionally holding up a photograph so that he could see it more clearly.

'Er — Inspector — ' Somers ventured at length. 'Did the Super say anything to you about the radium robberies?'

The Inspector pursed his lips and did not reply for a few moments.

'How much has he told you?' he asked in a cautious tone.

Faithfull always suspected internal intrigues and jealousies at the Yard, and while he steadfastly refused to be a party to them, he was nevertheless on his guard against being a victim. His colleagues had learned from experience that they would get little change out of Inspector Faithfull.

Somers was equally cautious in answering the Inspector's question.

'Well, the Super is putting me on it, and he said something about you as well — it's a hell of a job, you know.'

Faithfull nodded.

'I know. Quite an opportunity for a young fellow like yourself.'

His tone was still non-committal, and he finished looking at his photos and neatly packed them away in the file.

'You know, Inspector, I've a theory that these robberies are the work of a pretty big organization,' Somers began eagerly, and was about to enlarge upon this when Faithfull held up his hand.

'Just a minute, Somers. I've always liked the look of you, my lad, and I'd sooner work with you than anybody else here, if I've got to work in with somebody. But there's one thing you've got to get straight from the start. I have no use for theories. No use at all. I leave all that sort of thing to the newspapers. My way of working is to take one fact at a time, turn it inside out, relate it to the other evidence, and then put it in its proper place in the general set-up. Sometimes, it takes a bit longer, Sergeant, but it generally gets results.'

Somers nodded tactfully, and made no attempt to interrupt.

It was well known that Inspector Faithfull had this bee in his bonnet about his orderly methods, but that he only pursued them up to a point. When things were breaking rapidly in a case, Faithfull was as ready as the next man to go all out after his quarry.

He was continuing:

'It's just my way of working, I stick to facts and I use them in the proper way. I've been doing it for twenty years and I'm too old to change now.'

'I quite appreciate that,' Somers said seriously, but the other held up his hand once more.

'You're thinking I'm an old stick-in-the-mud; the sort of cop they make fun of in these detective novels; the poor old flattie who's so busy with what's under his nose that the vicar, a spinster aunt or a professor of entomology just walks in and puts a finger right on the criminal.'

Somers protested, feeling vaguely embarrassed by this fatherly lecture.

'No, really — '

'In real life, my boy,' Faithfull ploughed on, 'there's no spinster aunt and no professor of entomology. At least I've never come across 'em in my experience. There's just a crime and maybe a clue if you're lucky, and then a hell of a lot of routine work that has to be done to narrow down the field.'

Somers thrust his hands into his trouser pockets and tilted back on his chair.

'When I was on the Grimsby case — '

But the other again intervened.

'I read all about the Grimsby case. You made some pretty clever deductions after you'd found the trail while it was still hot. The publicity bureau did you well on that. I'm not belittling you, my boy; I'm only warning you that every case doesn't work out that way — you'll be dealt a different hand of cards every time. Why, I've landed a couple of murderers myself in less than a week. But they were open and shut cases; stood out a mile.'

'We have to take a lot of snap decisions nowadays,' Somers argued. 'The modern criminal is a pretty fast-moving bird. And he doesn't get any slower.' He hesitated, then decided to take the bull by the horns. 'If we work on this case together, Faithfull, you're the senior man, of course. But you can't stop me getting my own ideas.'

The Inspector grunted.

'Nobody wants to stop you. It's a free country as far as thinking your own thoughts is concerned.'

He took a dented gun-metal snuff-box from his pocket and helped himself to a generous pinch without offering it to the Sergeant. Faithfull suffered slightly from asthma and this was a special blend of snuff which cleared his head and helped him to think, or so he imagined.

Somers smiled.

'You mean you want me to keep my suggestions to myself?' he asked, feeling more at home now.

'I wouldn't say that. Different methods catch different crooks. Maybe yours will be right for this case. Maybe.' He sniffed hard and sneezed reverberantly. 'Naturally, I shall expect you to co-operate.'

‘But you don’t want me to go running off on any wild-goose chases of my own?’ Somers grinned.

The other shrugged.

‘As long as it doesn’t upset my lay-out, and it’s off the record, well, we’ll see.’

Somers leaned forward in his chair and with his elbows on his desk looked straight across at his colleague.

‘Inspector, I’ve a feeling we’re going to bust this racket wide open!’ he declared impulsively.

Inspector Faithfull’s face remained inscrutable.

He had secretly taken quite a fancy to the enthusiastic Sergeant Somers, but it would have been diametrically against his principles to have admitted it. He had been disappointed in so many people that he always proceeded warily where new acquaintances were concerned.

‘We shall see,’ he murmured in a non-committal tone. Then he put down the file he had been inspecting and said thoughtfully: ‘The first thing is to find out a bit more about radium.’

‘But we know what radium is. Any

schoolboy can tell you that,' Somers said in some mystification.

'All right, you tell me all you know.'

'Well,' replied the other, rather at a loss, 'it's a very valuable mineral, present in small quantities in uranium — a devil of a job to extract — you saw that film about the Curies?'

'I never have time for films. Go on about radium.'

'Well, it's used in experiments for splitting the atom, and for curing cancer of course — well, do we have to know any more than that?'

'You can't know too much about anything that's even remotely concerned with a case. If you're going after a gang passing slush, it's a help to know how the notes are forged, and what to look out for in the top attic.'

'I'm always ready to learn,' Somers retorted, with the barest trace of sarcasm in his tone.

'Aye, you'll learn all right. I've learned something from every case I've tackled — right from the day I pulled in the eldest son of the chairman of the bench for dangerous driving at Compton Magna over twenty years ago.'

Somers eyed him curiously.

'And what did you learn from that?'

With a barely audible chuckle, Faithfull replied:

'I learned the inadvisability of arresting the eldest son of the chairman of the bench. It set back my promotion at least five years.'

Somers laughed.

He found himself reflecting with some surprise that the old boy had a sense of humour after all. He said encouragingly:

'But you got there in the end.'

'Yes, my lad, it's dogged as does it.'

He was about to enlarge upon this apothegm when the telephone rang.

He took the call. Somers gathered it came from the Superintendent, though he was unable to glean from Faithfull's disjointed remarks what the conversation was about.

Presently the Inspector replaced the receiver and turned and said:

'That was the Super.'

Somers grinned.

'Is he still on the warpath?'

'Seems like it. I suppose it's understandable in a way.'

'You don't mean there's been more developments?'

'You might call it that. He's just heard another half-gramme of radium has been stolen.'

3

The Luxor Ballroom occupies a not very prominent site in one of the narrow streets huddled behind the Tottenham Court Road on the Oxford Street side.

Starting its career as a roller-skating rink just before the Great War, the Luxor had passed through many hands and fulfilled many purposes, varying from an auction room to a fun-fair.

Lately, however, it was enjoying a period of comparative affluence under the management of one Nicky Dulane, late of the Double Four Club in Dover Street. Nicky had the Luxor redecorated throughout at considerable expense. By dint of unremitting effort he had also contrived to obtain a wine and spirits licence. There was some speculation as to how he had worked this minor miracle, but Nicky kept his own counsel.

A lot of his acquaintances were also mystified as to why Nicky should leave a little goldmine like the Double Four and go in for a line of business with which he was less familiar. But soon after Nicky left, the Double Four was raided and was found to be the centre for a widespread distribution of cocaine. There was further speculation as to just how much Nicky knew about this state of affairs.

Once again, Nicky refused to talk.

He was a swarthy, lithe little man, very little different in appearance from the hundreds of foreign waiters who swarmed around the purlieus of Berwick Street. Perhaps his most striking feature was his piercing dark eyes, which somehow conveyed the impression of a shrewd brain swiftly assessing the place in the scheme of things of the person to whom he was talking.

Inspector Faithfull had made Nicky's acquaintance some time before the Double Four Club was raided, though it was extremely doubtful if more than two other people were aware of their meeting, which had taken place in a very respectable public house in Kensington.

During the ensuing conversation,

Nicky, who was only the manager of the club, had laid his cards on the table and told the Inspector just how much he knew. Then he had taken Faithfull's advice and given a fortnight's notice to the proprietor, taking a lease of the Luxor Ballroom almost at once.

Nicky was determined to raise the tone of the Luxor.

He did not intend that it should be exploited as the Double Four had been by dope-traffickers or any other type of shady gentlemen.

But it wasn't easy. The district was a difficult one; in fact a year never passed without a murder in that part of the world, and brutal assaults were almost commonplace. However, Nicky got his licence, made the ballroom more attractive and engaged a first-class band which began to attract dozens of smart young types with money to spend and a craze for dancing.

There were many rumours as to how Nicky financed all these improvements; it was said that there was a syndicate of moneylenders backing him. Once again,

Nicky kept his own counsel.

Every night Nicky Dulane mixed freely with his patrons, keeping his eyes, those piercing dark brown eyes, flashing around every corner of the hall, alertly sizing up every newcomer and assessing the possibilities of the remotest sign of trouble.

During the past week he had been worried.

On three separate evenings he had noticed a small group of men at a table in a corner of the dance hall, talking in animated fashion. They were somewhat sinister-looking individuals, and Nicky had immediately recognized one of them, Lem Knight, an angular man with a limp. Lem was always there, but the other members of the party varied on each occasion, and Nicky did not know them.

All the same, he had a shrewd idea that they were planning some coup or other, and not unnaturally he was anxious to discover whether the Luxor Ballroom was in any way involved in their plans. He seized every opportunity to walk past their table with ears alert to catch the merest snatch of conversation.

It was not until the third evening that he caught anything of importance, and that was the phrase, 'North London Hospital'. The next day when he read in the papers that a quantity of radium had been stolen from the North London Hospital in the small hours of the night. Nicky telephoned Inspector Faithfull without any hesitation.

When he had managed to stem the cascade of verbose broken English a little, Faithfull took a few brief notes and promised to put in an appearance at the Luxor that same evening. As Somers appeared to be at a loose end the Inspector asked him to accompany him.

The Sergeant insisted on their utilizing one of the new special cars which had been recently acquired by the Flying Squad, and after a lengthy telephone conversation with a certain Inspector Mayne, who, it appeared, had the cars in his care, Somers managed to make the necessary arrangements.

It was just growing dusk when they climbed into the black streamlined car, and Somers snapped on the illuminated 'Police' sign.

'You can put that off again,' growled Faithfull. 'We don't want to advertise ourselves to half the crooks in London!'

Somers grinned and switched off the light, then edged the car into the stream of traffic in Northumberland Avenue.

'Isn't she a beauty, Inspector?' he asked, as he manœuvred the car smoothly through the crowd of theatre traffic.

'I prefer my old pushbike when it comes to pleasure trips,' grunted the Inspector, who liked his presence to remain as unobtrusive as possible on such visits as this. 'And mind how you're going,' he added, as the other suddenly accelerated to take advantage of a gap in the traffic, and the speedometer needle waltzed round the dial in an alarming fashion.

'It's all right,' smiled Somers reassuringly. 'I was trained at Brooklands, you know.'

Faithfull said dryly:

'I can well believe it. As we don't happen to be chasing smash and grab bandits, I think it might be safer if you took a little more time. We're in no great hurry.'

Sergeant Somers relaxed a trifle.

'This man Dulane,' he said presently, as they pulled up at the traffic lights, 'is he the fellow who used to manage the Double Four Club?'

'You know him?'

'I came across him once or twice when I was doing dress-suit stuff in the West End. Not a bad little cove from what I remember — always seemed anxious to keep on the right side of the police.'

Faithfull nodded.

'That's why he rang me up. Nicky can smell a crook a mile off. He didn't say much over the phone, but I gathered that something was happening at this Luxor place that he doesn't altogether like the look of. He gave me a hint it was some connection with the radium job; otherwise I'd have passed it on to one of the outside men.'

Somers accelerated a little and the car shot into the Tottenham Court Road, where they presently turned left at the

Inspector's direction.

'Don't tell me you're a dancing man, Inspector,' Somers murmured with a twinkle in his eye.

Faithfull shook his head.

'I've known this dump since it was Swan Street Auction Rooms,' he grunted.

They swung round a corner and saw the word 'Luxor' in large neon lettering.

Somers found a parking-place for the car so that it would be quickly available — a part of his Hendon training. After he had shut off the engine they sat there for a minute or two surveying their somewhat sordid surroundings and getting the lie of the land.

'What do you think is going on here?' the Sergeant asked curiously.

'I don't believe in making wild guesses before the facts come to hand.'

Inspector Faithfull took out his gun metal snuff-box and helped himself to a pinch.

'Then what might be happening?'

'Well, if you'll think for a minute, Sergeant, you'll appreciate that the people who steal this radium have got to get it out of the country if they're going to realize on it.'

'Of course,' replied Somers rather irritably. 'The Super gave us no end of a lecture about that.'

'I'm glad you remembered. Well now, judging by the district, I should say this place is patronized by a large foreign element — a pretty mixed crowd. People who are coming into and going out of the country. And a pellet of radium wouldn't be too difficult to conceal.'

'Are you sure we can trust Nicky?'

'We can't trust anybody when the stakes run as high as they do in this case. But I've found him pretty reliable in the past. It's fifteen years now since he served twelve months for running a gambling-room at the Toreador, and it seems to have taught him a lesson.'

'Maybe you're right. But I'm always a bit suspicious when these blokes are so patently anxious to play in with the police. There must be a motive of some sort.'

Faithfull murmured:

'It could be that he doesn't want to lose

his licence. After all, it's his living. Anyhow, let's go and see what's going on.'

As they left the car they could hear the distant sound of the brass section of a dance-band attacking a popular dance tune in a crisp fox-trot tempo. Inside the foyer of the Luxor they saw a large photograph of Harry Bexford and his Boys, all grinning like Cheshire cats over their white shirt fronts.

Somers, who knew a little about such matters, flung a passing glance at them and commented:

'That must set Nicky back three hundred a week!'

Sensing they were not the usual type of patron, a smart uniformed attendant came forward to meet them with a polite inquiry, but Faithfull curtly informed him they had an appointment with Mr. Dulane. He directed them to the office at the top of the heavily carpeted imposing flight of stairs, which led to the balcony.

As they approached Nick's office, the Sergeant said: 'How would it be if I wander around a bit and see if I recognize anybody?'

The other hesitated, then nodded.

'So long as you keep out of the way. You might sneak into the balcony through the door yonder and keep behind one of the palms or whatever they've got littered about. And don't be more than five minutes.'

Somers strolled over to the door indicated, paused and casually lighted a cigarette before pushing the door half open and disappearing.

Faithfull waited a moment, then rapped sharply upon the door of Nick's private office.

There was no reply.

The Inspector waited a few seconds then repeated the knock.

No reply.

No sound save the distant dance-band and the swish of a thousand feet on the polished floor.

After knocking once more, Faithfull turned the handle and opened the door a few inches.

'You there, Nicky?'

There was no reply.

Inspector Faithfull put his head round

the door. The room was a fair-sized outer office, with a small desk, on which was a typewriter and letter basket, with a filing cabinet nearby. It appeared that the room was also used as a store for chocolates and cigarettes, with which several shelves were tightly stacked. The light was still burning there and also in the inner office, the door of which stood open a few inches.

The Scotland Yard man at once crossed over to the other door and looked into the second office, which was apparently Nicky's own private room.

It had obviously been the scene of some sort of struggle, for a chair was overturned, a number of papers lay scattered on the floor and a large ornamental inkstand lay on its side with the ink flowing over the edge of the desk.

Faithfull walked quickly over to yet another door in a far corner of the room, opened it and looked out. He saw the iron platform and stairs of a fire-escape. Closing the door, he heard a sound and swung round quickly.

It was only Somers, who had just come

into the inner office.

'Hallo, what's been going on here?' asked the Sergeant with a low whistle.

'Some sort of struggle.'

And the Inspector's bushy brows were almost meeting in an intense frown.

Sergeant Somers set the chair on its feet and gingerly righted the inkstand. Then he wandered out into the other office.

'I say,' he called presently, and when the Inspector joined him he indicated that the receiver of the telephone which stood on a corner of the mantelshelf had not been replaced in its socket, as if the last call had been interrupted.

Somers picked it up with his handkerchief and called:

'Hallo!'

There was no response, and he cradled the receiver.

In the meantime, Faithfull had also used his handkerchief and grasped the handle of the wall safe in the inner office, which appeared to be soundly locked. Robbery did not appear to be the motive behind the violent scene which had been enacted here.

'Don't you think we ought to get hold of somebody, Inspector?' Somers asked. 'Maybe the doorman or one of the attendants could tell us something.'

'Wait a minute!' said Faithfull absently.

'But it may have only been the band boys larking about the place. You know what they are, break up any happy home in less time than it takes to tell.'

'All right,' conceded the other at last, and Somers turned to go. As he did so, he thought he heard a sound inside a tall cupboard which stood behind the door of the outer room.

With a warning look in Faithfull's direction, he quickly turned the handle of the cupboard door and flung it open. Obviously a cupboard which was used as a wardrobe amongst other things, for inside there were two coats, a mackintosh, the jacket of an attendant's uniform.

And deep in the shadows a slim, blonde girl stared back at him.

4

As Sergeant Somers opened the door wider the girl blinked hard, but did not seem unduly upset.

'What the devil are you doing there?'

She did not reply for a moment, but stepped out into the light, revealing an attractive figure, vivid red mouth which had a humorous twist at the corners, unusually deep blue eyes and a narrow fringe that gave her a slightly tough appearance.

'What were you doing in there?' Somers repeated.

She smiled and replied in a composed voice that had an attractive husky quality:

'Just playing hide and seek. No harm in that, is there?'

She had obviously overheard their conversation and gathered from it that they were police officers.

'Who are you and what's your game?' snapped Faithfull, confronting the girl, almost elbowing Somers into the background.

'I told you, the game is hide and seek. And I'm a dance hostess here. The name is Georgia Nash. You can call me Georgie if you must.'

She leaned negligently against the office table, her slim arms showing to advantage.

'What made you go in that cupboard?'

She folded her arms and smiled at the Inspector somewhat whimsically.

'Well, it's quite a story,' she began, still showing no sign of distress.

'Make it as short as you can,' said Faithfull, who had a feeling the trail was getting colder every minute. 'What was your reason for being in this room at all?'

She lifted a neatly manicured hand to smooth her blonde curls which had become slightly ruffled in the cupboard.

'I came in here to see Nicky about new dance shoes,' she informed them. 'A pair hardly lasts us a fortnight.'

'Go on,' put in Faithfull impatiently when she was about to launch upon further details. 'What happened when you came in?'

'Nobody heard my knock, so I walked in. There was somebody in there — ' she nodded towards the inner office, 'because I could hear some sort of scuffle. I stood by the door here for a minute, wondering what to do. The door to the inner office was open about six inches and I caught a glimpse of two ugly looking customers rushing out through the door on to the fire-escape — and they seemed to be carrying a body.'

'You didn't see whose body?'

'No. But I wouldn't be surprised if it were Nicky. I can't think who else.'

'Did they see you?' queried Somers.

She favoured him with a smile that stirred that young man's pulses.

'No, they were half-way out, and pretty busy with the job in hand.'

'How long did all this take?'

'Not more than a minute I should think. Almost before I realized what was going on, they had slammed the outside door.'

Faithfull said:

‘Why didn’t you scream or give the alarm?’

She shook her head.

‘And get a bullet or a knife for my pains? Not this child! Besides, if I had screamed I doubt if it would have been heard. And even if it had, I don’t suppose anybody would have acted on it. Nobody goes round looking for trouble in this place; there’s quite enough pushed on to your plate as it is. So I decided the best thing I could do would be to telephone the police, and I was just going to do so when you knocked on the door. So I dropped the receiver and hopped into the cupboard.’

‘Why?’

‘On an impulse,’ she confessed. ‘I was beginning to get really scared, and I thought it might perhaps be an accomplice of the tough gents who’d just gone out.’

Faithfull nodded thoughtfully.

The story seemed plausible enough; particularly as she hadn’t had much time to think one up. Not that he really liked the looks of the girl. She was pretty, almost beautiful, but he had seen so many pretty girls on the wrong side of the law, invariably trying to right matters with a tearful display, that he always suspected the type.

'How long ago was it when you first came in?'

'Not ten minutes — you can judge that for yourself — you know when you knocked.'

He nodded again. It seemed to fit in, and in that case there was no time to be lost.

'Did you know Nicky very well?' he asked.

She shook her head.

'I've only been here a month.'

'And you can't call to mind anything else? You didn't hear those men say anything?'

She pouted her attractive lips as if she were making an effort of memory.

'As a matter of fact, I did catch one bit,' she admitted. 'It was just a tag end of a sentence, not too clear, but I could have sworn that one of them used the words: 'before we get to Henley'.'

‘Henley!’ echoed the Sergeant, his eyes lighting up.

‘Just a minute,’ cut in Faithfull in a warning tone. ‘Now look here, young woman, if you’re trying to lead us up the garden, you’d better stop it right now, or you’re going to be very sorry for yourself in the end.’

Georgie Nash shrugged her elegant shoulders.

‘As far as I’m concerned, officer, you can forget the whole thing,’ she replied in a tone of complete indifference. ‘I’ve told you what little I know, and whether you make use of it is your own affair. If we never see Nicky again, I don’t think any of us girls will be exactly heartbroken.’

Inspector Faithfull eyed her shrewdly for five seconds without speaking. Then he suddenly swung round to Somers.

‘How much petrol have you got?’

‘Enough for a hundred miles. They’re always kept filled up before they’re sent out.’

Faithfull snapped:

‘Good. Then we’re practically ready to go. Better get your hat and coat, Miss Nash.’

For the first time, the girl seemed a trifle startled.

'You mean you're taking me?'

'That's right. We're not losing sight of you at this stage. Get your things.'

'But the girls' cloakroom is the other side of the building — behind the stage.'

'Sergeant Somers will go with you. I'll see you at the car outside.'

As they turned to go he gave Somers a look which the Sergeant interpreted correctly to the effect that he must not lose sight of the girl.

Inspector Faithfull went out through the front entrance, exchanging a few words with the assistant manager on the way and putting him wise to the situation. He also stopped at the entrance to the car park and fired a number of questions at the attendant in the little hut.

He was sitting in the car when Somers arrived with the girl.

'No time to lose!' he snapped as the Sergeant settled in the driving seat. 'D'you know the road to Henley?'

'Like the back of my hand. I used to

visit a roadhouse the far side of Henley quite a lot.'

Georgia Nash queried:

'The Houseboat Roadhouse?'

'That's it — how did you know?'

'I get around,' she replied with her unusual mysterious smile.

Inspector Faithfull was showing signs of ever-increasing impatience as they headed in the direction of the Marble Arch.

'When you've quite finished your lighthearted backchat, Somers, perhaps you'll listen to me.' He growled. 'As it happens, we've had a stroke of luck. The car park attendant at the gate tells me that there's only one car left the place during the past half-hour — most of them were arriving at this time. He thinks the car in question was a Maryland saloon, but he can't be certain. Anyhow, it was a large American model.'

'Good enough.'

Somers switched on the 'Police' sign over the windscreen, for he was out to avoid any undue delay.

When they got on to the arterial road,

the car swept along at seventy miles an hour and had more power in reserve. But Faithfull would not let the Sergeant open her full out, arguing that the car they were after may have been delayed, and they could easily pass it in the stream of traffic unless they kept their eyes wide open. It was by no means easy to examine every car they saw by the light of their headlamps, particularly at that speed.

'They must have at least twenty minutes' start,' mused Faithfull, 'but there's just a chance they got held up, or had to call at a garage. You can let her go a bit more now. There seems to be a clear stretch ahead.'

The speedometer needle shivered around ninety.

Faithfull turned and saw that the girl's knuckles showed white in the reflected light from the dashboard as she clutched her handbag.

'It's all right,' he told her dryly. 'The Sergeant here was trained at Brooklands.'

Somers made no reply and they drove in silence, the powerful headlights boring a glaring tunnel in the night ahead.

Presently, they picked up a black American saloon car.

'This might be it,' muttered Faithfull

Sergeant Somers leaned over and depressed a switch on the dashboard.

'What are you going to do?' asked Faithfull.

'Try an old trick,' was the reply. 'It generally works.'

He extracted a small hand microphone from the cubby hole in front of him, and after waiting for a few moments, spoke into it.

'Hallo car number TXN 4159! Will you please stop at once for police inspection?'

There was a slight pause, and Somers repeated his message.

Almost at once, the car in front began to slow down. Somers overtook and passed it without slackening pace.

'Dammit! Aren't you going to stop?'

'No time. In the first place, you saw it was a woman driving, and we're looking for two men. Secondly, we have to take the chance that innocent people always pull up.'

'Humph!' grunted Faithfull, slowly

working it out and trying to find a flaw in the argument, without success.

'I suppose this is what they call psychology,' came the faintly sarcastic tones of Georgia Nash.

Somers shrugged.

'Call it that if you like. As a matter of fact, it's about an even chance.'

'I once knew a psychiatrist,' mused the girl. 'He had the job of examining murderers to make sure whether they were sane. He went mad himself in the end.'

'Do you know any more bedtime stories?' grinned Somers.

He was beginning to take a fancy to the girl's mordant sense of humour.

'Keep your eyes on the road!' snapped Faithfull, who never relished superfluous conversation in ticklish situations.

Twice during the next quarter of an hour they repeated Somers's strategy, but the car pulled up each time and they shot past.

Inspector Faithfull began to look dubious and Georgia Nash more amused. She suggested:

'Of course, there's always the chance

that the people you're chasing may have heard of the trick.'

But the Sergeant went on doggedly talking into his microphone, and his voice boomed out of the small but powerful speaker over the windscreen.

He would not admit he was feeling discouraged, but when a large Maryland saloon loomed into the headlights he privately decided that this should be his last attempt, for they were less than ten miles from Henley.

'Car number TLM 1487 please stop at once for police inquiry!'

Sergeant Somers's voice boomed out through the speaker. The car ahead did not slow down; he almost imagined it drew away a little. He repeated his message rather more deliberately.

The car in front showed no sign of slowing down.

'They're not stopping,' said Inspector Faithfull.

'Maybe somebody who's a bit deaf,' the girl said.

'Give 'em one more chance,' ordered the Inspector.

And the loudspeaker boomed out again, but the American saloon was actually gaining a trifle now. Its rear window had the blind drawn down, so they had no clue to the occupants. Somers pressed his foot hard on the accelerator. He kept the Maryland well in range of the headlights, which was no easy task.

'Hang on to 'em,' urged Faithfull, narrowing his eyes and trying to focus the car ahead more clearly.

The Sergeant muttered between his teeth:

'They must know we're following 'em, even if they didn't hear the speaker.'

The girl had become very quiet.

Then the police car suddenly gained twenty yards in less than a mile, to the Sergeant's mystification. But the reason was soon apparent, for during the next few seconds there were four tiny spurts of red flame from the car ahead.

One of Somers's headlights went out. A bullet struck the windscreen, which was fortunately constructed to withstand it. Sergeant Somers gripped the wheel a little tighter and drove on.

Faithfull growled:

'No doubt about it now.' Then after a minute, he demanded: 'What the devil are you trying to do?'

'We can't let them get into a town — sure to lose them — got to try and get level somehow.'

The police car crept closer.

'We're gaining! Do be careful!' cried Georgia Nash as they lurched on a fairly steep bend. Then the road narrowed for a long stretch and Somers dared not draw too close to the other car.

'What the devil are they doing?' exclaimed Faithfull, suddenly, leaning over to get a better view of the offside of the car ahead. Through a window in the back door the head and shoulders of a man had appeared, picked out quite clearly by the police car's remaining headlamp.

Georgia Nash gasped:

'They're pushing a man out of the window!'

Somers exclaimed:

'My God! I believe it's Nicky!'

The head of the man drooped lifelessly.

'They're throwing him out!' said Faithfull. 'You've got to stop — or we'll be over him!'

'Damn!' Sergeant Somers reached for the handbrake.

The police car screeched to a standstill, swerving round the sprawling body in the road. Faithfull picked up a large torch from beside his seat and they hurried back to the unconscious man.

'Yes, it's Nicky — poor devil!' the Sergeant said as Faithfull shone the torch. They carried the unconscious man to the side of the road. The Sergeant went back to the car for a brandy flask.

When he returned he suggested:

'Maybe we could carry him to the car and still catch 'em?'

Faithfull shook his head.

'They'll be in Henley by this time, and they've probably got some sort of hide-out there.'

The girl had joined them by this time.

'Is he — ?' she whispered.

'He's in pretty bad shape,' replied Faithfull, cutting the ropes that bound

Nicky's wrists and ankles. Meanwhile, Somers tried to force some brandy through his bloodless lips.

'He seems to have had a pretty bad crack on the head,' murmured the Sergeant suddenly conscious of blood upon his fingers. Faithfull picked up Nicky's left arm and felt the pulse. It was fluttering very feebly.

'Try him with more brandy.'

'Let me hold the flask — you take his head,' the girl said, and they managed to force a few drops into Nicky's mouth.

'He's coming round,' she whispered. Nicky gave a tiny, shivering sigh.

'Better see if he can talk, Inspector. Might not get another chance,' Somers urged.

Faithfull nodded and bent over the little man.

'Nicky.'

Nicky's eyelids fluttered as if he were conscious of the summons.

'Nicky this is Inspector Faithfull — you remember — Faithfull.'

Nicky gave a little gasp.

'He's trying to say something,' breathed

Georgia Nash, who had noticed the lips moving slightly.

The Inspector bent his head lower.

'Nicky — who was it — who did this?'

Again the other's lips moved.

'Lucifer . . . ' came a strangled whisper. 'Look out for Lucifer . . . '

The weak voice died away into another gasp, and Nicky relapsed into unconsciousness. They stood looking at him helplessly for a few moments, then the two men picked him up and carried him into the car. As they made for the hospital at Henley, Somers asked humourlessly:

'Who the devil is Lucifer?'

'I haven't the least idea,' replied Inspector Faithfull unemotionally.

'Perhaps it suggests something to Miss Nash,' Somers observed over his shoulder.

'Why should it?'

'You mean it doesn't?' Faithfull queried incisively.

'Not a thing.'

'Then we're not much wiser,' the Sergeant grumbled.

'Oh, but we are,' insisted Faithfull.

'We're quite a lot wiser.'

In response to the other's inquiring look, he went on:

'It seems pretty reasonable to assume that that Lucifer chap is the master-mind of this organization we're after.'

'That's fairly obvious. But what does it tell us?'

'Think, Sergeant, think. In the first place, it tells us that this individual has the besetting weakness of all criminals — vanity. It's always the biggest chink in the armour, Somers. Crooks have always had a weakness for fancy names, but once they fall for it, then I've always found it's only a matter of time. Just a question of tenacity, efficient routine, waiting for the inevitable mistake.'

'You seem to have gone mighty confident all of a sudden,' grunted Somers, who was feeling more than a little depressed that he had not been allowed to continue his car chase.

'I wouldn't say that. I'm a bit relieved maybe. You'll find it's only a matter of time before this man lets his vanity run away with him, and then — '

'You seem to have overlooked one small point.' The Sergeant gave a meaning glance in Georgia Nash's direction. 'Bearing in mind what you say about vanity.'

'Well?'

'There's always a chance,' replied Somers softly, 'that Lucifer might be a woman.'

5

Inspector Faithfull thrust his hands into the pockets of his mackintosh, and studiously ignoring the commissionaire and reception clerks in the cathedral-like foyer of World House, moved casually towards the marble stairs.

He avoided lifts from force of habit, for staircases were less obtrusive when it came to making an unnoticed entrance and exit. Faithfull always felt vaguely uncomfortable in the huge buildings which housed the popular dailies of Fleet Street, and the home of the *Daily World* was possibly the most awe-inspiring of the bunch.

Still, when Inspector Faithfull had a job to do, he saw it through without considering his personal feelings.

Having toiled up to the second floor, passing innumerable copy boys carrying galley proofs, letter trays, cups of tea and various other impedimenta which seem indispensable to the daily round on a newspaper, he turned down a corridor and began leisurely taking stock of the names on the various doors he passed.

It was the editorial department all right, for he had visited the building on previous occasions, but there were always three or four new names on the doors every time he came. The *Daily World* had a reputation for skimming the cream off Fleet Street's most brilliant brains, then dropping them.

Faithfull was looking for two names. The first was that of 'Pa' Woods, who gave the *Daily World's* weekly crossword competition forecasts, and who had been enjoying an unusual run of luck which had boosted the circulation by several hundred thousand.

Second name he sought was that of Wister Hale, the crime reporter, whose inside revelations had been worrying Scotland Yard considerably during the past few weeks. Faithfull walked from one end of the corridor to the other and back again; he even tried another corridor which housed the art department on the off-chance that his quarry might have been accommodated there during a shortage of office accommodation.

He found neither name.

Several members of the staff passed him from time to time, but raised no query. They were accustomed to seeing far more peculiar specimens of humanity in the *Daily World* offices. At length, Faithfull came to a halt before a door marked: Jack H. Barrington, News Editor. He hesitated for a moment, then pushed the door open. At once he was greeted with a rattle of typewriters and a Creed machine which was ticking away busily in a corner. The Inspector walked in and passed through a little wicket gate.

'Mr. Barrington's expecting me,' he flung over his shoulder to the typist who looked up inquiringly.

Without further ado, he opened the door marked 'Private' and went in. He was always ready to risk a brusque reception as a penalty of such abrupt entrances, for it meant that he caught his man off his guard. He had picked up a lot of useful information in this unorthodox fashion.

But Barrington was not to be caught as easily as that. The life of a newspaperman consists mainly of interruptions. The News Editor looked up from a dummy of the next day's issue and grinned.

'Hallo, Old Faithfull,' he murmured affably. 'I've been wondering when you'd drop in. Chuck those papers off that chair and sit down.'

The other obeyed, eyeing Barrington shrewdly as he did so.

He could never quite weigh up this alert middle-aged man, who had a reputation of being able to smell a good story in its roughest embryo. He was something of a tyrant in his way and was often said to have sold his soul to the *World*, but he retained a certain dry sense of humour and extracted more enjoyment from his job than he would have derived from any other form of existence.

'This is an honour, Inspector,' he began seriously enough, though there was a twinkle in his grey eyes. 'Try one of Lord Tom's cigars.' Lord Thompson was the proprietor of the *Daily World*, plus a score more newspapers.

'I prefer my old pipe, thanks.'

'Better not let the boss hear you say that,' smiled Barrington.

'I say a lot of things your boss wouldn't like to hear,' retorted Faithfull, the merest trace of a grin twisting the corners of his mouth.

'Well,' said Barrington, leaning back in his chair, 'what is it this time?'

The Inspector looked round cautiously to make sure the door was shut, then leaned forward.

'This fellow 'Pa' Wood,' he began in a confidential tone. 'The bloke who tips the crossword results — '

Barrington threw back his head and laughed.

'Poor old 'Pa' — you don't mean the Yard are after him?'

'Not exactly. But I thought I'd like to meet him while I'm up here.'

'I'm afraid that's impossible, Inspector,' Barrington replied seriously. 'I know you're a crossword fan, but I'm afraid it's out of the question. Professional etiquette and all that sort of thing you know. 'Pa's' very touchy.'

Inspector Faithfull sighed. But he was not greatly surprised. These little ideas of his rarely worked out the way he had planned them.

'Sorry I can't oblige you, Inspector,' went on Barrington. 'But you might be able to oblige me with some dope about that fellow Nicky. The bloke from the Luxor Ballroom.'

'H'm,' snorted Faithfull, 'you seem to know as much about that as I do, judging by your front page this morning.'

Barrington laughed.

'I just thought there might be one or two tit-bits that Wister Hale missed.'

The mention of the name brought the Inspector on to the edge of his chair again.

'That's why I came here,' he announced, 'to see this Wister Hale.'

Barrington seemed more amused than ever.

'Then it'll puzzle you, I'm afraid, Inspector. We never see him ourselves. He's one of Lord Tom's discoveries, and they're the only terms he'll work on. Complete anonymity as far as the inside staff is concerned. He sends in all his copy by special messenger. It's just as much a mystery inside the office as anywhere else. My instructions are simply that his stuff is to be printed word for word without any sub-editing — and I may tell you that instruction applies to only half a dozen more people in the entire country so far as the *World* is concerned.'

'But dammit man,' exploded the other, 'we have a perfectly good Press Bureau at the Yard that will give you a square deal.'

Barrington lit a cigarette and puffed out a cloud of smoke.

'The trouble is, Inspector, the public has got tired of reading the sort of stuff one gets on official hand-outs. They want exclusive stories — behind the scenes stuff. And the *World* always gives the public what it wants, no matter what it costs. That's why our circulation is a million above any of the others.'

'All the same,' said Faithfull, 'I'm warning you that if you go on printing this man's stuff you're heading for trouble.'

'That's fine!' applauded Barrington. 'The *World* thrives on trouble. You can't keep four million readers without running into it.'

Faithfull was momentarily nonplussed.

'But this affair will only be a flash in the pan,' he argued. 'If Wister Hale wants to keep a regular job, he'd do much better to come round to the Bureau and — '

'I don't think Hale is very interested in a regular job,' Barrington interrupted. 'He just happens to have a lot of specialized knowledge about this case, and when it's over the boss will probably drop him. By that time, I should think he'll have made enough money to retire, from the rate we're paying him!'

'He'll never live to enjoy it if he keeps going on like this,' muttered the Inspector darkly. 'This gang we're up against will wipe him out as soon as look at him if they find him in the way just once.'

Barrington shrugged.

'That's his affair. I have my instructions from the Chief that Hale is to play a lone hand. There's no need to look so sore about it, Inspector. You know very well you plant your men in the underworld. Why shouldn't we do the same? It's all in the interests of law and order.'

'That's just what it isn't. I prefer to conduct my cases in my way — not Wister Hale's, or Lord Tom, Dick or Harry's.'

Barrington flicked the ash off the end of his cigarette.

'It's not a bit of use your going on at me, Inspector,' he said mildly. 'The Chief has the first and last word here, and after all it's his paper.'

Faithfull frowned angrily but could think of no answer to this. At last he leaned back in his chair and said:

'Tell me his real name, anyway, and I'll know how to deal with him.'

Barrington shook his head.

'Sorry, Inspector. It's as much as my job's worth.'

'It'll be as much as his job's worth,' muttered Faithfull.

'But I'll tell you one thing, Inspector,' grinned Barrington suddenly. 'I'll let you into a secret about 'Pa' Woods.'

'Eh?'

'There ain't no such person. The staff take it in turns to do the crossword forecast — last two weeks the office boy did it!'

To Inspector Faithfull, devotee of crossword competitions for eleven years, this was almost akin to sacrilege. With hardly another word he picked up his hat and left the office.

6

Outside the enormous white stone building Inspector Faithfull paused to buy an evening paper.

There was a report of Nicky's death in the Stop Press. Faithfull read it through twice, then jumped on a bus and was back at Scotland Yard in less than ten minutes. His office was empty and he gloomily turned over the contents of the 'In' tray.

These were mostly concerned with matters of minor internal routine, but there was a cutting from two morning papers concerning a robbery of a small quantity of radium from a large wholesale chemists. They were quite straightforward reports, both giving the impression that the raid had been carefully planned.

The Inspector grunted and flung them back in the tray. Then he put a telephone call through to the hospital at Henley to inquire if the man whom he had left in attendance there had taken any statement from Nicky. But the doctor in charge informed him that Nicky had not recovered consciousness again.

Feeling singularly frustrated, the Inspector slammed down the receiver and returned to his files. Then he rang up the Information Room to see if anything had been heard of the car they had pursued the previous evening. There were no reports in. Must have changed the number plates pretty quickly, or gone to ground, Faithfull concluded.

A few minutes later Somers came in.

Faithfull asked:

'Hallo, where've you been?'

The other threw his hat neatly on to its peg, thrust his hands into his trouser pockets and perched on the Inspector's desk.

'Amongst other places, I've visited Dent and Clarke's.'

Faithfull recalled that was the name of the wholesale chemists mentioned in the two newspaper-cuttings.

'Get anything?'

'Not a thing. Johnson's handling it.

He'll send us a copy of his report this afternoon.'

'Hmph! Don't suppose that'll be much help. I suppose they got clean away as the papers say.'

'Not a clue of any sort.'

Faithfull observed:

'The Super'll be delighted.'

'I hear he's calling a special conference to sort of ginger us up.'

The Inspector shrugged.

'Waste of time. Things have got to take their course. All we can do is to bide our time and be ready to pounce on the first false move.'

'The newspapers keep screaming for results.'

'Newspapers — pah!' scoffed the Inspector, who had seen quite enough of newspapers for one day. 'Anything else to report, Sergeant? Did you go round to the Luxor?'

The other nodded.

'I went there first. And I came across a little thing which might be very interesting indeed.'

'You don't say. What was that?'

'I managed to catch the assistant

manager and asked him one or two things about Georgia Nash.'

Faithfull nodded approvingly.

'Yes, there's something strange about that girl. Did you find out anything?'

'It was true that she'd only been there a month, and she'd kept pretty much to herself. There were no complaints from the management anyhow. Then I went round to the girls' room where I waited for her last night and asked the assistant manager if I could see her locker. It's a sort of small wardrobe where the girls hang their clothes. At a first glance, there appeared to be only a dance frock and a pair of shoes in there. Then I happened to notice this lying in a corner.'

He produced from his pocket a folded and rather grimy piece of paper, which proved on closer inspection to be an envelope. On it was written:

Fraser Mallowes, Esq.,
15 Bermuda Avenue,
St. John's Wood.

Faithfull examined it carefully. Then he said:

'I suppose this is her writing.'

'Well, it looks like a woman's writing,' the Sergeant said in a non-committal tone.

'No letter inside of course.'

'I should imagine that for some reason she didn't send the letter.'

'Fraser Mallowes,' repeated the Inspector thoughtfully. 'Wouldn't that be the professor who caused a lot of bother about those atomic experiments?'

Somers nodded.

'Supposed to be the greatest brain in the country in that field.'

'I remember now. He had some bee in his bonnet about it wiping out civilization completely.'

'That's the man. I understand he's very wealthy. Discovered several dye processes that have brought in a fortune. And I hear he still goes on with his atomic research — says he's out to show the world how atomic energy can be used for the good of mankind.'

Faithfull sniffed noisily.

'That's what he says. When you've lived to my age, you'll be very cautious about accepting public statements.'

Somers chuckled.

'My dear Inspector! I'm not all that naïve, you know.'

'Then you'll appreciate that there's nothing to prevent this man Mallowes from making a statement that he is conducting atomic experiments for the benefit of mankind, while in point of fact he may be doing the exact opposite.'

'You mean doing research into atomic bombs for some foreign power? Or even cornering our radium supplies.'

'There is that to be considered. With radium coming under international control, there's sure to be some attempt to develop a black market. The stakes will be high enough to tempt some of the best brains.'

'All the same, what I should like to know at the moment is why a hostess at a *palais de danse* should write to a distinguished scientist.'

'She might have been giving him dancing lessons,' suggested Faithfull humourlessly.

‘I thought he was an elderly cove — ’

‘A man’s never too old — ’ Faithfull stopped abruptly. ‘Anyhow, I dare say there may be some quite harmless and fairly obvious explanation. In that case he can enlighten us.’

‘You mean you’re going to see him?’ Somers asked in a mildly surprised voice.

‘Just a friendly call.’

‘I should imagine he’s the sort of man who might turn a bit awkward.’

‘It’s when people turn awkward that things come to light!’

He was about to enlarge upon this theory when the Sergeant, who had picked up a newspaper cutting from his basket, interrupted him to ask:

‘Have you seen this from the *World*?’

Faithfull’s face clouded.

‘I didn’t get that one. Is it something of Wister Hale’s?’

The other nodded.

‘Pretty graphic report of this affair at St. James’s Hospital late last night. You don’t think that little gang doubled back from Henley?’

The Inspector looked dubious.

'I should doubt it.'

'In that case, this organization appears to be quite a sizable one — plenty of men to spare. By the way, did you know we picked up Pike Bellamy?'

'Yes, that's in one of my cuttings. Seems that Pike's fine friends made their getaway and left him to face the music.'

'Poor old Pike,' mused Somers, studying the report. 'Pity he couldn't keep his fat red nose out of this business. I see the others had a car waiting — Pike was just the look-out man stationed outside, left to fend for himself. Wonder if Inspector Denby has got anything out of him.'

'I doubt it. Pike's a tough nut.'

'What about having him in here and trying to throw a scare into him?'

'Presently.'

Inspector Faithfull helped himself to a pinch of snuff and sneezed vigorously three times in rapid succession. When he had recovered he leaned his elbows on the desk and looked across at his colleague.

'We've got to establish some sort of routine in this case, and the sooner we get down to it the better. We all have to face up to a certain amount of routine — what else is Fingerprints Department and Criminal Records but routine, routine, routine. Theories are all very well up to a point, but if you're going to get your man, you've got to have facts, marshalled in their proper order, before you can act on them.'

'This is where we come in,' thought Somers, who was getting a little tired of this moralizing on the virtues of routine.

He asked, a note of grim amusement in his voice:

'What routine are you applying to this Wister Hale affair?'

Faithfull sniffed at the mention of the name.

'I'll get to the bottom of that business,' he snorted aggressively. 'Dammit, the man seems to know more about our own case than we do ourselves. It's — it's damnably irregular!'

The other grinned.

'Yes, I wouldn't mind ten minutes with the gentleman myself. Have you any idea who he is?'

'I've been after Barrington half the

morning trying to get it out of him. Seems he was engaged by Lord Thompson, and more or less has a free hand. I'm beginning to wonder just what's going on.'

'You don't think Wister Hale might be a *nom-de-plume* for some really big bug — or may be somebody at the Yard?'

The Inspector shrugged.

'Anything seems to be possible.'

'Well, the fellow certainly gets results.'

'Of a sort. The accuracy of the results is another matter. I wouldn't like to arrest anybody on the strength of the evidence in the *Daily World*.'

'Pity Lord Thompson can't hear you say that,' chuckled Somers.

'I'll take good care he never does. But it's true all the same. Anyhow, I'm not having this man Hale continually throwing a spanner in the works where my case is concerned.'

Sergeant Somers frowned.

'I can't think where he gets his information. Look at his stuff this morning — all about our affair at the Luxor — and St. James's job — here, you'd better have it.'

He passed over the cutting.

Faithfull scanned the clipping, then flung it into his basket with a tiny snort.

'Luckily that can't do much damage,' he commented. 'The gang will steer clear of the Luxor now in any case. I don't suppose they told Pike Bellamy very much; in fact I dare say he knows next to nothing. Just a cog in the machine — even crime is losing its individuality nowadays,' he added with a sigh.

'I don't know about Pike. He's a cute old bird. Shouldn't be surprised if Denby has rubbed him up the wrong way and he's keeping his mouth shut.'

'We'll see about that.'

Faithfull ran through his file quickly. Then he observed:

'We shall want the doctor's report on Nicky for the inquest.'

'Pity we couldn't have kept him conscious a bit longer. He might have told us a lot.'

'I doubt it,' the other replied dubiously. 'In fact, I don't think he knew quite what he was getting mixed up with when he telephoned me. All he had to go on was one or two stray snatches of conversation.'

He picked up the telephone, asked for Inspector Denby, and began a conversation on the subject of Pike Bellamy.

After some minutes, Inspector Faithfull replaced the receiver and turned to Somers.

'Pike Bellamy will be here in a few minutes.'

Somers nodded. The Inspector eyed him thoughtfully. Then the Sergeant said:

'Coming back to that girl Georgia Nash.'

'Yes? What happened to her last night?'

'She slipped away while we were at the hospital.'

'Well, I'll be damned!' muttered Faithfull. 'For all we know, she might have joined those blokes at their hide-out.' He shrugged. 'Oh well, we can pick her up at the Luxor.'

'That's just what we can't do. When you sidetracked me on to the subject of Professor Mallowes, I forgot to mention that Miss Nash telephoned the Luxor this morning to say she wouldn't be coming again.'

7

Inspector Faithfull whistled softly to himself, at Somers's announcement.

He had mistrusted that girl right from the start, and had no intention of letting her slip through his fingers without some further questioning if he could help it. There was no doubt in his mind that she knew considerably more than she had told the police, and if the radium gang were really using the Luxor, it wouldn't have been difficult for her to keep in contact with them in her position as a dancing partner. Any man could speak to her there without arousing undue suspicions. She might even be a go-between, conveying instructions from the master-mind to the minor members of the gang.

Yes, the Inspector decided, this Georgia Nash would have to be found and kept under observation. His train of thought was interrupted by a sharp knock on the door which heralded the arrival of Pike

Bellamy. Faithfull nodded to his warder to wait outside and then turned to the prisoner.

Pike Bellamy was a stubby little man with a hard, set face which was a great asset to him in the card-sharping racket which was his line of business. At the moment he looked none too clean and he also needed a shave. An untidy spotted yellow scarf was twisted round his neck and there were two buttons missing off his jacket.

Faithfull took all this in at a glance, then indicated a chair between the two desks.

'Might as well sit down while you're here,' he suggested in a mild voice.

Bellamy gave him a suspicious look before slowly lowering himself into the chair. He glared first at Faithfull, then at Somers, but did not speak, and his face was a mask set in a slight scowl. He knew Faithfull of old; Somers he had seen only once before. But Pike mistrusted all policemen, who, he considered, had only one aim in life — promotion at all costs! So it was hardly surprising that he lowered himself into his chair as if he expected it to play some strange trick on him.

'All right, Pike, don't look so sorry for yourself,' Faithfull could not refrain from remarking with some inward amusement.

Pike's scowl deepened the merest fraction.

'There's one or two I could mention who'll be sorry for themselves before the week's out,' he announced in a hoarse Cockney voice.

But the Inspector was having none of this.

'That'll do,' he snapped. 'I got you up here because I'm sorry to see you're mixed up in this business.'

'Not 'arf as bleedin' sorry as I am!' retorted Bellamy, adding quickly: 'But yer needn't think you can get anything outer me. I don't know nothink — see?'

Faithfull nodded slowly.

'That's a pity,' he replied in a casual tone. 'A great pity. Because you seem to have got yourself mixed up with a very strange crowd, Pike. I'm afraid the judge is going to take a pretty severe view of the case.'

'They always take a severe view of it,' snorted Pike, scowling rather more fiercely.

The Inspector did not speak for a moment or two.

'I don't see that you've much to lose by telling us what bit you know,' he said at last. 'And I might be able to put in a word.'

The other said savagely:

'I'll tell yer what I got to lose, Inspector. You said they was a queer crowd I got mixed up with. And by God you're right! I don't mind tellin' yer I wouldn't like to come outer clink and find them waitin' for me. Shouldn't wonder if they ain't runnin' the blinkin' country by the time I'm due out.'

'They'll have forgotten all about your little job by then — if they aren't inside themselves.'

'I ain't so sure about that. I tell yer this gang is goin' to get pretty big from the looks of things.'

'They left you in the lurch all right, didn't they?' suggested Faithfull in a conversational tone.

'Maybe they did — maybe they didn't. Maybe it was our arrangement. They paid me big money, cash down, and I've got it hidden away, where no dirty cop'll ever lay 'is 'ands on it — see?'

Faithfull exchanged a glance with Somers, who shrugged his shoulders and lit a cigarette without making any comment.

The Inspector went on:

'I don't see how they can know you ever told us a thing. We have other sources of information, you know. It might easily have come from one of the men we've got planted all over the place.' He hesitated, then added persuasively: 'Now, Pike, you remember I played fair with you on that Chelsea job. I give you my word I'll do the best I can for you this time.'

Pike Bellamy struggled with conflicting emotions, though his none too clean face remained as inscrutable as ever. At last he shifted uncomfortably in his chair and met Faithfull's keen gaze.

'Well, seein' as it's you, Inspector

— mind yer I wouldn't do this for anybody else. That swine downstairs has bin tryin' to pump me for hours.'

'You can rely on me to handle this affair so that you come out all right,' promised Faithfull in an encouraging tone.

'You can trust the Inspector, Pike,' said Somers, speaking for the first time. 'I'm a witness.'

Pike sniffed.

'I know what cops are worth as witnesses!' he retorted contemptuously.

Faithfull shot the Sergeant a warning glance, then set himself to the task of persuading Pike once more.

At last Pike said in a sullen tone:

'What is it yer want to know?'

'Oh, just start at the beginning and go straight on.'

'There ain't much to it really. I was down at the Three Sailors in Shadwell one evening, havin' a pint of old and mild by meself in the Snug, when in comes Lem Knight.'

'The man with the sand-papered fingers,' put in Somers softly.

The other nodded.

'That's Lem's racket. There ain't many 'peters' he can't fiddle open if you give 'im the time. So Lem comes up to me in the corner and says: 'Pike, you're just the bloke I'm lookin' for'.'

Faithfull frowned thoughtfully.

'I don't quite get that,' he said. 'If you bust 'em open and he fiddles 'em open, I should have thought you wouldn't have had much use for one another.'

'Never have done before,' replied Pike promptly. 'He orders himself a whisky and comes and sits down and starts to tell me 'ow 'e's got in with a gang what's doin' these radium jobs. He says as 'ow money's no object with them — they want to leave nothink to chance. So that if he can't open the safes, they want somebody to bust 'em. They'd asked him to look out for somebody, and 'e thought of me.'

'Very nice too, and was that all you had to do — just stand by in case Lem couldn't do the trick?'

'I had to keep a sharp look-out in case of trouble. But it was money for old rope — and they paid cash in advance!'

'Who paid the money?'

The Inspector threw in the question quickly.

'Lem Knight.'

'And how many jobs did you do?'

'One at Prince's Hospital, one at St. James's — that's all.'

Faithfull regarded the other sceptically.

'And you mean to tell me you never saw the other men on those jobs?'

'Not close to. I always met 'em on the job, but it was dark, and I had to stop outside the room — '

'How many were there besides Lem Knight?'

'Two. But they weren't the same two last night. I can tell yer that.'

'You're quite sure you didn't recognize them?'

'No, I tell yer. They looked like toffs to me. I didn't see their faces properly.'

Faithfull wondered if the man was telling the whole truth, or just as little as he possibly could to ensure a certain amount of clemency being meted out to him. He decided to try a shot at adventure.

‘Ever heard of a man who calls himself Lucifer?’ he demanded suddenly.

A casual observer might have noticed no change in Pike’s expression. But the Inspector was watching his eyes, and he could tell the shot had gone home.

‘Lucifer?’

Pike did his utmost to suppress any trace of surprise in his voice.

‘You’ve heard of him.’

Faithfull’s tone brooked no denial. Pike Bellamy hesitated, licked his lips somewhat nervously and looked round the room with a hunted expression.

‘I’ve ’eard the name,’ he conceded at length with some reluctance. ‘But I can’t tell you nothink about ’im except — ’

‘Except what?’

‘Except that the rate ’e’s goin’ on, you blokes at the Yard’ll soon begin to wonder if the Devil himself ain’t loose out of hell!’

8

'Steady on,' urged Inspector Faithfull as the police car pulled up with a jerk when the traffic lights flicked to amber, and Sergeant Somers grinned.

'Sorry, Inspector. Force of habit.'

Faithfull grunted, then folded the paper in which he had been trying to study the crossword competition. The light was none too good now, and he decided to postpone the effort until he was able to read through the column at leisure when he got back home.

However, it was doubtful if he would manage it that night, for he and the Sergeant had a busy evening before them. They were on their way to the address in St. John's Wood which Somers had discovered scribbled on the envelope belonging to Georgia Nash. Both of them were somewhat dubious as to what sort of reception they would get from Professor Mallowes, but they were determined to make the attempt.

Presently the Inspector observed:

'I think it's a turning off here.'

They were sweeping along a broad road of dignified Georgian mansions. He had a good rough and ready knowledge of the London landscape, and his guess proved correct, for they found the road they sought and were soon pulling up outside a large house which was approached by a drive and was partly screened by large elm trees.

'Drive on another twenty yards.'

The other obeyed. The car came to a standstill, and as he switched off the engine, Somers asked:

'Have you decided how you're going to tackle him, Inspector?'

Faithfull folded his paper again and thrust it carefully into his mackintosh pocket.

'I stopped making cut and dried plans for interviews a good many years ago, Sergeant. I found out that they never work out the way you expect. The thing is to keep an eye open for an opportunity and make the most of it.'

'Oh,' said Somers, 'I thought you favoured a cut and dried routine.'

As he said it, he realized that he should have known better. Inspector Faithfull turned a penetrating, reproving glare upon him.

'Routine — in the office, yes,' he said with considerable emphasis. 'But outside . . . well . . . you have to keep your wits about you while you're on the job. Routine will take you a long way — far enough to catch most crooks — '

'Er — yes, of course,' Somers interposed hastily. 'I was just wondering whether you're going to tell the Professor right away that we're from the Yard.'

'We'll see. We'll see.'

Faithfull slowly levered himself out of the car and carefully closed and locked the door.

They walked up the uneven drive which seemed to need weeding and presently came out opposite a large front porch.

The Inspector pulled Somers back into the shadow of the large elms, and they stood surveying the house for a few moments, trusting to luck that in the falling dusk they would not be seen from inside. The house looked as if it sadly lacked a coat of paint, and its plastered walls were crumbling slightly in places. They walked quietly along the front of the house, still keeping in the shadow of the trees. There were no lights in any of the windows, or indeed any sign of life.

At the far end there was a single storey room built on to the gable in the manner of the billiard rooms which were so fashionable fifty years ago.

'I expect he uses that as his laboratory,' hazarded Somers, noting that the windows of this room were curtainless.

As they came level with this room, Faithfull paused for a moment, then moved quickly across the drive, the Sergeant close on his heels. He walked from one window to the next, peering inside and confirming his guess that it was a laboratory. In fact, it looked a very ordinary sort of laboratory, and as far as Somers — who had taken science in his higher certificate — could discern, there was no strange apparatus.

In his anxiety to make sure of this Somers approached a little too near the window and caught his foot in what appeared to be a length of wire.

Almost at once an alarm bell rang loudly in a distant part of the house.

'What the devil's that?' snapped Faithfull.

'A burglar-alarm, I think.'

They hesitated in some uncertainty for a second or two, and then heard a quick, light footstep. Then a beam from a powerful torch almost blinded them.

'Stay where you are — both of you!' ordered a thin, precise voice.

'We have no intention of running away,' replied Faithfull curtly, shading his eyes from the glare with his hand. The beam of the torch dropped, and they were presently able to distinguish the outline of the rather elderly looking man who was holding it.

Somers said quickly:

'As a matter of fact we mistook our way in the dark — we must have walked past the front door.'

The man with the torch sniffed as if he

were somewhat sceptical of this explanation.

'I can hardly believe you would blunder into my burglar alarm unless you had approached the window with some purpose in mind,' he replied in a suspicious tone.

'It was an accident — '

But the other cut Somers short.

'To what am I indebted for the honour of this visit?' he wanted to know.

Faithfull stepped forward a pace.

'We're from Scotland Yard,' he announced bluntly.

The little man looked from one to the other, then said:

'I'm afraid I shall have to ask for some evidence of that.'

The Sergeant produced his warrant card, which the little man accepted, then backed away a step to examine it by the light of the torch. Presently, he handed it back with the remark:

'Such things shouldn't be very difficult to forge, of course.'

'Look here, sir,' began the Sergeant in a somewhat heated voice, 'I'm Sergeant

Somers and this is Inspector Faithfull — and if you care to telephone the Yard — '

The little man waved aside the protest.

'I'll take your word for it. Now perhaps you'll tell me why you're here — you haven't a search-warrant by any chance?'

'What should we want with such a thing as that, Professor?' demanded Faithfull amiably, adding as an afterthought: 'I take it you are Professor Mallowes?'

'I am. And you'd better come inside if you really want to see me about anything important. I'm only wearing thin slippers and I feel the cold.'

He led the way round a corner and opened a side door which led into the laboratory.

They were greeted by the usual acrid smell of intermingling chemicals and Mallowes snapped on a couple of lights before he took them into a small office in a corner of the large room.

'You are my second lot of visitors this week,' he informed them, indicating a couple of plain wooden-seated chairs.

'Indeed?' queried Faithfull, raising his eyebrows. 'You mean you've had burglars?'

'They were cleverer than you, Inspector. They managed to get inside the lab.'

'Inside the lab!' echoed Somers. 'Did they take anything?'

'Fortunately, they did not. I have a quantity of valuable stuff on the premises.'

'Meaning radium?' put in the Inspector in a casual tone.

Professor Mallowes did not reply for a few moments, but finally gave a tiny shrug and said:

'I suppose the entire London underworld is aware of it, so there seems to be no point in denying the suggestion.'

Somers repressed an impulse to smile, and Faithfull went on:

'Where did you get this radium, Professor?'

'I bought it through legitimate sources. I can show you a record of the transactions if you're interested.'

'I'll take your word for it. Now about this burglar — or burglars. You say they got inside?'

'They avoided the wires outside the windows which one of you gentlemen tripped over, but they took it for granted that those were my only line of defence. I have amused myself by contriving all sorts of precautions, and before they got to my safe they would have to avoid at least four little traps. These gentlemen fell foul of the invisible rays which set an alarm ringing the moment the ray is broken. Quite an elementary device, but invariably effective.'

'Very ingenious.'

Faithfull nodded appreciatively and glanced round the room as if he expected some new gadget to spring out upon him at any moment. 'What happened when you heard the alarm?'

'I called my man, Turner, and we went down at once.'

'There are only two of you here?'

'At night, yes.'

'Did you see these men who'd broken in?'

The other shook his head.

'Not very clearly. Naturally, they'd heard the alarm as well, and they were naturally making a getaway. I did just catch a glimpse of one of them as he went out through a window.'

'Could you describe him?'

'Not accurately. That was why there seemed so little point in notifying the police. I'm afraid I haven't very much confidence in the minions of the law.'

Faithfull coughed. Then:

'I always say there's nothing like speaking your mind. Can't you tell us any more about this man you saw?'

'He seemed to be of average build — perhaps a little on the slim side. I didn't see his face, but I'm fairly certain that he ran with a distinct limp.'

'Lem Knight — !' exclaimed Somers involuntarily.

'Steady, Sergeant, Lem Knight isn't the only crook with a game leg.'

Inspector Faithfull turned to the Professor once more and frowned.

'That piece of information,' he said, 'would have proved very valuable, Professor, if you had notified us at the time. And besides that there might have been fingerprints or some other clue.'

The Professor made an impatient gesture.

'I happen to be working about fourteen hours a day, Inspector, and I've no wish to be interrupted by red-nosed constables barging around my delicate apparatus looking for fingerprints.'

The Sergeant's face slipped into a grin and he turned his head and pretended to examine a row of bookshelves beside him.

'I only said there might have been fingerprints,' Faithfull replied in a surprisingly mild tone. 'Though from what we know of these people it is rather unlikely.'

Somers turned from the bookshelves and nodded.

'You're right there, Inspector.'

The Inspector went on:

'Still, now we are here, Professor, I think you ought to tell us the whole story.'

'There's nothing to tell. And I really am getting tired of these interruptions,' protested the other in a peeved voice. 'If they don't stop soon, I shall have no alternative but to start taking steps on my own account.'

Faithfull said gravely:

'I don't think that would be very wise, sir. It might land you in a lot more trouble in the end. The law's a very peculiar thing, you know, Professor — catches different people different ways. Now, if you could just spare five minutes to give me one or two ideas about what's going on, it might help to work things out without any further bother.'

Professor Mallowes tapped his desk rather impatiently with the end of a silver pencil he had picked up, and no one spoke for a few moments. Then the Professor said somewhat abruptly:

'I rather like the look of you, Inspector. You have an honest face — for a policeman!'

'Thank you, sir,' replied Faithfull, quite seriously. Then he leaned forward in his chair and murmured in a confidential tone:

'I do hope you won't go doing anything outside the law, sir. Self-defence is one thing, but anything in the nature of harmful assault — '

His voice trailed away and he shook his head dubiously once again.

The Professor fumbled in a drawer of his desk and produced a cardboard box filled with cigarettes which he passed over to his visitors.

After he had lighted one himself, he said:

'All right, I'll tell you what little I know about this affair.'

9

Professor Mallowes blew out a cloud of smoke and began:

'I dare say you saw some of the publicity I had in the newspapers a couple of years ago when I decided to have nothing more to do with the work on the atomic bomb.'

'I remember it well,' put in Somers.

The other nodded slowly and then went on:

'Of course, I was completely misrepresented. I had no particular objections to working on the atom bomb, but the research I did convinced me of the far greater possibilities of the use of atomic energy in the commercial field. That was what I wanted to concentrate upon — it was a constantly developing field, you understand?'

'I can see what you mean,' said Faithfull slowly. 'But it must take a lot of money to work on your own — specially when you're competing in a way with the government.'

Mallowes nodded.

'Exactly. But I happen to have made more money than I'll ever need for my personal use from certain other inventions. So I was able to fit up this lab and buy a certain amount of radium.'

Sergeant Somers said:

'There was quite a commotion when you resigned, Professor. I remember some M.P. saying in the House that you have the best scientific brain in the country, and the country couldn't afford to let you go.'

There was a gleam in the Professor's pale blue eyes as he nodded and said:

'So I have. But the country will benefit just the same in the long run. However, there's no point in arguing about that.'

'Quite so, sir,' Faithfull murmured, beginning to wonder exactly what bearing this had upon the present case.

The Professor lost no time in enlightening him.

'Almost from the day it was known I had resigned,' he continued, 'I have been pestered incessantly by all sorts of people — some of them who don't even know the atomic weight of radium.'

Inspector Faithfull didn't know it himself, but he nodded encouragingly.

'The usual approach from these people is an offer to employ me by some private company — companies I've never heard of, and which probably hadn't even been formed.'

Somers queried:

'You mean there was something shady about these offers?'

'I never troubled to investigate them, but I should be very surprised if one tenth of them were genuine.'

The Inspector said:

'Did these people want you to work on atomic experiments, Professor?'

'They left no doubt about that. Several mentioned the atomic bomb as their only objective.'

Faithfull rubbed his chin with his hand as he turned over this information in his mind. There seemed to be no end to the tentacles of this organization they were up against, nor to the agents whom they employed. Some of them might even have been acting in good faith.

'Did you ever get anything in writing from these people?' he inquired.

Mallowes shook his head.

'Oh no. It started with telephone calls. Then they began to call and see me here, representing themselves as agents of some mysterious company. But they refused to reveal the names of their principals unless I was ready to talk business.'

'Then you don't think these callers were crooks?'

The other waved his cigarette in a nonchalant gesture.

'My dear Inspector, I don't know enough about crooks to recognize them on sight. But my impression of these people was that they consisted chiefly of the more shady type of lawyer. Though I never took very much notice of them — my main interest was in showing them the door!'

'You wouldn't have any idea as to whether they represented the same organization,' suggested Somers.

'I'm practically certain of it.'

Mallowes replied in a casual tone, as if he were not particularly interested.

'Why do you say that?' Faithfull asked.

'Just straws in the wind. There was a distinct similarity in their line of talk. They all offered me a free hand — no limit to expenditure — they all wanted me to leave England and work in a specially equipped lab — some mentioned South American countries. They all flashed a bundle of bank notes at me — the last man had three thousand pounds — '

Inspector Faithfull whistled softly. Then an idea struck him.

'I suppose it's possible, Professor,' he said slowly, 'that one of the big chemical combines might have something to do with these mysterious offers.'

Professor Mallowes nodded emphatically.

'Certainly it's possible, Inspector. Some industrial concern may have become interested in some game of international politics.' He stubbed out his cigarette and added with a shake of the head: 'I spend most of my time in a laboratory, but I hear quite a lot of what goes on behind the scenes.'

'Then supposing it is some such company, would you connect them in any way with this attempt at robbery?'

'I don't know about that. It is possible that, having tried all the legal approaches, they may think they'll drag me into their research department by depriving me of my own supplies of radium.'

The Inspector shook his head slowly. He mused:

'H'm . . . it's a bit far-fetched, though. I doubt if any concern would dare to take the risk of such a thing being exposed.'

The Professor smiled and nodded.

'Ah, I can see you're a man after my own heart — a man of caution.'

'I never believed in jumping to conclusions.'

'Quite right, Inspector. We scientists never assume anything unless we have tested it right up to the hilt, and we find ourselves applying the same principles to everyday life in many cases.'

'Exactly, Professor. Personally, I think we'll have to go pretty carefully over this case. I sincerely hope it isn't any firm behind the affair.'

The Professor smiled grimly as if he appreciated the Inspector's line of thought.

'Personally,' he remarked, 'I'm not particularly interested as to who is responsible for all these interruptions I'm getting. My main concern is that they should cease at once. And the next time it happens, I shall certainly take the law into my own hands. If people come trespassing on these premises, then they must take the consequences.'

'I hope you won't do anything you'll be sorry for, Professor.'

The Sergeant, who had been strolling round the room, was peering curiously at a strange piece of apparatus in a far corner. It was unlike anything he had seen before, consisting mainly of a number of meters and control knobs, grouped around a chair-shaped cavity about two feet from the floor.

The apparatus was almost completely enclosed by a plastic material, so it was difficult to form any idea as to its purpose.

'I take it this is part of your experiments, Professor,' Somers said curiously.

The Professor slowly rose and walked over to the Sergeant. Faithfull also got up and joined them.

'This is practically the entire focal point of my experiments,' Mallowes told them.

They stood for some seconds looking at the machine without speaking. Then Somers asked what the apparatus was exactly.

Professor Mallowes's manner became slightly more impressive.

'That,' he announced, 'is my own development of the cyclotron.'

Faithfull reminded him:

'You must remember you're talking to two laymen as far as science is concerned. Perhaps you'll give us some idea as to what a cyclotron is exactly.'

The other smiled as he replied quite casually: 'It's just a piece of apparatus used in splitting the atom. Rather complicated to the layman, perhaps, though its original layout seems a bit crude to us now. I've developed this apparatus so that it will now disintegrate most of the heavier minerals.'

Somers frowned thoughtfully.

'You mean they just vanish?'

The Professor made a slight gesture of impatience.

'No, no, nothing ever vanishes; they are simply transferred into energy which is storable in the condensers. If you're really interested, I'll switch on the machine and give you a small demonstration.'

He disappeared for a moment, and there was the sound of clicking switches. A deep hum began to penetrate the quiet of the room and Faithfull imagined he felt a faint vibration of the floor. A strange bluish-white light was reflected from the back of the machine.

The Professor returned with a lump of dark substance about the size of a walnut, which he placed in the cavity of the machine. Then he turned two knobs at the side and the buzzing note slowly changed. Faithfull and Somers moved closer to the apparatus to get a better view, and as they watched they saw the dark brown substance slowly disappear before their eyes.

The whole operation took rather less than two minutes; meanwhile Mallowes studied the dials and made some slight adjustments to the control knobs. When the last fragment had disappeared, he twisted the knobs and the original humming note was resumed.

'I don't often give these demonstrations,' he told them, 'but at least this serves the purpose of satisfying your curiosity and also demonstrating the progress I have made to outside witnesses, just in case of any accidents.'

This last phrase rather puzzled Faithfull, but he made no comment.

'It's — it's amazing!' stammered Somers who was deeply impressed. 'You mean this machine changes the solid substances into electric energy or something?'

'That's roughly the idea,' Mallowes nodded. 'As it improves, I hope in time to be able to disintegrate almost anything.'

'Even a living body?' queried Somers, favouring him with a shrewd glance.

The Professor hesitated.

'That might be possible,' he conceded at length.

Faithfull chuckled.

'When you do that, Professor, you'll have discovered the way to the perfect murder,' he announced.

Mallowes smiled slowly.

'Even that might have its uses.'

He disappeared again for a few moments and switched off the power. The weird penetrative humming stopped and the silence that followed seemed more pronounced.

Then Professor Mallowes reappeared, soothing his silvery grey hair at the back of his head.

'I think that's about all I can do for you gentlemen,' he announced quite pleasantly. 'I've told you all I know about our little burglary, and I hope you'll be able to arrange for me to be left in peace from now on.'

The Inspector shrugged expressively.

'As long as you're dealing with radium,

Professor, I'm afraid you're bound to come in for some attention. We can't very well stop these people calling on you and making you offers — unless we can catch them in the act of putting up some illegal suggestion. By the way, you did say that these visitors were all men, didn't you?'

The other nodded.

'Yes, though there was a woman who telephoned — some time last week I think.'

'She didn't give her name?'

Mallowes shook his head.

The Inspector eyed him shrewdly and suddenly asked:

'Have you ever heard of a girl called Georgia Nash?'

The Professor looked puzzled.

'Not that I can remember,' he replied. 'Is she anyone in Science or Research?'

Faithfull took the shabby envelope from his pocket.

'D'you recognize that writing?'

He passed it over to Mallowes, who held it about two feet away from him.

'I'm afraid I've left my glasses in my

sitting-room,' he explained. 'I dare say I can manage . . . '

He screwed his eyes up for a few seconds, then he announced confidently:

'Yes, I know this writing.'

10

Somers stifled an exclamation, but Faithfull showed no sign of surprise at Professor Mallowes's announcement.

'And you're quite sure you've never heard of Georgia Nash?' he persisted.

'Of course not. This writing is Helen Winton's.'

'Helen Winton?'

'She was my secretary for about two months. I had a large accumulation of notes to transcribe.'

'Then you can recall what she was like to look at.'

Mallowes gave them a description which undoubtedly applied to the girl who called herself Georgia Nash.

'How did you come to know this woman?' the Inspector asked, returning the envelope to his pocket.

'I got her through a secretarial bureau. She was highly recommended and I found her most efficient. It was specialized work, you understand, and she had a very intelligent grasp of all the jargon.'

'But she's a dance-partner,' Somers could not refrain from interjecting.

The Professor favoured him with a whimsical glance.

'I did not inquire into the manner in which she employed her leisure,' he retorted mildly. 'I only know her work gave every satisfaction.'

'And you haven't heard from her since she left?'

'There was no reason why I should.'

'Perhaps not — but she had evidently addressed an envelope with a view to sending you a letter.'

'It might not have been a letter,' the other pointed out in a reasonable tone.

'That's true. Then you've no idea what this woman may have intended to send you?'

'Not the slightest. It may have been a simple inquiry as to whether I was requiring her services again. I told her that I might when she left. In fact, I was very sorry that I couldn't offer her a permanent position, but my work is peculiar in that respect. She would have had practically nothing to do for weeks while I was busy in the lab. I always find it preferable to engage a secretary for short periods to clear off an accumulation of notes and correspondence.'

'I see.' Faithfull tried hard to detect some flaw in the Professor's suave explanations.

'Well, there's no accounting for blondes,' muttered Somers, the piquant features of Georgia Nash still playing tricks with his imagination.

Faithfull sniffed and turned towards the door.

'You don't know the address of this secretary of yours?' he queried as Mallowes showed them out.

'I understood she had a flat in town somewhere, but of course I should contact her through the agency. They're called Express Secretarial Bureau — you might try them, though I hardly see how Miss Winton can be in any way involved. She seemed a highly respectable girl.'

He seemed frankly puzzled, but Faithfull did not offer to enlighten him at all about Georgia Nash.

They left Professor Mallowes reconnecting his burglar alarm outside the laboratory, and made their way back to the car.

Neither said very much until Somers had turned the car and they were heading in the direction of the East End. Presently, the Sergeant deftly contrived to light a cigarette and blew out a cloud of smoke. He mused:

'Looks fishy about that girl.'

Faithfull frowned.

'How often have I warned you about jumping to conclusions?' he growled, winding up the window on his side, for the night air was chilly.

'But look at the facts,' insisted Somers. 'First, this girl is on the spot when Nicky is taken for a ride; then we hear she's left her job and vanished; and finally we know that she acted as secretary to a man who's doing atomic research. If she isn't mixed up in the business somewhere — '

'It's all purely circumstantial so far,' Faithfull reminded him with an emphatic gesture.

The other changed down as they approached some traffic lights, and merely grunted by way of reply. Somewhere, deep down, he hoped that Georgia Nash was not criminally implicated in any of these activities. He was a susceptible young man, and the girl's face was already vivid in his memory.

He realized he had hardly given his girl friend, Carol, a thought during the past twelve hours. He had hoped to meet her this evening, but had now given up the idea with no more than a momentary pang. There was something intriguing about this Nash girl, something attractive too. Somers had had very little experience of women crooks, and they were still invested with a certain amount of glamour in his imagination.

Resolutely, he put Georgia Nash out of his mind for the time being, and glancing at Faithfull out of the corner of his eye, he casually inquired:

'What d'you make of the Professor bloke? Think he's holding anything back?'

The other rubbed his rather bristly chin.

'I'm not trusting him,' he announced. 'It never pays to trust anybody until the guilty party is safe in the cells. I've always conducted my investigations on that principle,' he added solemnly.

Somers nodded approvingly.

'You think he might be in league with the Nash girl?' he suggested, as the car sped through the traffic-free streets of the City and headed in the direction of the Shadwell Basin.

'He would be in an ideal position to control the type of organization we're up against. We have to remember that,' was the reply.

'He sounded pretty genuine to me. And there was no need for him to have made up that story about the robbery. Or was there?'

Faithfull shrugged.

'Once the mind turns into criminal channels, there's no telling what it won't invent in self-protection. It's no use following these theories too far, but one has to keep all the possibilities in mind. His story is feasible enough, I admit.'

The Sergeant slowed down to avoid a

woman who dashed across the road.

'The gentlemen we're up against would be only too pleased to have a man like Mallowes at their disposal,' he said. 'He'd be worth a hundred thousand a year to 'em. Or even more than that. Those blokes think in millions from what I can see of it.'

They began to meet a stream of heavy dock traffic, and Somers did not speak for some minutes as he steered past the oncoming lorries which thundered at them and vanished into the night.

'No need to hurry,' grunted Faithfull. 'We'll be there before the pub shuts, and that'll be time enough.'

Somers nodded, then bit his lower lip — something was obviously worrying him.

'I don't altogether trust that girl,' he murmured at last. 'She seemed sort of tough — it may have only been a sort of act for our benefit, but all the same — '

'She may have had a tough life,' Faithfull said. 'That often has a toughening effect.' He spoke as seriously as any social investigator about to deliver a lecture on the effects of environment. 'All the same, you've got to be very careful about judging by appearances, as I think I've said before.'

'Frequently,' grinned Somers, who was beginning to get a lot of quiet fun out of these little lectures from his superior.

The other mused:

'I was just thinking of a case that came up when I was up North. When I got there, the Deputy Chief Constable wouldn't let me in on it. Said he had it all sewn up. And he got his verdict all right. Murder it was. Two hours before the execution, a woman turned up to prove the convicted man was innocent. That taught me a lesson.'

'I wonder what it taught the Deputy Chief?'

Faithfull fumbled for his snuff-box and took a pinch.

'He was very upset. Never really believed it. Thought it was some sort of frame-up. Still, they had to let the man go, and we never found the real murderer. Myself, I thought it was suicide, but I couldn't prove it — '

He broke off with an exclamation as the car suddenly lurched. As he tried to straighten it out Somers became conscious that the wheel did not respond. He transferred his foot from the accelerator to the foot-brake at once, but the car had swung into the centre of the road right in the path of a large five-ton lorry which was lumbering towards them at twenty miles an hour. Somers spun the wheel viciously with some slight effect. There was a screaming of brakes and a splintering of metal.

It had been impossible for the lorry to stop, but the driver, sensing that something was wrong, had managed to slow down considerably. The car struck the lorry a glancing blow, and the vehicles came to a standstill within ten yards of each other.

Somers and Faithfull, who had been flung against the windscreen with the impact, sorted themselves out, gingerly feeling their faces for any possible cuts. However, apart from a few bruises the two Scotland Yard men were unhurt. They looked up to see the scowling face of the lorry driver thrust in at the window.

'What the 'ell's goin' on? Ran slap into me, you did. Never give me time to pull up — '

'It's all right,' Somers assured him. 'Something's gone wrong with my steering. It wasn't your fault.'

He took out a torch and began to inspect the steering column.

'That's all very well,' grumbled the driver, 'but I'm reportin' this to the police.'

'We'll see that a report is made,' replied Faithfull a trifle testily.

'I've only got your word for that. I'm not movin' from 'ere till I've seen the police,' sniffed the driver, wiping his grimy forehead with his shirt sleeve. 'Might have been somebody killed — bashin' into me like that.'

'This steering has been tampered with,' muttered Somers to Faithfull in an undertone, which the driver happened to catch.

'That's all very well,' he grumbled, 'but the police have got to 'ear all about — '

'We are the police!' snapped the

Inspector impatiently.

The lorry driver looked sceptical, whereupon Somers switched on the illuminated 'Police' sign over the windscreen, which was undamaged.

'Satisfied?' he asked, switching the light off again.

The driver gaped and the Inspector got out of the car and took a note of the lorry's registration number. A small crowd had gathered by this time, and as they were anxious to avoid any more attention than was necessary, the detectives pushed their car into the gutter. Somers went to telephone the Yard from a nearby callbox, arranging to have it towed back to its garage.

They were less than half a mile from their destination. A brisk walk down gloomy side streets soon brought them to the cobblestoned corner on which stood the Three Sailors. It was a Victorian public house, whose decayed walls looked as if they would benefit by a coat of paint.

Shabby red blinds were drawn over the windows and a decrepit piano was tinkling in one of the rooms. The two police officers stood for a moment on the cobblestones which a fine mist from the river had turned greasy, and made quite sure they were not being watched. They were also taking a shrewd survey of the landscape in case of emergency. An elderly man in shabby clothes lounged past, giving them a suspicious glance, then passed down an entry at the side of the public house. A tug's siren hooted dismally on the river.

'Come on,' said Faithfull abruptly. 'I could do with a drop o' something. Hope we'll be lucky!'

They pushed open the swing-door leading to the saloon-bar and were greeted by a gust of tobacco smoke and smell of stale beer. The small bar was fairly full. Noisy conversation almost drowned the tinkling of the piano. Inspector Faithfull found a vacant chair in a corner and prepared to take stock of the customers. The Sergeant elbowed his way to the counter.

The barmaid stood with her back to him as he approached, his ear turned to catch a snatch of conversation from his neighbour. Then the barmaid pushed a drink towards a customer and faced Somers.

'Yes, sir? What can I get you?'

It was Georgia Nash, smiling at him pertly.

11

Miss Carol Collins leaned back in her chair, extended a long, slim elegant leg and peeled off a gossamer nylon which she flung on the dressing-shelf in front of her.

Slowly repeating the operation with the other equally slender leg, she suddenly glanced in the mirror at Miss Val Harris, with whom she shared this particular dressing-room at the Regal Theatre.

'It sounds marvellous, darling,' she murmured, 'but what does he *do*? Nobody gets as much money as that nowadays for doing nothing. I mean what with taxes and all that, it just can't be true.'

Miss Val Harris paused in the act of slipping off a frothy scrap of lingerie preparatory to putting on a costume designed to display her figure to the utmost advantage in the 'Bathing Belles' scene of the revue *Ever Since Eve* in which the girls were appearing five times a day, from twelve o'clock until eleven.

'He says he's got a system,' explained Miss Harris, insinuating her lithe figure into the meagre costume. 'You know — the dogs. He says he backs 'em by the number of the trap, not on the form of the dog. It's a sort of — what do they call it? — mathematical formula.'

'Oh yeah?' Miss Collins sniffed sceptically, a wealth of innuendo in her tones, implying she had heard many such stories before. In fact, this was a very studied pose which Miss Collins was wont to affect quite frequently. It was a popular one among the show girls at the theatre; and in many cases it was not entirely a pose, for some very queer types found their way to the stage door of the Regal.

'Have you ever been with him to the dogs?' pursued Carol persistently.

Val made an impatient gesture.

'Now, darling, what time do we ever have for going to the dogs; when we're stuck in this darned palace of pleasure almost every hour God gives us?' She repaired one or two minor defects in her make-up and emphasized the already over-generous Cupid's bow of her lips.

Carol rose and began to undress further, sorting out her own bathing costume which was suspended on a hanger behind her. It was only a tiny room, and the girls found it paid in the long run to be tidy. They were lucky indeed to get a room to themselves away from the ten other show girls in the revue. They had got it through Miss Collins's influence with the stage manager — there had been a phase of her life when she had been upon rather more than familiar terms with him. In fact, she could have probably achieved a dressing-room to herself, but she declared that she preferred a limited amount of company, so she magnanimously allowed Val to share — a favour of which she never tired of reminding her.

'You can say what you like, Maurice is a good sort,' insisted Val. 'Why, only yesterday he gave me a radiogram for the flat — you ought to see it! Must have cost best part of hundred and fifty.'

Carol sighed, 'Considering you've talked about nothing else all day.'

'But you ought to see it, darling. It does practically everything but put you to bed.'

'I expect Maurice manages that all right,' sniffed Miss Collins. Val giggled.

'You do say awful things, darling. But I wish you could see it.' She hesitated, then swung round and faced the other.

'Why don't you pop round with me after this show?' she suggested. 'I've got to fetch those things for the cleaners. And I hate going by myself. We can do it in five minutes and have time for a quick cup of tea.'

Carol considered this with a frown, then decided to accept, for her stage manager friend often chose this long break as opportune for becoming a little more than friendly, and to tell the truth Carol was tired of his somewhat arrogant advances, which compared unfavourably with the rather more cultured manner of Detective-Sergeant Somers, who at least treated her as if she were a lady. Besides, it would be a breath of fresh air, and the theatre was very stuffy tonight.

'All right,' she agreed. They brilliantined their hair and added a last dab of wet white to their arms, then joined their scantily costumed colleagues who were waiting in line at the side of the stage. Presently on their cue they flashed on their automatic smiles for the benefit of the elderly gentlemen in the front stalls as they swung on to the stage. In perfect rhythm they moved with quite flawless precision. Which was hardly surprising, for they had performed those identical actions in this particular dance on 452 previous occasions. For four minutes, Carol and Val were cogs in a smoothly functioning machine. Then the girls broke up and draped themselves against odd bits of scenery to dress the stage while various principals engaged in romantic or comic interludes. On such occasions, Val and Carol had developed a technique for conducting a *sotto-voce* conversation behind their steadfastly maintained toothy smiles.

'There he is again,' muttered Val. 'Second row — next but two to the gangway left-hand side.'

Carol took a peep at the first opportunity and espied the elderly peer who was causing a certain amount of scandalous comment among the girls by reason of his attentions to Miss Trixie Malone, who was seizing every opportunity to flaunt her admirer's lavish gifts before her envious fellow chorines. He had sat through two shows a day for the past month with absolutely tireless devotion. Miss Malone was one of the girls who posed artistically in two scenes under subdued lighting. She had allowed her hair to grow until it reached half-way down her back, and he told her (she passed on the information) that he had singled her out at once for this reason. She reminded him, it seemed, of his dear wife. If he could have heard the profane howl of laughter (including his beloved's) which greeted this announcement in the chorus dressing-room, he would have been rather more cautious with his endearments in the future.

The reflection from the strong stage lighting in the 'Bathing Belles' scene lit up the bald pates of the ancient stalwarts in the first few rows who usually formed the nucleus of the Regal audiences. In fact, it happened quite frequently that there was not a woman in the house.

At the end of the show, Val and Carol hurriedly put on their outdoor clothes, removed a little of their lavish make-up, but not very much, and made their way down the half a dozen flights of stairs which separated their dressing-room from the street level. They wore scarves over their heads, and exchanging a couple of swift wisecracks with stage hands clustered round the stage door, they passed into the night.

Val's flat was just nearby. Very convenient for the theatre, but according to her, the only trouble was the dubious class of people who inhabited the immediate neighbourhood. Rarely a day went by without her relating some hair-raising incident of the night before.

The flat was on the second floor above a gown shop, and they entered by a door at the side of the shop and mounted three flights of stone stairs. Val rushed to switch on the radiogram and demonstrate its tricks, and it was not until it was in the middle of the second record that she thought to run into the kitchen and fill the kettle for their tea.

'For heaven's sake watch the time!' implored Val, rushing around looking for the milk and the biscuits. 'You know I was fined last week.'

She made the tea and they sat sipping it in front of the electric fire.

Carol asked, 'Where's the boy friend — at the dogs?'

'Of course, darling. He's there every night.'

'That's what he tells you,' thought Carol, but made no audible comment.

She was accustomed to Val's boy friends by this time. None of them lasted more than a couple of months, during which time they made themselves at home in her flat until she succumbed to the inevitable fit of 'temperament', after which they usually walked out with anything valuable they could lay hands on. Rarely did they make any such generous contribution as a radiogram to the hearth and home. ('He can't very well pick that up and walk out with it,' thought Carol.) It certainly was a handsome instrument. Must have cost at least eighty pounds.

The strains of the latest dance-record filled the sitting-room as they drank their tea. Suddenly, a thought struck Carol.

'Val, darling, you don't think it's serious this time? He hasn't mentioned getting married?'

Val laughed.

'What d'you take me for?'

'Well, I've thought about marriage quite a bit lately. There's one of my boy friends — '

'You mean the policeman?'

'He isn't a policeman. He's a detective.'

'Pooh — six pounds a week. Wouldn't keep you in undies!'

'I could go on working. Not that he's ever said anything about wanting to be married,' she added as an afterthought.

'No, he's one of the smart ones — never says a thing till he means it in case it lands him into something. I could see that clearly enough. I weighed him up that night he came to the dressing-room.

There are no flies on that cop!'

Carol shrugged. 'Oh well, there are plenty more at the stage door any night. But I did like him rather specially.'

'You must have. Never heard you talk of settling down before. Time enough for that when your figure's beginning to droop!'

She stubbed out the cigarette she had been smoking, put her cup and saucer on the mantelpiece and switched off the radiogram.

'Time we were getting a move on,' she announced. 'I'll just go and get the things for the cleaners.'

She went off to the bedroom on the other side of the narrow hallway. Carol leaned back in her chair and finished her cigarette, toasting her toes at the electric fire. She had just puffed out a long stream of smoke when there was a scream from Val in the other room.

Carol leapt to her feet.

'What in God's name — ' she began, then saw Val in the doorway, her face drawn, her eyes wide with fear. Carol ran across and clutched her.

‘What is it, Val — what is it?’

‘It’s Maurice — he’s in there — on the bed — ’

‘Well, good heavens, that isn’t the first time he’s lain on the bed,’ snapped Carol, giving her a little shake. ‘Pull yourself together. He’s probably been on the binge and — ’

‘Shut up!’ screamed Val. ‘He’s dead, I tell you! Maurice is dead!’

12

Carol Collins pushed past the other girl and went to the door of the bedroom. One glance at the man on the bed sufficed to tell her that if he were not dead he was desperately wounded. He had apparently been shot through the temple. She closed the door and returned to the hysterical Val.

'Here — got any brandy or whisky?'

Val indicated a cupboard in one corner of the sitting-room. Carol poured two half-tumblers of whisky.

'Come on — drink that quickly!' She tossed down the contents of her own glass, then went across to the telephone and rang Sergeant Somers's private number. He was out. She telephoned Scotland Yard and was told that he was expected back sometime later. She gave the sergeant the number of the flat and also that of the stage door at the theatre, with an urgent message for Somers to ring there as soon as he got back. Then she turned to Val.

'Come on!' she urged. 'We're going back to the theatre. Pull yourself together now — there's nothing we can do for him — it's a job for the police. And my boy-friend always told me be sure and never touch anything in cases like this. So we'll give it a wide berth till the police get here.'

But Val refused to be pulled together. The shock had apparently been too much for her.

There was nothing for it but to telephone the theatre and ask to speak to her friend the stage manager, to whom she rapidly explained the position. Carol added that the police were detaining them at the flat for the time being, just to make quite certain that no unnecessary blame could be attached to them. Then she set herself to the task of calming down her companion. And the temperamental Val was making the most of the situation, declaring her undying love for the dead man, that life was no longer worth living, and vowing vengeance upon whoever had killed her lover.

Carol tried more whisky, and when this had no effect she took Val by the shoulders and shook her vigorously, then slapped her face. This treatment was more successful and after a series of gulps Val stopped her screaming, which must have been heard in the street. However, no one made any effort to inquire as to the source of the commotion.

Carol was more than a little relieved when at half-past ten the telephone rang and she heard the familiar voice of Sergeant Somers.

He sounded a trifle irritable. He had received similar urgent messages from her on other occasions which were a prelude to nothing more than an invitation to take her to a party. The one or two actresses he had known seemed compelled to dramatize the most minor incidents in their lives. He supposed it was understandable, but it became more than a little annoying at times. His voice on the telephone had a challenging note, for this had been a hectic evening, and he wanted to get back to a hot bath, a stiff drink and then bed.

'Is anything wrong?' he snapped.

'Wrong!' she echoed. 'You'd better grab a taxi and come round at once.'

She gave him the address, but he seemed inclined to argue.

'Now, darling, if this is just a party,' he began, but she cut him short.

'It may be your idea of a party,' she snapped, 'but it certainly isn't mine.'

'What d'you mean?'

She told him grimly.

'Somebody's been playing 'Murder' round here with a loaded revolver!'

13

If Georgia Nash was surprised to see Somers, she certainly showed no sign of it.

On the other hand, the Sergeant was rather more taken aback than he would have cared to admit. He chose to consider himself an experienced detective, thoroughly hardened to all the variegations of human nature. When he had recovered a little he elbowed nearer to the counter and spoke to her in a low voice.

'What the devil are you doing here?'

The corners of her mouth curved slightly.

'I may be wrong,' she replied imperturbably, 'but I have an idea I'm serving drinks to a couple of plain-clothes policemen.' She nodded in the direction of Inspector Faithfull. Her voice rang out above the din in the bar, and one or two suspicious-looking characters favoured the detectives with dubious glares.

'Give me two double brandies,' Somers said hurriedly.

'No brandy — only Irish whisky.'

'That'll do.'

Somers felt he must drink something that was fiery to the taste, though he had never been able to cultivate a liking for Irish whisky.

While she poured the drinks he tried hard to think of some remark which would convey to her that his was a business call. But she seemed to be very popular, carrying on three or four conversations almost simultaneously, and he dared not say anything that would be likely to attract undue attention.

When she brought the drinks he handed over the money without a word and she slapped his change on the damp counter as she was in the midst of a chat with another customer.

The Sergeant returned to Faithfull carrying the drinks. The older man accepted his whisky without comment, and tossed it down with a couple of gulps. He had spotted Georgia Nash, but gave a non-committal grunt when the other asked him what he thought about her presence at the Three Sailors.

'That's better!' was his only remark, regarding his empty glass. 'I must say that little accident shook me up a bit. I'm not as young as I was to stand up to these shocks.'

'That steering was tampered with!' Somers asserted emphatically. He paused, then added quietly: 'You don't think she had anything to do with it?' He nodded in the direction of Georgia Nash.

'How could she?' asked Faithfull unemotionally. 'She can't act as barmaid and go round messing with cars as well.'

'I wonder what the devil she's doing here,' mused the Sergeant. 'There's something pretty fishy about the way she keeps popping up in a fresh job every few weeks.'

'There's no law against it,' the Inspector pronounced reasonably enough. 'But as you say, it's queer how she gets mixed up in jobs where this gang goes to work!'

'She's so damn brazen about it all. That's what gets me,' exclaimed Somers with certain anger. At that moment, the new barmaid looked over in their direction and smiled.

'I think she's taken a bit of a fancy to you,' remarked Faithfull drily.

Five minutes later they noticed that the room was emptying rather quickly. The word had got round that the strangers were plain-clothes police. Having finished their whisky, the policemen now drank beer. Somers went out and took a look round the other bar, but did not see the man he sought. Meanwhile, Faithfull sat imperturbably in his corner, reading the crossword competition in the paper again, and looking up from time to time.

Once, he caught Georgia Nash's eye and stared at her stolidly for a few seconds before she turned to busy herself at the bar once more.

'Looks like we've drawn a blank,' murmured Somers returning from a second trip to the other bar. 'Pike Bellamy said we should find him here practically any night,' he continued in a disappointed tone. Then he suddenly looked thoughtful. 'Inspector, you don't think he's got a job on tonight?'

The other shot him a warning glance, then carefully folded his newspaper and thrust it into his mackintosh pocket. It was five minutes to ten, and there was only one man left in the bar. He was obviously a small tradesman, decidedly respectable-looking. Georgia Nash came from behind the counter collecting empty glasses.

'You two have certainly done the business a bit of no good tonight,' she commented as she came to their table. 'And it doesn't look as if you've done yourselves much good either.'

Inspector Faithfull looked up at her.

'We have,' he retorted imperturbably.

'But there's been no sign of Lem Knight all evening.'

'Who said we came to see Lem Knight?' he asked in a level tone.

She shrugged as she picked up some more glasses.

'At any rate,' the Inspector continued, 'we have had the pleasure of renewing your acquaintance. We were rather worried about you when you vanished from the Luxor. In fact, we shall want you to give evidence at the inquest.'

She smiled at him.

'Well now, you know where to find me.'

'Yes,' was the slow reply, 'we thought we could always find you at the Luxor.'

'Just a temporary job to tide me over,' she parried.

'Now look here,' Faithfull said, 'we know quite well that during the past three months you've been a private secretary, a dance hostess and a barmaid. What conclusion d'you imagine I'm liable to draw from that?'

'You might conclude that I'm a versatile sort of girl,' she replied brightly.

The other grunted.

'I might conclude a lot of other things, too. It's as well for you I'm not the sort of man who jumps to conclusions.'

She eyed him levelly.

'Isn't that lucky?'

'Time, gentlemen, please!' came the landlord's voice, and Faithfull slowly rose to his feet.

'The inquest is at three tomorrow afternoon — quite a convenient time for you,' he informed the girl. 'I'll send a man along with the subpoena just in case of accidents.'

'You'd better send Sergeant Somers, then there won't be any accidents,' she replied with a meaning look at that worthy. 'And talking of accidents reminds me of a nasty jolt I had this evening.'

'What was that?'

'Coming down here, my handbag was snatched just as I was getting off the bus at Fenchurch Street. There was a big crowd — it was the rush hour — and I didn't even see the man who did it!'

'Anything valuable in it?' Somers asked.

She hesitated for a moment, then said, 'Nothing very much. About thirty shillings in cash — the usual odds and ends — make-up and so on.' She paused. 'The only thing of any value was a small Resto automatic — a point two-two.'

She noted the two men's eyebrows which had raised the merest fraction.

'Yes, I have a licence for it,' she informed them sweetly.

'Isn't it a little unusual for a young lady like yourself to carry such a weapon?' Inspector Faithfull queried mildly.

'I carry it in case I should have to scare someone. I've never actually used it. But it's rather a wicked-looking little weapon, and in these parts a girl never knows.'

Her voice trailed away. She dumped her glasses on the bar counter.

'So if you should see a Resto .22 lying round,' she concluded, 'there's quite a chance it may be mine.'

Faithfull asked her, 'Was it loaded?'

'As a matter of fact it was.'

He nodded.

'All right, I'll keep it in mind. I hope we'll be seeing you tomorrow. We may have some news for you then.'

He turned to Somers and nodded in the direction of the door.

The landlord, a burly individual in shirt sleeves, was waiting to close it after them. He looked them up and down very suspiciously. However, he made no comment and the door banged after them with a reverberation that echoed down the misty street.

Faithfull and Somers found their way back to their car to find the repair squad busy. The front wheels had been jacked on to a low platform behind their small lorry and they were almost ready to move off. They gave the two detectives a lift as far as their garage, where Somers signed the necessary forms.

'They won't be so keen to let you have their special speedsters in future,' commented Faithfull a trifle grimly as they walked back to the Yard.

The other nodded abstractedly.

'I wonder if that girl will turn up at the inquest,' he said as if suddenly speaking his thoughts aloud.

Faithfull shrugged.

'It isn't very important, really,' he grunted. 'Main thing is we want to keep track of her. I've a feeling she may lead us to something.'

'She's damned attractive,' the other mused. 'I don't like the idea of her being in that awful pub. Can't think what made her — '

'That,' declared Inspector Faithfull, 'is another thing we have to find out.'

The official on duty stopped them as they entered the Yard and gave Somers the message from Carol Collins.

'She sounded as if it was pretty urgent, sir,' he added.

Somers sighed.

'All right, I'll phone from my office.'

The Inspector went up with him to see if there were any late reports which he could digest overnight. While Somers was telephoning he ran through half a dozen memos, answering two of them. When the other replaced the receiver, the Inspector looked up and asked:

'Did I hear you say something about murder?'

Somers looked slight embarrassed.

'It's a girl I know — she's rather excitable. Maybe nothing in it after all. She wants me to go along to this place right away.'

He tapped the slip of paper on which he had scribbled the address.

Faithfull rose to his feet.

'I'll come along with you,' he announced, 'I used to know Soho pretty well in the old days. I can do with a bit of a walk.'

'But you won't get home till God knows when.'

'I'll get a bus up till eleven-thirty. And the wife's away at her sister's, so there isn't much point in getting back early.'

Actually, although he did not admit it, the word 'murder' was like the trumpet to a warhorse where Faithfull was concerned.

They started walking briskly and reached the flat in less than ten minutes.

'I hope to God it isn't a wild-goose chase,' Somers said as he rang the bell with some urgency.

Carol opened the door to them herself, and led the way into the sitting-room. The police-officers could see from the expression on her face and on that of Val Harris, that something tragic had occurred. Before leading them into the bedroom, Carol and Val told them how they had come to discover the body.

Somers asked: 'How long have you known this man, Maurice Preston?'

'He's been living here nearly two months,' replied Val.

'What is he? What's he do for a living?'

'She doesn't quite know,' put in Carol. 'He's told her that he makes all his money at the dogs. He's bought her this radiogram — he does pretty well.'

'When did you last see him?'

Val Harris replied:

'This morning.'

'You're sure you haven't seen him since? No idea where he was going?'

'He said he might go down to Harringay.'

Val sniffed and seemed likely to burst into tears at any moment. The Sergeant looked across at Faithfull and suggested:

'Shall we go and take a look at him, Inspector?'

Faithfull nodded.

He had made little attempt to interrupt Somers, and was secretly intrigued to note how he was handling the case. He was a little surprised that the sergeant had not demanded to be shown the body before this; in fact these were his own tactics — the cautious and thorough approach and careful questioning.

Carol led the way into the bedroom, motioning to Val to remain where she was. Carol switched on the light and Somers walked in quickly after her.

Faithfull stood at the door, peering at the figure slumped across the bed, the blood soaking into the pale green eiderdown and congealing in unsightly clots. The man's head was almost buried in the eiderdown and they could not distinguish his features immediately.

Then Carol noticed something which already caught the detective's eyes but which had escaped her previously.

'Look!' she cried, 'he's holding a revolver.'

Somers walked round the bed. The gun was almost concealed in the hand that was farthest from the door. Stepping up to the bed, the Sergeant turned the body over so that he could see the face.

He caught his breath in sudden surprise. He exchanged a brief glance with Faithfull who now came into the room, then said to Carol:

'What did you say this man's name was?'

'Maurice Preston. Why?'

'Because,' Somers explained slowly, 'the Inspector and I have always known him as Lem Knight.'

14

Carol Collins did not seem unduly surprised at the Sergeant's remark. She had known many of Val's boy friends, and there was invariably something fishy about them. In fact, she could not recall one who had worked at a steady job.

Val was the sort who attracted that type — young wasters and elderly roués, most of them with money to burn and a fixed idea of what they expected in return for it. As often as not, the type who gave you another name because they were married and didn't want you to trace their address.

Somers picked up the hand which held the revolver and examined it, while Inspector Faithfull moved to the foot of the bed and looked on curiously.

'Probably a plant.'

He had noted that there were no burn marks on the dead man's face. Somers nodded, for he had noticed the same thing.

'Hardly the type to commit suicide, specially when he's doing so well for himself,' the Sergeant said. With some difficulty he managed to extricate the revolver from the dead man's grasp.

It was a Resto .22 automatic.

With a grim face, Somers passed it over to the Inspector who took it gingerly by the end of the barrel. He raised a questioning eyebrow in the direction of Carol to indicate they would discuss the ownership of the weapon later on. Somers felt pretty sure the girl caught the gesture, but she made no comment. In fact, her behaviour came as rather a surprise to the Sergeant. She had coped with the situation extremely capably, had refused to give way to panic in face of very trying circumstances. It wasn't like the Carol he knew, the irresponsible show girl who never knew her own mind for two consecutive minutes.

The suspicion drifted idly into his mind that this new mysterious Carol might be holding back some information, something of vital importance to the case. But his thoughts were distracted again by the Inspector who had begun to run through the contents of the dead man's pockets.

He said to Somers:

'You might as well telephone the doctor.'

Carol showed him where the telephone was.

Meanwhile Faithfull rapidly emptied the dead man's pockets and laid the various articles on a sheet of newspaper spread upon the bedside table. He noted there were no apparent signs of a struggle in the room. It was almost as if Lem Knight had been shot from a hiding-place of some sort, or suddenly taken unawares. The Inspector switched on the bedside-lamp to give him a little more light as he examined the room.

It seemed typical of a show girl. There was an expensive triple-mirror dressing-table with a glass top, a large modern wardrobe, luxurious carpets. A couple of brightly dressed French dolls were lying grotesquely across each other at the foot of the bed. Faithfull noted that the windows were closed but not fastened, and they led out on to the platform of the fire-escape.

Very carefully, he gathered together the odds and ends on the sheet of newspaper and carried them into the sitting-room. Carol and Val were in the kitchen making the third lot of tea that evening, and when Somers joined his superior, Faithfull was slowly turning over the small articles on the newspaper.

There was a wallet containing eighteen pounds in notes, a handkerchief, a penknife, a cigarette case, a latch-key, a small case containing an assortment of small calipers and a piece of indiarubber. Also a small black notebook which as far as the Inspector could judge contained nothing but a list of bets upon racehorses and greyhounds with a record of the resulting financial transaction.

Faithfull slowly turned the pages, but it appeared to be no more than a typical punter's notebook. Finally, he flung it back on the paper and picked up the wallet, which in addition to the pound notes appeared to contain only a couple of betting slips.

He was pushing a finger through a corner of the lining when the two girls came in with the tea. While Carol was pouring it out, the Inspector fished around in the lining and produced a scrap of paper, which he looked at carefully, then handed over to Somers.

The Sergeant saw scrawled upon it in pencil:

'16 Shanklin Avenue, Sydenham.'

That was all. There was no name on the paper.

'What have you got there?' demanded Carol curiously, as she passed Somers a cup of tea.

'Just a bit of paper.'

'Anything important?'

'Just one of those odd bits of paper that get tucked into wallets,' added Faithfull, slipping it inside his own notebook.

They were half-way through their tea when the front door bell sounded. Carol went to let in the police surgeon, a very business-like young man who had only been with the Force a year. Somers took him into the bedroom right away, while Faithfull stayed and talked to the two girls. Val seemed to have almost completely calmed down by now, and even made half-hearted attempts at conversation.

'I've always been interested in the show business,' Inspector Faithfull informed them. Carol, to whom this opening was only too familiar, smiled to herself but merely nodded encouragingly.

'Not that I've ever had much to do with it,' the other went on. 'In fact, the only dancer I think I've ever met before you two was a girl named Georgia Nash. You wouldn't have come across her by any chance?'

He looked from one to the other quizzically, but they gave no sign.

'Girls often change their name in our business, Inspector,' Carol informed him. 'They think it brings them luck. In fact, lots of them are certain their luck's changed when they've used a different name. What was this girl friend of yours like?'

'I wouldn't exactly call her a friend,' Faithfull said hastily. 'She's a blonde, fairly tall, hair cut in a narrow fringe, rather a husky sort of voice.'

He broke off as he saw the girls smiling at each other.

'There's half a dozen at the theatre that might apply to,' said Carol. 'What theatre was she playing last?'

'Not exactly a theatre. It was a sort of dance palace — '

'Oh, a dance-hostess. That's another side of the profession altogether.'

'Yes,' sighed Faithfull. 'I suppose it would be. I don't know very much about such things.'

Actually, he knew far more than he would have admitted to them. He always believed in leaving other people guessing as to his exact knowledge of any subject. If they happened to underestimate it, then it often gave him a trump card to play at the correct moment.

Carol asked thoughtfully:

'This girl you're talking about — she wasn't mixed up in anything — any crime, was she, Inspector?'

'Depends what you mean by 'mixed-up'. We haven't been able to prove anything against her so far.'

The girls lighted cigarettes, but Faithfull refused one, preferring to content himself with the inevitable pinch of snuff.

He looked at his watch and noted that it was twenty-past eleven. He glanced at the bedroom, frowning impatiently.

'I wish the doctor'd hurry,' he murmured. 'I'll have to be getting on if I'm to get my last bus.'

As if in answer to his wish, the doctor and Somers appeared. It seemed the doctor wanted to remove the body at once, so that he could conduct a post-mortem. The bullet was apparently embedded in the head. The Inspector nodded his permission. A small calibre bullet might well have struck a bone after doing its deadly work.

The doctor went off to make the arrangements. Faithfull thanked the girls for the tea, told Somers to supervise any necessary arrangements about removing the body, and went off to catch his last bus.

Inspector Faithfull, who did a lot of quiet thinking on his bus journeys, surveyed the events of the evening.

To start with, who could have tampered with the steering of the car while they were at the Professor's? Of course, it was possible for somebody to slip out of the house while Mallowes was talking to them. Or had they been followed there? Or yet again, had someone contrived to discover they would be at the professor's that evening?

He didn't know quite what to make of Mallowes. On the face of it, he seemed like a one-track scientist, intent only on his job, as 99.9 per cent of them were. But there was always that Machiavellian mind that seemed to crop up every fifty years. Yet Professor Mallowes hardly seemed that type.

All the same, that machine he was working on might be put to very unpleasant uses. If only to disintegrate valuable evidence of a crime. And if ever he did get round to playing the same trick with a human body, well, it was going to give them a few headaches at the Yard. It was difficult enough to prove your case even when you could produce the body!

Yes, if that machine fell into the wrong hands they were in for lively times.

The conductor came for his fare. Next, Faithfull found himself trying to discover some rhyme or reason in the recent exploits of Georgia Nash. That young lady was a mystery all right, but she had a way of looking at you that made you think it was just devilment and love of adventure. But there, you could never tell with women.

The Inspector was never very comfortable when the feminine element intruded in his cases. Women had so little regard for logical facts and measured deduction. And they lied so easily and with such a straight face that he doubted if even the lie-detector would show any evidence of such fabrications. Faithfull cross-questioned women suspects as cautiously as any leading counsel. Very occasionally he managed to trip them up, but the female thus ensnared would either recover with a rapidity which left him breathless, or would fall back upon the age-old alternative of tears. And once a woman started crying you might as well put her in a cell and leave her to calm down.

It was no doubt a mere coincidence that Lem Knight had been killed by a Resto automatic and that Georgia Nash had lost one the same evening.

But why should she go out of her way to tell them about it?

What possible point could there be in that? Of course, that girl had her wits about her. She was up to some queer business, and this might be part of a plan she had worked out. On the other hand, somebody might be out to play Georgia Nash a dirty one. They might have known she'd gone to the Three Sailors to contact Lem Knight. It was his 'local' and someone might have taken the opportunity to throw suspicion on the girl. Faithfull had never liked the look of the Three Sailors. Before its present tenant took over, it had been 'cleaned up' by the police on several occasions for various reasons. So far they had nothing against the present mine host, but Faithfull was not very impressed with him. Of course, appearances might be deceptive.

Whistling lugubriously under his breath, Inspector Faithfull took a half-sheet of pale blue notepaper from his pocket and, holding it by the extreme corner tips, frowned thoughtfully at the straggling block lettering in startling green ink. It read:

'A WISE MAN KEEPS HIS OWN COUNCIL
LUCIFER.'

15

Faithfull held the paper steadily before him for a long time.

He had told no one about it yet; not even Sergeant Somers.

When he was running through the dead man's pockets, he had found it tucked away just under the top of his waistcoat. It had probably slipped down there. He was rather surprised Somers hadn't spotted it, but the Sergeant had been concentrating rather more upon the bullet wound.

Somehow, the Inspector felt the misspelling of the word 'counsel' was not consistent with a master-mind of the calibre of Lucifer. Of course, we all had our blind spots so far as spelling was concerned, but this was a very elementary mistake, the sort one would expect from a child or a very poorly educated adult. Not from a person with the intelligence to devise a scheme for cornering the world's supply of radium.

Still holding the paper by its corners, Faithfull carefully replaced it inside his wallet. It was, of course, extremely unlikely that it would yield any fingerprints. The slip of paper they found on Nicky Dulane had shown nothing in this direction and the person responsible was pretty certain to have been wearing gloves. However, it was a matter of routine, and Faithfull was the last person to overlook any such item.

As he put his wallet away the conductor yelled out his stop. Slowly he dismounted the stairs and made his way to his empty house and cheerless fireside. Before going to bed, he made himself a cup of cocoa, spooning in plenty of sugar, and sipped it, sitting in front of the gas-fire in the sitting-room, still ruminating upon the case.

When he had finished the cocoa, he went to his mackintosh and extracted the folded newspaper from a pocket. Laboriously he began filling in the squares of the crosswords, occasionally consulting the paper's expert, though judging by his muttered comments he often scorned these prognostications. Having completed his usual number of entries for the competition he filled in all the other details and placed them in an envelope and sealed it. He would post it in the morning.

Faithfull took a final pinch of snuff and made his way to bed. By way of a small consolation for his wife's absence, he lighted the gas-fire in his bedroom, which she would never have countenanced if she had been at home.

Most men who have had a narrow escape from serious injury, and later encountered the aftermath of a murder, might well lie awake until the small hours. But it is to be recorded that Inspector Faithfull was snoring in regular sonority as the clocks struck midnight.

The following day he was rather surprised to receive an early visit from the alert young police surgeon, who placed a bullet on his desk.

'Thought you'd like to see it,' he said.

Faithfull picked it up and examined it closely.

'This isn't a point two-two. It's bigger.'
'You're quite right,' the doctor nodded. 'I had them check it up — it's a .33.' He smiled and nodded, then added pleasantly: 'Looks like an interesting case.'
'Any idea how long he'd been dead?'
'At a rough guess, I should say he was killed somewhere between three and four o'clock in the afternoon.'
'As early as that? H'm . . . '
Faithfull considered this for a few moments, scribbling thoughtfully on his blotting-pad. At that moment, Somers came in and the Inspector passed on this new development.
Somers was plainly taken aback.
'Are you positive about the time?'
The doctor shrugged.
'I couldn't say to an hour either way with absolute accuracy.'
Faithfull rolled the bullet between his fingers.
'It's this that worries me,' he said. 'Knight is shot with one revolver, and another is found in his hand of a different calibre.'
'He could have been trying to defend

himself with it,' Somers pointed out. 'There was one spent cartridge.'

The Inspector said slowly: 'That theory is rather upset by the fact that the gun was in Knight's right hand.'

The others said nothing. Faithfull indicated a folder on the desk before him and added:

'According to this dossier, Lem Knight was left-handed. Whoever planted that gun in his right hand must have forgotten that.'

Somers asked him: 'Then you think it was a plant?'

'I don't go in for theories, Sergeant, as you well know.'

There was a note of disapproval in the Inspector's tone. The police surgeon looked from one to the other, then with a little shrug moved over towards the door.

'I'll leave you two to fight it out. You know where to find me if you want to know anything else. In any case I'll send you a detailed report just as soon as it's typed.'

He shut the door quietly and went off whistling along the corridor. Somers waited for some moments, flicking through a batch of memos in his tray. Then he looked across at the Inspector.

'What makes you think anyone would plant that gun to implicate Georgia Nash?'

Faithfull went on scribbling tiny designs on his blotter. At last he said:

'If you'll think a minute, it doesn't really implicate her if her revolver is found in the hand of a dead man.'

'It might look as if she planted it there, rather than get rid of it.'

Inspector Faithfull shook his head a little.

'But we know now that Knight was killed by a bullet from a completely different revolver.'

'Have you had the Resto automatic tested for prints?'

'I did that first thing. Nothing definite to show for it — except Knight's prints of course.'

He passed over the gun.

'You'd better take that over to the Three Sailors with you and bring Georgia Nash back for the inquest. Maybe if the pub has no beer she'll let you take her out to lunch.'

Somers grinned as he pocketed the revolver.

'Before you go,' continued Faithfull, 'tell me a bit about this Regal Theatre. They start at twelve I believe?'

'That's right. The girls get there about eleven-thirty.'

'H'm . . . And this Miss Collins of yours. What do you know about her?'

'Carol? Oh, I've known her for quite a while — off and on, as you might say. Met her first when I was doing the dress clothes stuff — she was at some night-club in those days. She gets half-a-dozen jobs a year — as much work as she wants, but she has a lazy time every now and then. I don't know her terribly well.'

'My mistake — I thought I heard her call you 'darling',' the other said drily.

Somers laughed.

'Good lord, Inspector! Actresses call their bitterest enemy 'darling'. It doesn't mean a thing.'

'I know, I know,' retorted Faithfull a

trifle impatiently. 'It was the *way* she said it.'

'You must have been imagining things.'

The Inspector eyed him shrewdly.

'Then you don't think she's likely to be mixed up in this business in any way?'

'Who — Carol? Good lord, no! She only happened to go along with Miss Harris to see her new radiogram — you heard them explain all that.'

'Maybe it's true enough . . . but what about this Miss Harris?'

The Sergeant hesitated.

'I don't really know much about her,' he confessed. 'In fact, I'd only met her once before, when I picked up Carol at the theatre one night. And I must say I didn't like the looks of Miss Harris at all that night. At first, I thought she'd been drinking. But there was no smell of drink of any sort. Then I took a good look at her eyes.'

'Ah.'

Faithfull regarded him with curiosity.

'I haven't had much experience of the dope racket, Inspector. But I could have sworn she'd been sniffing cocaine. It stood out a mile. I tried to pump Carol about it after, when we were having supper, but she's loyal in some ways, and she wouldn't breathe a word. I had to content myself with giving her a lecture, warning her to keep off it herself. I've been meaning to drop in on Miss Harris again, but somehow there hasn't been time.'

Faithfull rose to his feet.

'Well,' he said, 'this is where we make time.'

'You mean we are going there now?'

'I am going there — you're off to Shadwell Basin,' the Inspector reminded him. 'Before we start, is there anything else about this Harris girl you can think of?'

Somers frowned thoughtfully.

'Carol would never say very much about her. She joined the show about a month back, I think, and Carol rather took a fancy to her and had her in to share her little dressing-room.'

'You've no idea what she was doing before she went to the Regal?'

'Oh, she's been in and out of the

profession for years, I believe. And I think Carol said something about her being a photographer's model. Lots of the girls do that of course.' Somers regarded the older man a little anxiously. 'You wouldn't like me to come too?' he suggested. 'These stage folk take a bit of handling, and I wouldn't trust the Harris — ' He broke off, then went on abruptly: 'She was living with Lem Knight of course. So she may know a hell of a lot more than she's told us. Better watch your step.'

'Thank you, Sergeant, I'll follow my own nose if you don't mind. You'll have your hands full with Miss Nash, I'm thinking. Perhaps it's I who ought to be warning you. When you've had to do with the opposite sex as many years as I have.'

He sighed and took a pinch of snuff.

The Sergeant grinned.

'We'll just have to keep our fingers crossed and hope for the best. But keep a sharp eye on Val Harris's fingernails. They must be an inch long, and I should imagine they could do a bit of damage. You can't be too careful with these tawny-headed women. And don't forget she's an actress, so you automatically take off fifty per cent from everything she says.'

Faithfull gave a snort, but made no further comment. Eventually he went off in the Soho direction. It was only just a quarter past ten, and he had to ring several times before Val Harris wearing a very becoming black négligé, chosen no doubt to suit the occasion, let him in. She picked up the bottle of milk that was standing outside her hall door, tossed her attractive tawny locks from her face and smiled somewhat sleepily at him.

'Just a few inquiries about your friend, Miss Harris,' he began tentatively.

She smiled at him.

'Of course. Won't you come inside?'

She closed the door and led the way into the sitting-room.

'Is there any more news? Have you found out who?' she began, then halted as if she were a little embarrassed.

'We have discovered one or two things,' replied Faithfull evenly. 'For instance, the bullet that killed him was not fired from the revolver in his hand.'

She was unable to check an involuntary gesture, and he thought for a moment he saw a flicker of fear in her grey-green eyes.

But her voice was quite controlled when she said:

'That was pretty smart of you, Inspector. You found the bullet?'

The Inspector settled on a straight-backed chair and placed his hat on the floor beside him. Then he put a hand on each knee and looked at her intently.

'Yes,' he said, 'we found the bullet — and one or two other things as well.'

She gripped the back of a chair until her knuckles showed white.

He continued imperturbably:

'I've been thinking that there are one or two more little things about Lem Knight you might be able to tell me.'

16

'I can't think of anything important.'

There was a note of defiance in Val Harris's voice as she faced him.

'Maybe I can help you for instance, you say you didn't see Knight after breakfast yesterday.'

'That's right. You see the show starts at twelve, and we don't get much chance to leave the theatre. We take our meals in the canteen. So I didn't go near the flat again till the middle of the evening when Carol came with me.'

'And you never left the theatre till then?'

She shook her head.

He deliberately folded his arms and regarded her sadly.

'Miss Harris, I'm afraid your memory isn't very good,' he informed her reproachfully.

She was on her guard at once, but Faithfull continued remorselessly:

'On the way here, I looked in at the

stage door and saw the door-keeper. A most methodical man — keeps a book with all your company's comings and goings in it, all timed to the minute. A very neat bit of book-keeping indeed — I complimented him on it. But it makes things a bit difficult for you because the book shows you were out of the theatre between five-forty-two and six-four yesterday evening.'

'Oh yes,' she replied quickly. 'I went out to do a little shopping — we don't get much chance — I suddenly remembered I had no food in — '

'But you didn't come back to the flat?'

'No, I took the stuff back to the theatre with me. There wasn't time to come here. I brought it back when I came up with Carol after the end of the next show.'

Faithfull rubbed his chin thoughtfully for some moments. There did not seem to be any way of proving her statement true or false at the moment. He tried another tack.

'No doubt you noticed I discovered a slip of paper in the dead man's wallet. There was a bit of writing on it, and I'm rather anxious to discover whose it was. However, whoever wrote it probably won't be so willing to admit doing so. The only plan seems to be to ask everyone remotely connected with the case to give me a specimen of their writing.'

She regarded him suspiciously.

'That's rather a roundabout way, isn't it?'

'Can you suggest any other?'

'Well . . . No.'

'For the simple reason that there is no other. Well now, I take it that you don't object to giving me a specimen of your writing.'

'I don't see why I should.'

'If you aren't in any way involved, there is no reason why you shouldn't.'

'Of course I'm not involved,' she retorted.

She went to a bureau and came back with a blue writing-pad, picked up a fountain-pen from the mantelpiece, seemed to change her mind suddenly and put it back again. She returned to the bureau, discovered a stump of pencil and demanded:

'What do you want me to write?'

'Anything will do. An old proverb perhaps.'

He hesitated for a moment, then:

'What about that old saying — 'A wise man keeps his own counsel'?'

Without a sign of emotion she began to write at once. Deliberately he helped himself to a pinch of snuff and slowly replaced the box in his waistcoat pocket. She came across with the paper.

'Will that do?'

He took the paper and examined it carefully.

'Why didn't you write in ink?' he demanded.

The question seemed to upset her a little.

'Er — the pen's run dry,' she stammered. 'I've been meaning to get some ink for days.'

He took the pen from the shelf and unscrewed the cap.

'Really, Inspector, can't you believe anything I tell you?' she cried in a sudden protest. Her voice had grown high-pitched.

He ignored her, but picked up a discarded newspaper and scribbled upon it with the pen in question. It wrote quite easily with a steady flow of bright green ink.

'Give it to me: How dare you!'

'Certainly,' he agreed calmly, 'it's your pen, and it seems to be in perfect working order.' He shook his head a trifle wistfully. 'It would save a lot of time if you didn't lie to me, Miss Harris,' he suggested in the tone in which a parent admonishes a recalcitrant child.

He took the slip of paper from his pocket. The inks matched perfectly, but there was no means, of course, of accurately checking the writing at a casual glance. The first slip had been written in block capitals. But there was one other very marked resemblance.

In both cases, the word 'counsel' had been mis-spelt. Holding one slip in each hand he looked up at her.

'Now, Miss Harris,' he said softly, as if waiting for a further explanation.

'Look here, you can't prove it's my writing on that slip you found,' she blurted out angrily. 'It was written in block capitals.'

'And how did you know that?'

'I — I — caught a glimpse of it last night?'

'Then why didn't you point it out to us?'

When she did not reply, he rose and placed a hand on her shoulder. She recoiled, but his grip tightened.

'If you don't stop telling me these foolish lies, and give me the truth, this case is going to be a very serious one for you.'

There was terror in her eyes as she shook herself free and looked wildly round the room as if seeking a means of escape.

'I didn't kill him! I tell you I didn't!'

'But you wrote that note,' he challenged her in an insistent tone.

She collapsed on to the settee.

'Yes, I wrote it.'

Her voice was a strangled whisper.

He went and leaned against the mantelpiece, replacing the fountain-pen as he did so. Val Harris lay back in her chair, long-drawn hysterical sobs convulsing her slight figure. For a moment, he felt sorry for her; then he pulled himself together. She had told him a string of lies already, and she would go on lying as far as it suited her purpose.

He noticed that the muscles at the side of her face were twitching slightly and that she puckered her lips nervously. He pulled out his cigarette case.

'Better have a cigarette and tell me all about it quietly,' he suggested.

With a hand that shook slightly she accepted one and he lit it for her.

'What made you write that note, Miss Harris?' he demanded after a pause.

'Because I was made to,' she replied sullenly.

'I'm afraid I shall want to know a bit more than that. Who made you do it?'

'I had my orders.'

'Can I see them?'

'No, I got them by telephone.'

'Pity. If you had them to show me in writing they might have helped quite a lot in several ways. Who sent them to you?'

'Oh, I suppose I'd better tell you the

whole story as far as I know,' she said wearily, puffing hard at the cigarette.

'I've told you I didn't kill him, and it's true. I've been dragged into this business right from the start against my will. I've got nothing out of it. No money, that is.'

Faithfull made a shrewd guess that her reward had taken the form of drugs, until she was so much in its grip that she had to go on obeying orders on pain of having the supply cut off.

'It makes no difference what this gang has got on me,' she went on in a helpless voice, 'I've had to do as I was told. So when they wanted Lem Knight to change his address I had to put him up here.'

'When was this?'

'About five weeks ago.'

'And you'd no idea what his game was?'

'I knew he was a crook of some sort. Opened safes, didn't he?'

'That's right. Did he tell you anything about his jobs?'

'Never mentioned a word.'

'Yet you were — shall we say more than friendly with him?'

'I've known him for over a year,' she answered defiantly. 'Don't you go making me out a tart, because — '

He made a pacifying gesture of reassurance. Strange, how anxious these women of easy morals are anxious not to be written off as professional prostitutes, he reflected. Couldn't be more touchy if they were royal ladies-in-waiting.

'It's all right,' he interjected quickly, 'all that is your private affair unless it directly concerns Knight's death. Do you know who killed him?'

'No, no! If you'll let me tell the story in my own way. This gang has got something on me, and I have to do as I'm told. I had no idea that he'd been talking. That the gang were going to wipe him out.'

'Well, he hasn't talked to the police,' said Faithfull shortly.

'I wouldn't know anything about that. All I know is that somebody telephoned me at the theatre yesterday afternoon, told me to go back to the flat — '

'So the door-keeper was right.'

'Of course. I had to go back. I was told I'd find Lem Knight's body in the bedroom, and that I was to write that piece to put on it. I was scared to death. It put me in a proper spot. I couldn't drag the body out of the flat.'

'You didn't recognize this voice over the telephone?'

'No. It was a man; that's all I can tell you. He made me repeat it over twice — it was a lucky thing for me the stage door-keeper was out at the time — '

'Then nobody overheard you?'

'Not likely! I came back to the flat, and it took me a bit of time to pluck up courage to go in the bedroom. But I wrote out that message, and after a while I went in — and came out pretty quick. The sight of blood always turns me a bit queer. The man on the phone said I was to notify the police, but I was frightened. Then I hit on the idea of asking Carol Collins to come back with me after the next show, and I thought she'd — well — you know — sort of witness that I had nothing to do with it. Anyhow, I couldn't stand the idea of being there on my own when the police came. I thought Carol being friendly with a man from the Yard she might somehow help.'

Faithfull sighed.

'I appreciate all that; but it doesn't take us much farther, now does it?' he demanded. 'I'm inclined to believe this story of yours, but you might just as well have come back here after tea, met Knight, had a row, shot him, and planted all the other evidence. You've told me nothing to disprove anything like that. In fact you've nothing at all to prove that you did not kill Lem Knight.'

She looked at him defiantly.

'What had you got to prove that I did?'

He reminded her:

'It happened in your flat — at least the body turned up there. You can't get away from the fact that circumstantial evidence is pretty strong against you. I think you'd have great difficulty in convincing any jury he was murdered by the agent of a mysterious gang.'

'But you know there is such a gang,' she protested.

'Of course I know. That, again, doesn't help very much.'

'But I told you they've got something on me — '

'You can't tell me what exactly?'

'No. It wouldn't make any difference.'

'All right. Tell me what you know about the gang — that's if you want me to be convinced. Surely, during all those weeks Knight must have let some clue slip.'

She shook her head decisively.

'You must know *something*,' he urged. 'You have been in touch with these people; you must have come across somebody — met them somewhere.'

She bit her lip.

'I expect it does sound a bit far-fetched, but all I get is a sort of password and instructions who to contact. Sometimes it's a man in a pin-table saloon, or a fellow hawking toys in Regent Street. The only information I can give you is an address that these orders come from.'

Faithfull's brain was busy. He guessed that these agents supplied the girl with fresh quantities of dope. But the address interested him. Of course, she might say the first thing that came into her head, just to stall him off and give her breathing time so that she could contact the gang again and get further instructions. Still one had to give her a chance. He said:

'Right, let's have the address.'

She regarded him from beneath her eyelids and after a moment's hesitation replied: 'It's in Sydenham. 16 Shanklin Avenue.'

He whistled softly and took a scrap of paper from his wallet. It was the address he had found on the dead man — and it was the same address.

'I'm inclined to believe you,' he announced deliberately. 'Do you happen to know who lives at this house?'

She shook her head.

'I've only been there twice and I saw a fellow through a sort of service hatch, and he was wearing one of those masks made out of papier mâché. There wasn't much light in the room, so I couldn't even tell you whether he was tall or short — he might have been standing on something the other side of the hatch. They don't give much away, I can tell you.'

'So I gather. But surely you can give me some idea how you came to get mixed up with this crowd.'

She stubbed out her cigarette with a vicious gesture.

'That doesn't come into it,' she snapped. 'This gang is big; organized like a city company and just about as impersonal. From what I can see of it, none of 'em know quite who . . . '

She hesitated.

He said gently:

'You mean nobody in the gang knows who Lucifer is?'

'I wouldn't say that. But I doubt if anyone except his two or three right-hand men know who he is.'

She answered him almost casually, unaware of the subtlety of his question.

'Then you have heard of Lucifer?'

She nodded.

'Lem used to talk about him sometimes. That was about the only thing to do with the racket he would talk about. We used to try and fathom out who Lucifer could be. Waste of time, of course. Anyway, his gang's damned well organized,'

'What do you know about such things?'

She shrugged.

'I've told you before, I don't know anything definite. I only heard odd remarks here and there. And there's not only the gang itself. There must be dozens of people they've got something on, and whom they can blackmail into doing just what they want. Like they've done with me. Put me in this spot with a murder in my flat, and I can't move a finger to do anything except call the police. They could have got the body away if they'd wanted to, but they don't give a damn about me. If I hanged for it, they'd hardly notice.'

Her voice was bitter, each clipped syllable acidly venomous.

'So now you see why I'm talking, Inspector. I've got no use for the police as a rule, but this time — '

'And supposing they find out you've talked?'

'I haven't told you anything that you didn't know already — at least, nothing very much. They take pretty good care that folks like myself can't give much away.'

She found another cigarette and lit it.

He regarded her levelly. She went on:

'Seems to me, Inspector, you're up against a hell of a proposition, no matter which way you look at it.'

She puffed nervously at the cigarette. Still Faithfull did not speak, and at length she asked in a defiant tone:

'Well, what are you going to do?'

He placed a hand on her arm.

'Officially, you are under arrest for the murder of Lem Knight.' She gasped. He went on quickly: 'Unofficially you'll be in a certain nursing home out of harm's way, and receiving some new treatment that I think might help you a lot, from what a doctor was telling me the other day.' He patted her shoulder reassuringly and said, 'Come on now, get your hat and coat.'

She shook herself free.

'Don't you see, Inspector, that's just what the gang will want. If they think they've fastened the murder on somebody else, that'll fit in with their plans.'

'Exactly,' nodded Faithfull. 'And it's always fatal to underestimate your enemy — as many a crook has discovered to his cost.'

17

'Somehow,' Georgia Nash said, 'you don't look like a policeman.'

'Any more than you look like a barmaid,' Detective-Sergeant Somers replied. 'Let's have the trifle — it's always good here.'

He had brought her to a small restaurant he knew in Cheapside where they retained considerable pride in the luncheon they provided for the business men from the neighbouring offices. On every side, burly stockbrokers and bank managers were busily devouring substantial cuts off the joint, and the place had a warm, reassuring atmosphere.

Somers felt particularly pleased with himself, for his companion was subjected to many covert and openly envious glances. She was dressed in a neat two-piece which enhanced her startling good looks to the fullest degree. In fact, she couldn't have seemed less like a barmaid. However, he had never taken her job at the Three Sailors very seriously. What really worried him was the reason for her being there.

They dealt with their trifle, and he ordered coffee.

'I can't think what makes you take all these crazy jobs,' he told her presently. Their conversation over lunch had revealed her as a person of a considerably wider experience than she had at first given him the impression. She could talk with surprising intelligence upon a variety of subjects, and had apparently travelled abroad quite extensively. In fact, she seemed to possess all the assurance of a highly sophisticated young woman who spends her life getting around.

'You're not scared about this inquest, are you?' he asked as they stirred their coffee.

She shook her head.

'As long as they don't ask me to identify the body.'

'Ever been to one before?'

She hesitated for a moment before replying.

‘Some time ago.’

‘Whose?’

‘An acquaintance of mine who fell a victim to the dope habit.’

He looked up quickly.

‘I suppose you wouldn’t know a girl by the name of Val Harris?’

Her eyes narrowed a trifle as she made an effort to concentrate.

‘No,’ she said at last. ‘I don’t think so. Who is she?’

‘A show girl at the Regal — lived with Lem Knight — if that’s any help.’

Her face cleared.

‘You mean Nancy Dane,’ she told him. ‘At least, that’s the name I know her by. Slim girl, good figure, tawny hair.’

‘That’s the girl,’ he nodded. ‘What do you know about her?’

‘Not very much. She used to be a mannequin, and got mixed up with rather a tough night club set — that was in the days before the Pink Rat was raided and reopened as the Caliente. Remember it?’

‘I remember — in fact, I helped to raid it,’ he informed her with a slight smile.

'So Nancy's changed her name again — she was always doing it,' she said thoughtfully. 'I've lost track of her this last year or so. Now tell me what *you* know about her.'

'Rather less than you do, I should imagine.' He paused before adding: 'Apart from the fact that she's shot to the eyes with dope — '

'I'm not surprised to hear that.'

'And that Lem Knight was found dead in her flat last night,' he continued, flicking the ash off his cigarette.

'H'm, that doesn't surprise me very much either,' she replied in a casual tone.

She puzzled him more than ever.

But her attractive features remained inscrutable beneath the artistically applied make-up. She had accepted one of his cigarettes and was smoking it with evident enjoyment.

Somers shifted in his chair.

'Look here,' he said abruptly, 'what exactly do you know about Lem Knight?'

A tiny smile lifted the corners of the shapely mouth.

'I know,' she replied slowly, 'that he is a

safe-breaker — or rather he was. That he has a weakness for chorus girls. That he's been mixed up with something rather peculiar these last few weeks.'

'How did you get to know all this?'

Once again she smiled enigmatically.

'I picked up one or two tips when I was at the Luxor, you know. And I got around a fair amount before then. It's wonderful what a girl hears if she keeps her ears open.'

'You have such very nice ears.'

'Thank you. It's nice to find that the police can be human.'

He took a sip of coffee, then returned to the attack.

'All the same, you can't expect me to believe that you've taken that barmaid's job for the fun of the thing.'

'Lots of girls do,' she informed him. 'There's Jess Black, the novelist. She always takes a new job for a few months, then writes a book about it.'

He said:

'I don't think even Jess Black would venture into the Three Sailors.'

She smiled at this, revealing even, white

teeth, which gave the final touch to her vivid charm.

'There's no accounting for tastes,' she said.

'Please don't beat about the bush. I don't like the thought of your being at that dive. They're always having trouble there.'

'It's all right,' she assured him. 'I know exactly what to do when a rough house starts. I dive under the counter.'

'Have you had a rough house then?' he asked quickly.

She laughed.

'I've only been there two days — give me time. Anyhow, the boss is pretty strict. I don't think anything much could start while he was there.'

'H'm,' he nodded dubiously. 'I don't know very much about the gent. We've got nothing against him yet.'

He regarded her with a worried frown. He said:

'I do wish you'd come across and tell me why you're getting mixed up in this racket.'

She shook her head.

'Informing to the police isn't in my line. Don't you think we'd better be getting along?'

She gathered her handbag and gloves and he called for the bill.

A dozen male heads were raised and admiring glances followed them as they left the restaurant.

They reached Henley five minutes before the inquest started, and found Inspector Faithfull already there. He exchanged a non-committal greeting with them as they filed into the court room. The proceedings lasted only twenty minutes, the verdict being: 'Murder by person or persons unknown.'

Georgia Nash caused a slight flutter among the reporters when she entered the witness-box, but her evidence was merely a corroboration of the police reports, and the coroner only asked her a couple of minor routine questions.

As they came out of the court room, a batch of evening newspapers had just reached the stands. Somers bought one.

ARREST IN SOHO MURDER CASE

The banner headline ran across the front page.

'Well!' exclaimed Georgia Nash, peeping over his shoulder to read, 'that was quick work!'

Somers rapidly scanned the brief report, then turned to the Inspector.

'You never told me you were going to arrest Val Harris,' he said in a mildly reproachful tone.

'I wasn't quite sure about it myself. It was only when I had verified certain evidence that I decided it would be the safest plan, taken all round.'

He shot a warning glance in the direction of Georgia Nash, who was sitting in the car behind them.

'It kills several birds with one stone,' he added cryptically.

'I don't quite understand.'

'All in good time. At any rate, it gives the gang the idea they've got away with it, and it puts the girl out of the way of any possible reprisals. What's more, it gives her a chance to — well — to recover from you know what.'

He shot another significant glance

towards the back of the car.

'Don't mind me,' said Georgia Nash quite affably. 'I'll put my fingers in my ears if you just say the word.'

A fleeting expression of annoyance flickered over Faithfull's features.

'It would be expecting too much of any woman!' he commented with a contemptuous snort.

The girl laughed.

'Then you don't think Val Harris is guilty of the murder of Lem Knight?' she asked sweetly.

'I can't think that my opinions should be of any interest to you,' the Inspector retorted severely.

She said no more, but subsided behind the copy of the evening paper which Somers had passed over to her.

The remainder of the journey passed with no more than a few occasional remarks between the two men. When they reached London, the Sergeant offered to drive the girl back to Shadwell, but she insisted that she could easily get a bus to land her back there well before opening time. As he had a feeling that Inspector

Faithfull had further news for him, Somers eventually agreed, and she left the car at the top of Charing Cross Road.

As they drove down towards Trafalgar Square, Faithful asked:

'Did you get anything from her?'

'Not a thing. Stood her a large lunch, and got her to talk all right. The only trouble was she didn't say anything — except that she knew a thing or two about Lem Knight.'

'You didn't mention that gun?'

'No — I thought you wanted to hold that until — '

'Yes, we'll keep it up our sleeve a bit longer.'

'I can't for the life of me think what her game is,' Somers said in a puzzled tone. 'I'm pretty certain she's somehow mixed up with this radium gang, but it seems to me she's just as likely to be against them for some reason or other.'

'We shall see,' the other nodded, as Somers parked the car.

They went up to their office.

Almost as they entered, the telephone rang and the Inspector took it.

'For you,' he said.

The Sergeant took the receiver.

It was Carol Collins, apparently in a considerable state of worry.

'You can't do this to Val, darling,' she protested over the line. 'I know she hasn't done a murder. She isn't the type. I wouldn't have her sharing my room if I thought for a minute — '

'Look, darling,' he interrupted, 'we haven't proved that she actually did it yet.'

'I should just think not! Why I'd have known right away if she'd gone out and done a murder.'

'Did you know she was taking dope?' he asked her.

There was a moment's hesitation at the other end.

'Well — well, I thought once or twice — '

'You thought!' he echoed sarcastically. 'My dear Carol, you've been dressing for months with a dope-fiend and you tell me that — '

'Don't you start on me!' came her indignant voice. 'You'll be trying to pin the murder on me next.'

Somers laughed and rang off.

Faithfull was sitting at his desk, stolidly looking through a sheaf of forms, from which he sorted out a couple of reports.

'Not much help from Fingerprints,' he grunted, detaching the slip with the address in Sydenham on it from one of the reports.

The Sergeant examined the slip which the other had passed on to him.

'It looks a respectable sort of address. Do we know anything about it?'

'Yes,' the Inspector replied slowly. 'We know who lives there. I got through to Sydenham and made some inquiries.'

'And who is the party? Anyone we know?'

Inspector Faithfull answered:

'A gentleman we know very well. A Mr. Osbert Strang.'

Somers gave a long, expressive whistle.

18

The career of Mr. Osbert Strang has already filled two books, one written by a Fleet Street hack in the days of Mr. Strang's opulence: the other, written by Mr. Strang himself to while away the time during five years in prison, had never been published. In fact, Osbert Strang had caused the police more trouble than any of the most notorious murderers. His crimes had been far more subtle and difficult to trace, though their effect upon the community had been widespread and demoralizing.

You would have found it perhaps a little hard to believe this if you had sunk your foot into the carpets in Mr. Strang's magnificent suite of offices on a corner of Park Lane.

After acting as a sort of general clerk in his father's paint factory for two years, Osbert Strang, realizing that a small paint firm stands a considerably poorer chance of obtaining business than a large one, obtained his father's permission to turn the company into a public one.

Such was his skill at presenting the prospectus and talking his way into the private offices of a well-known firm of under-writers, that the issue proved highly successful, and the future of the new company was rosy indeed.

But Osbert had tasted blood, and was looking for fresh fields.

He had that peculiar type of brain which grasps the main issues of high finance and never overlooks any likely opportunity. It was not long, then, before Osbert Strang had made what appeared to be a sensational offer to the proprietors of Mother Martin's All-cure Tonic. He bought them out, lock, stock and barrel, for a quarter of a million, promptly floating a public company with a share capital of half-a-million, and netting a matter of £100,000 clear profit on the deal.

One of the secrets of Osbert's long run of success lay in the fact that he always saw that his associates in any deal had a lavish rake-off.

Often it made all the difference between success and failure.

So he passed on to other undertakings of every description — gramophones, toys, bicycles, electric fires. Anything for which he saw consumer possibilities.

Sometimes, he was running a dozen companies simultaneously; then his interests would drop to perhaps only three or four, all within a couple of months. He developed a technique in handling an antagonistic meeting that was unequalled in the financial world.

He came to know the value of every 'guinea pig' director in the financial firmament. He knew exactly what men he wanted for every company he floated, and what they were worth to him in attracting the hard-earned savings of the millions.

He bought a Rolls-Royce and a couple of expensive but slightly smaller cars as well. He had a large country house in imitation where his week-end parties became famous.

Then, like so many financiers before

him, Osbert Strang began to lose his sense of money and think more and more in terms of power. Slowly, the idea began to formulate that Osbert Strang was something of a law unto himself, that his actions were quite independent of the best interests of the community or any other particular individual.

The police began to get complaints from disgruntled shareholders and participators in certain of Strang's financial ventures. But the ways of high finance are a world of their own, and it calls for considerable skill to produce sufficient evidence upon which to arrest a mogul of Strang's standing; one false step and he brings an action in which damages can run to five figures. The police were very cautious, and it was over a year before they acted.

But they made no mistake.

In his high-handed manner, Strang had decided to take over a small firm manufacturing a new type of tin-opener and amalgamate it with one of the leading companies. He had been so confident that this absorption was merely a matter of form that he induced two financiers of integrity to 'go in' with him, telling them that all was cut and dried and generally misleading them in several directions. He was quite taken aback when the proprietor of the small firm refused to sell out, thus throwing a considerable-sized spanner into the financial machinery which had advanced too far for any retraction at that stage. How it all leaked out to the police, he never quite discovered, but he found himself in court on a charge of 'false pretences'. That was the beginning of his downfall. He had spent the greater part of five years in gaol. Emerging to a strange world of controls he had not found the going too pleasant.

At first, he had dabbled somewhat vaguely in the black market, but he had lost some of his nerve, and overcautiousness did not make for a large turnover. He had salted away a small fortune when he went to prison, but its value had dwindled considerably with the passing years, so he hesitated to use this money. However, he finally decided to buy a partnership in a small firm of outside stockbrokers, and as far as the police could trace his activities had so far been on the right side of the law.

But the police had by no means lost trace of Osbert Strang, or even lost interest. They knew that during the past few months he had twice visited Switzerland and had once vanished from his home for over a fortnight without the police being able to trace his movements at all.

He had returned as suddenly as he had gone and resumed his business at the office as if nothing had happened. Perhaps nothing *had* happened, nevertheless certain police officials were none the less curious.

Among them was Inspector Ashton, a tall, middle-aged man with a high forehead and a shrewd knowledge of the shady side of financial circles. Faithfull lost no time in seeking out Ashton, whom he discovered in the library, checking over a list with the help of some files of financial papers.

Ashton looked up and pulled his spectacles down his nose to gaze rather quizzically at Faithfull.

'Hallo,' he grunted. 'Haven't seen you lately. What have you been up to?'

Faithfull offered him a pinch of snuff, which the other accepted. He was one of the few men among Faithfull's colleagues who appreciated his special brand of snuff.

'What do you know about Osbert Strang lately?' he asked, without answering Ashton's question.

The other frowned thoughtfully.

'I've got an uncomfortable feeling about him,' he admitted. 'He's acting too blatantly respectable for my liking.'

'Found out anything yet about the trip to Switzerland, or where he vanished to after that?'

Ashton shook his head.

'Nothing very much. The Switzerland trip was supposed to be something to do with an amalgamation with a film company out there, though I have my doubts about it. Anyhow, there's been no amalgamation yet as far as I can trace. As for that vanishing stunt, well, your guess is as good as mine.'

Inspector Faithfull took a pinch of snuff himself and sniffed several times before he spoke.

'Know anything about this place of his at Sydenham?' he asked at length.

'Not much. Apparently, he bought it soon after he came out. It was bomb-damaged, but that's been put right now. I asked the local station to keep an eye on the place and report anything at all out of the ordinary. But there hasn't been much. He doesn't seem to get many visitors, or if he does they come after dark or when our men miss 'em. As far as we can tell, he lives a very quiet life. That's what I'm not too comfortable about. Osbert Strang isn't the type.'

'Maybe his five years inside quietened him down.'

Ashton shrugged. He clipped a tiny square out of a newspaper.

'I don't think his nature would change like that,' he decided. 'He had a fairly easy time — library work and so on, from what I hear. I think his spirit is a very long way from being broken. And it's fairly certain now that he had a few thousand salted away — that's how he bought himself into that firm and got the house too.'

'Doesn't anyone live there with him?'

'Only a housekeeper — two have been and gone already, I believe. Nothing exceptional about that these days of course.'

'And there has been nothing suspicious about the place?'

'As far as the local men can judge, it's just the ordinary sort of house of a typical city man.'

'Wasn't there ever a Mrs. Strang? I seem to have a vague recollection — '

'Yes, of course. They had been married ten years. She divorced him just before the trial.'

'That must have been a bit awkward if he had any money invested in her name.'

'We're not altogether sure it wasn't a trick of some sort. Although they are divorced, she visited him in prison several times.'

'Did you discover any particular reason for these visits?'

'We had a man listening pretty carefully, but he couldn't detect anything unusual. It seemed just a friendly chat about old times. Of course, they may have had some sort of code. I wouldn't put anything past that bird.'

'What happened to his ex-wife while he was inside?'

Ashton shrugged.

'Well, there didn't seem to be much point in keeping a close check on her. She's been abroad a certain amount, I believe. Living in *pensions* and such places. Over here, she took a flat at one of the south-east coast places. St. Leonard's, or Angmering, or somewhere. I can't recall it off-hand. I've had her mail opened several time, but that seems to have been innocent enough.'

'Did she write to him in prison?'

'Occasionally. Nothing wrong there either. So far as we could see. They were mostly about the book he was writing.'

'Was that book ever published?'

The other man shook his head.

'No publisher would touch it. Scared of libel and Lord knows what else besides! I heard at one time Strang was thinking of starting a publishing company himself, but that seemed to fizzle out. Maybe he thought better of it. He's always threatening to dabble in all sorts of things — brought off quite a few coups on the Stock Exchange that way. He still can't resist the temptation.'

'All the big swindlers had a bit of luck using the same tactics,' Faithfull said dryly.

He had read most of the literature authored by and about the infamous crooks of the past many years. He had drawn a deep breath to enlarge upon this theme, when he was interrupted by Somers, who came in with a letter.

'I've been looking everywhere for you,' he announced, handing over the envelope. 'This came by a special messenger who said it was urgent.'

While Faithfull was slitting open the envelope, the Sergeant turned to Inspector Ashton and said:

'By the way, Inspector, didn't you have something to do with the Strang case?'

Ashton smiled.

'I've already been over that little matter with our friend here. We've practically emptied his snuff-box while we were talking it over.'

'Then I won't waste any more time. I dare say the Inspector will give me the dope,' said Somers, turning to go.

But Faithfull called him back.

'Just a minute, Sergeant. This letter came by special messenger, you say.'

'That's what the man said when he brought it in. He also said there was no reply. Why — is anything wrong?'

Inspector Faithfull pursed his lips and read the letter for the fourth time.

'It's from a woman named Lydia Powers — seems quite an educated type,' he informed them. 'She says: *If you will meet me at the above address tonight at nine p.m., I will give you some information that may help solve your radium mystery, and at the same time level one or two old scores.*'

Ashton said:

'I suppose she means her own old scores.'

'Sounds worth looking into,' Somers

commented. 'Where does she want you to go to meet her?'

Faithfull slowly folded the piece of notepaper.

'The address,' he said, 'is 16 Shanklin Avenue, Sydenham.'

19

At four o'clock that afternoon the Assistant Commissioner called a conference of all engaged upon the radium case. It was actually more of a pep talk than a conference. He briefly outlined progress to date and stressed the urgency of obtaining speedy results.

He informed them:

'Public feeling about this business is pretty strong as you know. The Press keep repeating panicky stories, which doesn't help. That's no concern of ours of course, gentlemen. But you know how politicians like to shift their troubles on to other shoulders at times. And if we don't look out they'll give the baby to us to hold.'

His subordinates eyed each other somewhat uncomfortably. A sergeant took out a packet of cigarettes, then thought better of it and returned them to his pocket.

The A.C. resumed his lecture.

'I don't want you to think that you're not getting any outside help in this business. I've had the guard at sea and airports doubled — trebled at some of the important points. Whoever is taking this radium won't get it out of the country as easily as all that.'

'I take it that no one has been intercepted yet, sir?'

The query was in the dry tone of Inspector Faithfull from the back of the room.

It was obvious that the Assistant Commissioner was none too pleased at the interruption.

'There have been no arrests, Inspector,' he replied shortly. 'But you can take it from me that this tightening-up is known to the organization we're up against by now, and it's going to cramp their style quite a bit. They may try some fresh moves to distract us from this watch on the ports. On the other hand they may experiment with some other way of getting the stuff out of the country.'

Faithfull looked somewhat sceptical.

'A million pounds' worth of radium can be smuggled out in a box of pills,' he observed in a flat tone.

'Yes, yes, I'm quite aware of that,' retorted the Assistant Commissioner brusquely. 'But every person leaving the country now has to pass a very sensitive electroscope which would at once detect the presence of the most minute particle of radium. I've had 'em installed everywhere.'

It was the Inspector's turn to appear slightly uncomfortable, though he betrayed the fact by the merest lift of his bushy eyebrows.

He recovered almost at once and asked:

'Wouldn't it have been wiser to let the gang find out for themselves about the electroscopes?'

The other shook his head.

'We've thrashed that out, and decided that it would be quicker to put the news round the underworld right away. We're hoping it will force them into some change of tactics which will give us an opening. Everything has to be considered from the time angle,' he added in a patient tone as if for Faithfull's special benefit.

Inspector Faithfull nodded and said no more for the rest of the session.

When the Assistant Commissioner asked for reports and suggestions, Faithfull was almost the only officer present who appeared to have no contribution to make. The A.C. noticed this, but refrained from any comment, having long since reached the conclusion that it was futile to attempt to jolt old Faithfull out of his own particular method of routine of worrying things out. There was always the odd chance that he would stumble on something useful.

'I think that's all, gentlemen,' said the Assistant Commissioner at last. 'But bear in mind everything I've been telling you. This is the A1 priority job at the Yard until we've seen it through. Follow up anything that offers even the faintest chance of giving you a line on the case.'

The men drifted out talking amongst themselves.

Faithfull beckoned to Sergeant Somers and they went off down to the canteen.

There, the Inspector sipped a cup of rich brown tea, made specially strong for him. The other crumbled a stale bun, offering small pieces to the canteen cat who sniffed disdainfully.

Presently he said:

'You didn't tell the A.C. about tonight.'

'No,' Faithfull replied, almost nonchalantly. 'I thought it could wait till after. Maybe a wild-goose chase after all, and I don't see that he could do any more than I'm doing myself.'

He paused, then lowered his voice still further as he went on:

'I've arranged for six men, besides ourselves, including a couple from the local station to give us the lie of the land. They say the house stands in about half an acre, with a shrubbery at the side, so we'll have to keep a sharp look-out.'

'We'll need a couple of cars,' said Somers thoughtfully. 'I'll see to that.'

'Fix it for eight-fifteen sharp, then we'll have time to look round.'

'D'you think six men will be enough?'

'Heaps. We don't want 'em falling over each other, and what's more we don't want to attract any more attention than we can help.'

'Anyhow, it'll be dark at that time. Did you tell the locals to bring torches?'

Faithfull shook his head. 'Don't want lights flashing all over the place. You and I will take a torch apiece, and that ought to be enough.'

Soon after eight-thirty, two police cars made their leisurely way past Dulwich College playing fields and along the leafy by-ways in the direction of the Crystal Palace.

Shanklin Avenue proved to be a turning off Sydenham Hill, and consisted mainly of substantially built houses of the late Victorian period. Number sixteen was smaller than most of its fellows and appeared to be in total darkness as the police cars drove slowly past.

They went on to the end of the crescent-shaped avenue, which led them back to the main road, and eventually parked in another side-turning which was overshadowed by enormous elm trees. There, they found one of the local policemen awaiting them.

He had nothing of importance to report. He had been watching the house with his colleague for the past three hours, and had seen no one enter, not even Osbert Strang himself. Nor had there been any signs of life in the house; no rooms were lit up unless these were obscured by a very efficient black-out.

'You might say the place was shut up, sir,' concluded the constable respectfully.

Inspector Faithfull nodded and began to dispose of his men as inconspicuously as possible. His plan was to enter the house himself, leaving Somers in charge outside, with orders to intervene only in certain agreed circumstances.

Under cover of darkness, the task of stationing the men at intervals around the house presented little difficulty. Three of them slipped through the shrubbery at the side and made for the back garden. The local man who had been on duty showed them the way.

A neighbouring clock was striking nine as Faithfull went to the front door and rang the bell. He could hear it echoing shrilly somewhere at the back, but there was no sign of any movement inside. He waited a minute or two, then rang again. Not a sound disturbed the silence, except a rustling of wind in the trees of the shrubbery and the whine and clatter of a nearby electric train.

He rang once more, and when there was again no response, walked slowly round the side of the house, flashing his torch twice downwards to the ground as a sign to the policemen who were watching.

He passed two windows which he examined cautiously, and came to a third which appeared to be open a few inches at the top. It was the ordinary sash type of window, and he carefully lifted the bottom half so that it slid upwards noiselessly. The window opened enough to allow him to wriggle through, which he proceeded to do with surprising agility for a man of his build.

He stood for quite four minutes without moving, then pressed the button of his torch for a second. He seemed to be in a small pantry, the door of which was partly opened. He moved over towards it a step at a time, opened it a few more inches and looked out. No doubt about it, the house seemed quite deserted.

Very cautiously, he walked along the corridor, keeping close to the wall and moving as silently as possible. Twice he switched on his torch for a second, still pointing it downwards.

Suddenly, he paused and listened intently. He had imagined that he had heard a slight bumping noise some distance away. After a minute or so, the noise was repeated. It sounded rather like two muffled knocks. He moved cautiously in the direction from which it came, which was towards the front of the house.

As he came to a door apparently leading into one of the main rooms the knocking was repeated once more, and this time it came from what appeared to be the other side of the wall. Suspecting a trap, he silently turned the handle of the door and opened it a couple of inches. Almost at once he heard a peculiar animal-like sound which he could not immediately recognize.

Opening the door about a foot, he called sharply:

'Who's there?'

Again the strange sound, which seemed to come from a corner of the room. He took a chance and slid quickly through the door, at the same time switching on his torch and, holding it well away from him, flashed it round the room.

It came to rest on the figure of a dark-haired woman, who was tied to a chair and was also quite effectively gagged. She had obviously been trying to attract attention by kicking the wall, which she could just reach.

Faithfull closed the door, pulled the window curtains and switched on the light. Then he went across and removed the woman's gag, after which he released her arms. Her legs were not tied.

A little sigh escaped her as he untied the gag, and for a moment he thought she was going to faint. But she recovered quickly and presently managed to speak in a low whisper. She was a distinctly attractive woman, with high cheek bones and smouldering grey-blue eyes.

As she chafed her hands to restore the

circulation, Faithfull noticed that she was very smartly dressed and wore two expensive diamond rings.

'Feeling better now?' he asked presently.

She nodded.

'Much better, thanks.' Her voice was little more than a whisper.

He looked round the oak-panelled room with its imitation antique furniture and neat brick-built fireplace.

'Well?' he said curiously.

She gazed somewhat anxiously towards the door.

'I — I think we ought to put the light out perhaps — they may still come back,' she said rather nervously.

'You mean the people who tied you up?'

'Yes.'

'All right — if it'll set your mind at rest,' he agreed. 'I've got my torch in case of emergency.'

He went across and switched off the light, drawing back the curtains once more and letting in just enough light to show the furniture of the room in very faint outline. He could see the dim figure of the woman crouched on her chair in the corner.

'Who are you?'

'I'm Lydia Powers.'

20

Lydia Powers's voice came in soft, liquid tones which many men would have found fascinating.

'H'm . . . the woman who wrote to me.'

'You're Inspector Faithfull?'

'I am. Why did you write to me?'

'I saw your name in the paper.'

'What made you ask me to meet you here?'

'I happen to have a key to this place, and I knew it would be empty.'

Her manner was quite self-possessed.

'Then you know Osbert Strang?'

'I used to live here. I still keep in touch, and I knew he had been called abroad at short notice. His housekeeper is staying for a few days with some relatives. I thought we could talk quietly here.'

'And what happened?'

'I came by bus, getting here about eight-thirty, and let myself in. As I did so I thought I heard a suspicious noise somewhere at the back of the house. When I turned to close the front door after me, this handkerchief was suddenly pulled round my mouth and my arms were pinioned. Then I was hustled into here and tied to this chair. Luckily they didn't fasten my legs, so I managed to wriggle over and kick the wall.'

'Did you see these people?'

She shook her head.

'It was all confused. All I can tell you is that there were two men. One had a very harsh voice.'

'Didn't you see their faces?'

'They wore pâpier maché masks.'

'You only heard one of them speak?'

She nodded.

'It's all such a jumble. I was very frightened. I still am. They may come back any minute and — '

'Don't worry about that,' he told her, reassuringly. 'I've got half a dozen men outside.'

'Can't we get out of here?'

'I'd prefer to stay and have a good look round. This place interests me. So does Mr. Strang.'

'But you haven't got a search warrant?' she queried. He eyed her shrewdly through the gloom, but could not discern her expression.

'No,' he replied slowly, 'I haven't got a warrant. I really came on a friendly visit, you know. But I like to take precautions as far as possible. Now, perhaps you'll tell me as quickly as possible why you wanted to see me.'

She appeared to hesitate for a few moments, then leaned forward in her chair.

'I've read all about these radium robberies,' she began nervously, 'and the other day when I was down at one of the shipping offices I happened to overhear a conversation that seemed — well, rather important. There was a show-girl — '

She went on to give a reasonably recognizable description of Val Harris.

Then she continued:

'This girl was talking to a little man with a scar from his left eye down to his mouth. She called him Denny, I think.'

Denny Fox, thought Faithfull at once.

'Go on. When did this conversation take place?'

'It must have been nearly a week ago.'

'Then why didn't you get in touch with us before?'

'I — I didn't quite know what to do. Then I saw that this girl had been mixed up with a murder of a man named Lem Knight.'

'I see. And what was the man saying to this girl?'

'He said she was to bring him some stuff from Knight and that it had got to be sent out of the country right away.'

'He didn't say how?'

She had just started to reply when Faithfull imagined he heard a slight creaking noise behind him. He turned quickly, to be met with the blinding light from a powerful torch.

'Don't move,' said a curt, harsh voice. Two men were standing in the aperture left by a section of the bookshelves which had swung away from the wall on a hinge.

The torch swung over to the woman, who had given an involuntary gasp.

'Better come quietly,' the second man

told her in a low tone.

Faithfull was now able to see that they were both armed with revolvers. The woman was bundled into the opening in the wall, where a third man grabbed her. She started to scream but a hand was quickly placed over her mouth. At the same moment, Faithfull was conscious of a revolver barrel poking him in the ribs. Again the light was flashed in his eyes, and he was pushed into the chair deserted by the woman.

In less than a minute he had been efficiently bound and gagged. He tried to get a glimpse of his assailants, but as the woman had said, they wore masks.

'Don't try any tricks — and let this be a warning to you to give us a wide berth in future,' snarled the man with the harsh voice. 'We shall deal with this woman as we do with other people who interfere in our affairs. Remember Nicky?'

'I remember,' replied Faithfull, quite equably.

'It would have been a simple matter to leave a small bomb under your chair,' continued the man with the harsh voice as he backed towards the opening. 'But we think you're pretty harmless, Inspector Faithfull.'

'That's very nice of you.'

There was a rattling on the front door and the bell was rung several times.

'Open up there!'

The voice sounded like Somers's.

The man in the mask dropped the gag which he had been about to fix and made a rapid exit through the aperture in the wall, pulling the bookshelves to behind him with a distinct click.

Faithfull whistled shrilly.

It was a trick he had learned as a boy and it had stood him in good stead on many occasions. That whistle could be heard half a mile away in quiet surroundings. The Inspector repeated it two or three times, and it was not long before he heard footsteps running along the corridor.

'Are you all right, Inspector?' came the slightly anxious tones of Somers at the door.

Faithfull called out.

'Come in quickly!'

The lights were switched on and the Inspector quickly freed from his bonds. He went over to the bookshelves and fingered the wall at the side, explaining to Somers what had happened.

'See that the men outside keep a sharp look-out,' he ordered. 'This passage or whatever it is at the back of these shelves is almost sure to lead out of the house somewhere.'

He went on pressing the wall, and Somers ran to the men outside and passed the word along as instructed.

When he returned, Faithfull was still fumbling around the shelves and muttering imprecations.

'Which way did it open?' Somers asked.

Faithfull showed him.

Somers nodded.

'All right. Let's put our shoulders to it — here.'

He indicated a likely spot, and the other agreed.

At the second attempt, they felt something give. At the next assault the shelves swung inwards.

'Switch off the lights!'

Faithfull realized that they would present an easy target against the light in the opening. Somers complied at once, and they slowly widened the aperture. There was no sign of any movement on the other side of the shelves.

Faithfull stood to one side and flashed his torch inside the opening. As he had suspected, it was not a room, but a low tunnel, descending a gradual flight of steps and then an incline and apparently turning sharply about twenty feet away.

'Come on, Somers,' snapped the Inspector.

'Half a minute.'

The sergeant took a chair and propped the bookshelves open in case they had to make a hasty retreat.

The passage smelt somewhat damp as they went down somewhat cautiously in single file. Somers had to bend his head from time to time, and when they came to the turn the passage degenerated into a roughly constructed tunnel with earth walls, which showed some signs of fairly recent digging.

There was still no evidence of their

quarry and they moved on at a good pace. The tunnel went on for some considerable distance, and the ground was now very soft underfoot.

Faithfull had to use his torch almost all the time now. Soon both men were crouching to accommodate themselves to the height of the tunnel, which was only just over four feet. It seemed interminable, and Faithfull estimated they must have scrambled some seventy feet before he felt a breath of cold air which signified they might be nearing the exit.

'Careful now,' he whispered over his shoulder, 'they might still have somebody waiting outside.'

He switched off his torch, and they moved a foot at a time, feeling their way. Presently, he encountered what seemed like a strip of canvas blocking the way. Very cautiously, he pulled it aside and they felt the night air on their faces. Inspector Faithfull waited a few seconds before putting his head round the strip of canvas.

Fifty yards away to the right he saw a red light abruptly turn green, and there was the sound of an approaching electric train.

Somers gave a surprised gasp.

'Good lord! We're on the railway embankment! Anyone about?'

'Keep your voice down!' urged Faithfull, rapidly taking his bearings.

They were about ten yards from the top of the embankment. The exit from the tunnel, covered by the strip of green canvas, was obscured from anyone down on the railway line by a large hawthorn bush which provided an excellent screen, and it had obviously been planned to utilize it.

Faithfull was a trifle puzzled as to which way their quarry would have gone, but he decided that they would have tried to get back to the road.

There was no moon, and it was difficult to discern any signs of a path. The two detectives walked straight to the top of the embankment until they came to the garden wall which ran along the back of the houses in Shanklin Avenue. Almost immediately they were challenged by one of the local men who was patrolling there.

Having made himself known, Faithfull at once asked:

'Seen anyone pass this way?'

The man shook his head.

'No, sir — no sign of anybody.'

'Can you get out to the main road at all along this back wall?'

'Oh yes, sir. It brings you out in Morleigh Road that backs on to the Avenue.'

'Lead the way.'

But, as he expected, it was too late. There was no sign of anyone but a couple of stray pedestrians in Morleigh Road, and they were recognized by the constable as local residents. Nor was there a car to be seen in the road.

The Inspector told Somers:

'No use wasting any more time here. Call the men together.'

This took a little time, as Faithfull did not believe in using a police whistle for such purposes except in an emergency. They left one of the local men on guard, telling them the whereabouts of the tunnel and with strict injunctions to telephone the Yard at the least sign of anything suspicious.

On the way back, Faithfull told Somers about the kidnapping of Lydia Powers. At the mention of the name of Denny Fox, Somers said quickly:

'But isn't he one of our blokes?'

'That's right. We've had him planted down at that place in Wapping for nearly three weeks — as soon as these robberies started he was sent there.'

'Think anybody suspects anything?'

'I don't know. Denny's a queer bloke. Always works in his own way and never comes near us until he's got pretty near as much evidence as will close the case. That's probably why he hasn't split anything about Val Harris — if it's true that he has seen her, as the Powers woman said.'

'There couldn't have been much in that, or he'd surely have given us the tip-off.'

'It's tricky for Denny. Once he's blown the gaff, it's none too easy for him to go back. That's why he likes to come out with a fistful of information that's worth pretty big money. Then he lies low for a year before he takes on another job. We were lucky to get him this time — he had to be persuaded. It was only six months since his last job, but we told him that this gang was a new outfit who wouldn't know him. I hope to God it's true,' he added, as he lit a cigarette Somers had given him.

'But do we have to wait for him to contact us?'

'No. This time, I'm going to take a chance and see Denny. For one thing, I have a feeling that somebody in that radium gang might be wise to him.'

'What makes you think that?'

'I don't know. There's quite a possibility that those blokes heard the woman mention his name. In that case, Denny's chances of getting away with a whole skin aren't going to be any too healthy. I think we shall have to withdraw him from this case, just to be on the safe side.'

'You mean he might get some phoney information passed on to him?'

'That's possible. Though from what I've seen of this gang, they wouldn't bother doing things like that with small-timers like Denny Fox. Their tactics are to wipe out anybody who gets under their feet.'

'They might change their tactics for once in a way.'

Somers steered deftly past a tram and shot the Camberwell Green cross-roads on the amber traffic signal.

'In any case, I'm afraid Denny's out of the running in this set-up,' Faithfull decided. 'But until I can get hold of him, he's a danger to us and none too safe where his own skin's concerned.'

'Where can we get him?'

'He drops into the Three Sailors for a drink soon after eight every Thursday, but we've only to contact him there if it's really urgent.'

'This seems to be urgent enough all right.'

Somers pulled up with a jerk at the next set of traffic lights. He said: 'I suppose you'll go along tomorrow night.'

Faithfull smiled at him shrewdly.

'And I dare say you'll be interested to see your barmaid friend again.'

Somers let in the clutch and said:

'Might be an idea to see what he's up to. She's no more a barmaid than I'm Charley Peace. That girl's got something up her sleeve. I wish I knew what.'

The other told him:

'I shouldn't let it worry you too much. She doesn't look the criminal type.'

'H'm . . . Neither do lots of 'em,' the Sergeant murmured, dubiously.

21

The next morning, the Assistant Commissioner sent for Faithfull.

It was obvious to the Inspector that his superior was considerably annoyed about something, and it was not long before his guess was confirmed.

The A.C. fumbled amidst a pile of daily newspapers on his desk and flung a copy of the *Daily World* in front of Faithfull.

'That damned Wister Hale has been at it again. Have you seen it this morning?'

'There was nothing of any interest in the one I got on my way here.'

'This is the last edition. See — in the Stop Press there . . . '

RADIUM ROBBERIES REVELATION

Our special reporter, Wister Hale, has now discovered how the gang behind the radium robberies is smuggling the stolen radium out of the country. Quantities have been taken by a clever crook who is masquerading as a hostess on one of the big air lines.

* * *

Faithfull sniffed, folded the paper and passed it back to the Assistant Commissioner.

'That fellow gets around,' he commented.

'Where's he get his information, that's what I want to know?'

The Inspector shook his head. 'Sounds a likely tip-off, all the same,' he mused. 'I suppose there's nothing come to light at the air ports?'

'No — I'm having the hostesses searched, of course. Haven't you found out any more about him yet? I thought you went down to the *World* office and put the fear into them — '

'I went down there, sir, but there was nothing doing.'

'You haven't tried 'em again?'

'No, sir.'

'But dammit all, this can't go on.

Haven't you any idea who this man can be? After all, he must cross our path sometimes to pick up all this stuff.'

The Inspector shifted to a more comfortable position in his chair.

'I've got my suspicions, sir,' he said in a deliberate tone, 'but I don't see how I can move in the matter. After all, we've got nothing against this Wister Hale.'

'Obstructing the course of justice.'

Faithfull shook his head.

'Lord Thompson would have something to say about that. If we brought a case, there'd be plenty of unpleasant publicity — '

The other interrupted him with an irritable nod.

Reluctantly, he had to admit the other was right. Lord Thompson was capable of making himself very awkward indeed in half a dozen different ways, each more unpleasant than the last. They simply could not afford to take the risk of upsetting him.

'Very well, Inspector, you'll have to handle this in your own way. Better warn the others that if they come across this man Hale they're to warn him off in a nice way — no rough stuff.'

Faithfull nodded.

'I'll see to it, sir. Have any of the others reported anything about Hale, may I ask?'

The A.C. shook his head slowly.

'He seems to be a complete mystery packet. Manages to keep out of people's way in some uncanny fashion.'

'We probably see more of him than we're aware, sir. The name is just a cover of course.'

'Yes, it must be. Otherwise, somebody would surely have had his suspicions aroused.'

'The only thing that worries me, sir,' continued Faithfull deliberately, 'is that we're going to find Wister Hale's body one of these days.'

The Assistant Commissioner frowned.

'Yes, there is that. The fellow's letting a few cats out of the bag, and the odds are this radium gang is even more anxious to find him than we are.'

Inspector Faithfull murmured:

'Whoever he is, he's certainly got a nerve, playing a lone hand against one of the most dangerous bunches I've ever come across. Perhaps his boss doesn't realize that, sir, or he'd call him off.'

The other shook his head.

'I had dinner with Thompson last Saturday. He seems to know exactly what this business involves. He says he's paying out thousands and the fellow's taking a sporting gamble.'

'In that case, sir, I don't see there's much else we can do about it, except keep a sharp lookout.'

The Assistant Commissioner nodded and opened a file that lay on his desk.

'Just pass the word round. And don't forget, every minute counts on this case.'

Faithfull quietly withdrew and walked thoughtfully along the corridor and up a flight of stairs on the way to his office. He met Somers in the top corridor and the sergeant turned back with him into their office.

'There's a phone message just come through from Sydenham. A young woman has been to the house, stayed about twenty minutes and left again.'

'Did they know who she was?'

‘No. They’ve never seen her go there before.’

‘Couldn’t the man give a description?’

‘Nothing much, apart from the fact that she was young, slim and fairly tall — and he didn’t seem too certain about that. He said she wore some sort of veil, and that hid her face rather — ’

Somers broke off abruptly as an idea struck him.

‘Inspector, you don’t think it could be that woman you saw there last night? She might have escaped somehow and gone back to the house.’

‘She might. But it would be rather like asking for trouble, wouldn’t it?’

‘We never discovered the real reason why she asked you to go to that house. She must be well in there, or she wouldn’t have known the place was going to be empty at that time.’

Somers sketched a neat picture of a woman in a brief bathing suit on his blotting pad. Presently he asked:

‘Do you think she has any connection with Strang?’

‘I’m quite certain of it,’ was the terse

reply. 'What I can't get quite clear in my mind is whether she's one of his underlings, or an ex girl-friend out to level some old scores.'

Somers whistled softly to himself and added a few more touches to the drawing.

'Surely we ought to be able to trace her,' he mused. 'Have you tried the phone directory?'

The Inspector nodded.

'Nothing doing there. In fact, I have a suspicion that Powers isn't her real name.'

'In that case there isn't very much we can do.'

'I sent the fingerprints people to see what they could get in that room, but they were out of luck. All they got were a couple of the woman's smudges, and they aren't in our records.'

Faithfull helped himself to a pinch of snuff and began looking through a new file that had just come in.

'Did the A.C. want anything special?'

'He seemed anxious to show me the morning paper,' was Faithfull's grunted reply.

Sergeant Somers grinned slightly.

‘You mean the *World*? Russell came in with a copy while you were out. This bloke Hale is certainly going it. Think there’s anything in that story of his about some mysterious air hostess?’

Faithfull sniffed.

‘I think there’s probably quite a lot in it. We’d have got round to the racket in a day or two. Too late now, of course. The gang will drop it like a red hot cinder.’

Somers was thoughtful.

‘It was quite an idea,’ he said. ‘These air hostesses are a new thing, and none of us ever gave a thought to their criminal possibilities. I shouldn’t have thought a girl in an interesting well-paid job like that would have wanted to take the risk of losing it.’

‘There’s always the possibility that the girl was a crook before she got the job.’

‘You mean the gang used its influence to place her so that she could get their stuff out of the country?’

Inspector Faithfull shrugged non-committally.

‘This organization has a lot of tentacles. However, now that outlet is stopped up, they'll switch on to something else. And we've got to be there waiting for 'em.'

'Point is — where?'

'That's what we've got to find out. Maybe Denny Fox will give us a line on it tonight.'

He reached for the telephone and gave a number.

'Is that Mr. Strang's office?' he asked presently.

A girl's voice said that it was, but regretted that Mr. Strang was away at the moment. She wasn't quite sure when he was expected back; it might be the end of the week or early next week. Mr. Strang was often called away on business for days at a time.

Faithfull put one question after another in a casual manner, but politely refused to state his business, and finally rang off saying that he would get in touch with Mr. Strang again. He did give his name.

'What's he up to this time?' Somers asked, as Faithfull replaced the receiver. He had listened to the Inspector with a speculative look in his eyes.

'That's another thing we've got to find

out,' said Faithfull, returning to his files.

'Think Ashton would have heard anything?'

Faithfull gave him a glance, then picked up the receiver again and got through to Inspector Ashton. He, however, could offer Faithfull no explanation of Strang's absence, but promised to set to work to see what he could find out from his contacts in the City.

Somers said:

'I have an uncomfortable feeling that there's something going on. The gang hasn't pulled off anything in the last few days.'

'Except a mere murder and a kidnapping.'

'I mean in the radium line.'

'Remember they've got to think up another way of getting it out of the country. Not much use lifting it until they've got that all lined up. So that gives us a day or two's breathing space. And we've got to make the most of it.'

'All right, what's the programme?'

'You can get hold of one of those fast cars, and we'll make a quick round of the places where they hold the largest quantities of radium. Check up the precautions they're taking.'

Sergeant Somers said briskly:

'I get you. But how do we know they won't switch to the provinces? There's a lot of atomic experiments at that new place near Oxford, and the laboratories at Uxbridge, and — '

The other cut in abruptly.

'I know all about them. The A.C. has been in touch with the local police and arranged for special guards to go on duty at night.'

Somers pulled a dubious face.

'I can't see the local cops coping with that gang if they organize a big hold-up.'

Inspector Faithfull grunted.

'We shall see. Meanwhile, let's see what's for lunch. We'll start immediately after.'

When they were heading for Shadwell once more that evening, Somers, who was as usual driving, turned and said:

'Well, Inspector, we don't seem to have got much further this afternoon.'

'No?'

Faithfull's reply was in a non-committal tone, which made Somers feel vaguely uncomfortable.

He sometimes got the impression that the Inspector had observed something that was not obvious to the casual onlooker, and was storing the knowledge carefully to produce at the opportune moment. It seemed he just went on plugging away at his routine inquiries which appeared to be yielding no result on the face of things. But he was always liable to put his finger on some detail which would tie up with an important new development in the case and lead him straight to the desired objective.

Yes, Somers decided, he was a queer bird — kept his own counsel — of course he was bound to be somewhat set in his own special methods — but with every day that went by Somers grew more convinced that old Faithfull was by no means the back number that some of his colleagues thought him.

Somers was a shrewd young man, who was not above learning a trick or two from his superiors and adding them to his own ever-growing repertoire. He had concluded some time ago that Inspector Faithfull and his methods were worth studying.

The car raced through the city streets, now almost deserted.

Somers asked suddenly:

'Think Georgia Nash knows Denny Fox?'

The Inspector did not reply for a few moments.

'That's rather a nice point, Sergeant,' he murmured at length. 'In fact, a very nice point.'

'On the other hand,' he went on thoughtfully, 'it may be that Fox knows Georgia Nash.'

'H'm. If he's found out any more about her than we know already, he's certainly earned his keep,' Somers commented somewhat sceptically.

They drove on in silence until the City was left behind and they were meeting the inevitable stream of traffic from dockland.

Outside the Three Sailors they ran into a shambling little man with a cap pulled down over his eyes and a shabby scarf knotted round his throat.

' 'Arf a minute, Inspector,' he whispered hoarsely.

Inspector Faithfull halted abruptly and looked at the man in the half-light reflected from the pub windows.

'Why, it's Tubby Coles,' he exclaimed. 'Haven't seen you around lately, Tubby. What have you been up to?'

'Never mind that, guv,' replied the little man, looking round cautiously to see if they were observed. 'I got a message for yer from Denny.'

'What sort of message?'

' 'E said to tell yer 'e'd gone to the Perfessor's — called away sudden like — so he couldn't give yer the meet — see?'

The Inspector nodded thoughtfully.

'Thanks, Tubby.'

The little man vanished as unobtrusively as he had appeared.

They stood looking after him for a moment, then Somers said:

'So now what?'

'I think we may as well go in and have a quick one.'

'But supposing they're after the Professor's radium — I take it he meant Professor Mallowes — '

'If Denny had been sure about that, he'd have passed the word. As it is, I've an idea he's gone up there to check up some sort of clue.'

'Good lord! You don't think Mallowes has something to do with the gang after all?'

'I think a drop of something wouldn't do us any harm,' replied Faithfull evasively as he swung open the door of the bar.

Somers suddenly thought of Georgia Nash and cheered up considerably.

But there was no sign of her in the bar.

Behind the counter stood a large woman in the late forties, who bore the unmistakable stamp of being the landlord's wife.

Sergeant Somers got the drinks, and as he paid for them said:

'Has your fair-haired barmaid got a night off?'

The other sniffed.

' 'Er? She's packed up and gawn! And a

good job too if you arsk me. Sight too 'oity-toity for this job, she was! Never liked the looks of 'er from the start. If it'd been left to me, we'd never 'ave 'ad 'er 'ere. But my ole man says the boys always go for a blonde.'

She sniffed again, even more contemptuously.

'Blonde! Packet of peroxide every other Friday — that's all it is. I says to my ole man, 'If she draws every bloke in Shadwell into 'ere, we ain't got enough beer to sell 'em, so all you'll get is a free fight.'

She slapped the change on the counter in a small pool of beer, and Somers moved away with the drinks.

'Well, what do you make of that?' he asked Faithfull. 'You heard what she said?'

The Inspector nodded and took a gulp at his glass.

'D'you think we ought to follow this up and try to find her?' Somers persisted.

Faithfull slowly shook his head, then tilted his glass.

'She'll turn up soon enough,' he said.

22

Sergeant Somers was still considerably puzzled by the absence of Georgia Nash, as he drove in the direction of St. John's Wood.

This trick she had of vanishing almost at a moment's notice was becoming more than a little disconcerting, and he felt it was bound to arouse Inspector Faithfull's suspicions. He couldn't think why he wanted to take her part against the Inspector, he should have been concentrating upon following her trail and seizing upon any shred of evidence that might implicate her.

However, Faithfull was not particularly interested in the girl at the moment. His thoughts were running in the direction of Professor Mallowes and Denny Fox.

'That Mallowes is a queer bird,' he burst forth. 'What did you make of him?'

The Sergeant dragged his thoughts away from a slim figure and dancing eyes and concentrated upon his superior's question.

'He seemed to put his cards on the table when we were last up there.'

The other sniffed.

'Aye, he put a lot of cards on the table, but he might have had a couple of aces up his sleeve. He struck me as a man who knows just how far to commit himself. That's a very rare quality these days. Most folk say too much or too little.'

Somers nodded.

'Maybe that's his scientific mind,' he murmured.

'That doesn't necessarily follow. Look at those scientists we hear on the wireless. They talk far too much, until everybody feels downright uncomfortable.'

Somers chuckled.

'I think we'd better put the car in a garage this time,' he decided. 'We don't want one of the Professor's minions popping out and playing tricks with it again.'

'We don't know that it was one of the Professor's — '

'No,' agreed Somers quickly. 'We don't

seem to be able to prove anything against him, but there's no point in taking risks. I got properly blown up by the Flying Squad people over the last little affair. They said we should have taken greater care of their precious property — you can't altogether blame 'em you know.'

Faithfull grunted.

'Never mind about us nearly being smashed to bits! They would worry about a tinpot car.'

He could never summon up much enthusiasm for the Flying Squad.

'Anyhow, where shall I leave it this time?'

'We'll get a man at the local station and leave him to keep an eye on it.'

As it happened, they managed to pick up one of the local men on his beat not far from their destination. The policeman was interested to learn they were going to the Professor's house.

'I've seen some rum-looking birds going in and out of that place,' he told them.

'Rum in what way?' Somers asked.

'Oh, foreigners and suchlike. Always

seem to be coming and going. Experimentin' with this radium stuff, ain't he?'

'Has the news leaked out then?'

'Oh yes, we've known that for a long time. Quite a character the Professor is in these parts.' They left the man sitting in the police car, with strict injunctions not to show himself or attract attention in any way.

This time they went straight to the front door, which was opened by the Professor's manservant, who ushered them into a small study. When Mallowes came in he was obviously in a not very pleasant humour.

'Well, Inspector, what is it this time?' he snapped in his thin, dry voice.

Faithfull fished out his cigarette case and proffered it, but the other refused. The Inspector said casually:

'I understand you've had a visit from a gentleman named Denny Fox.'

'Who the devil is Denny Fox?'

The Inspector eyed him searchingly for a moment, then said slowly:

'In a manner of speaking, he's a sort of glorified copper's nark.'

'Then I fail to see what he could want with me.'

Faithfull shifted in his chair.

'The point is this, Professor,' he said deliberately. 'Fox has come here following up some pretty important clue. We are quite certain about that. It only remains to find out what clue — or what person — he came after.'

'But I tell you no one's been here.'

Faithfull smiled.

'I very much doubt if our Denny would have come to the front door. He's inclined to be a bit — well — informal in his methods.'

The Professor kicked a piece of coal in the grate, and the fire blazed fitfully.

'If this man got in here he's the first to pass my alarms.'

'He's no fool.'

'Surely you don't rate his intelligence above your own,' said Mallowes meaningly, in oblique reference to the fact that the alarms had entrapped the Inspector.

'He has a degree of low cunning sufficiently developed to cope with any burglar-alarm I've come across,' Faithfull retorted imperturbably.

Listening to the two, Somers fretted impatiently, feeling that the Inspector was losing what might prove to be valuable time. He realized, of course, that they had no search warrant, and were therefore to some extent at the mercy of the Professor's co-operation. At the moment, Mallowes did not appear to be over-anxious to co-operate.

Faithfull leaned forward in his chair. He said in a serious tone:

'I don't think you fully appreciate the seriousness of this. I'm convinced that Denny Fox came here to anticipate a very much more dangerous visitor than himself.'

'I have seen no evidence of any visitor at all,' insisted Mallowes.

The Inspector appeared more than a trifle puzzled.

'Would there be any objection to us taking a look round?'

The Professor frowned.

'I've got a lot of stuff about the place,' he growled. 'And I'm in the middle of an experiment too. It's a confounded nuisance — '

'It'll be an even greater nuisance if your stock of radium vanishes and you are unable to complete the experiment,' was the reply.

The Professor uttered a tiny exclamation of annoyance, and led the way to the door.

'Very well,' he snapped, taking them in the direction of the laboratory. 'You're a persistent man, Inspector, and I suppose you'll hang about the place until you're convinced that there's no one here.'

He unlocked a small cupboard at a bend in the passage, opened it and depressed a switch.

He said:

'May as well put the alarms out of action while we look round. Otherwise there'll be bells ringing all over the place.'

He closed the cupboard door, but did not lock it, and continued down the corridor, pressing down a couple of switches as they neared the laboratory. Somers's right hand went involuntarily to his coat pocket, which contained a small automatic. There was an almost eerie stillness as they stood at the door of the laboratory, in which there was considerably more apparatus scattered round than on their last visit.

Some of it was covered over with dust sheets. But there was one complicated mass of glass containers and retorts linked by innumerable pieces of tubing which straggled along a bench which ran almost the full length of the room under the large windows. This was obviously an experiment in operation.

Mallowes clicked on another couple of lights and they stood in the doorway for some seconds, taking a careful look round.

The two detectives moved in different directions, peering under the working benches and opening the tall cupboards on one side of the room. These, however, proved to contain only more apparatus. With folded arms, and the merest flicker of a smile playing around his lips, the Professor watched them from the doorway.

Faithfull casually lifted a dust cover

and called across to Mallowes:

'I see you've moved the cyclotron affair in here, Professor.'

The Professor moved over to him.

'So you remember that, do you, Inspector?'

'I take it you've been working on it, eh?' the Inspector commented, letting the cover fall again.

'Practically night and day,' admitted the other.

Faithfull pursed his lips and stood deep in thought.

'I suppose you couldn't make a man disappear by this time,' he suggested presently in a diffident tone.

The other smiled and shook his head.

'No, Inspector, I couldn't have done that to Denny Fox or to any other man,' he replied pleasantly enough.

Faithfull made no comment.

He walked round the back of the apparatus. His foot kicked a light object and he stooped to pick it up. It was a cheap metal-cased penknife with a small ring at each end to open the blades.

'What is it?' asked Somers, who came

across at that moment.

The Inspector held the knife in his palm, then extended it to Somers and the Professor.

Scratched crudely on the case, probably with a pin, were the initials 'D.F.'

The Inspector said quietly:

'Well, Professor, are you still certain that Fox hasn't been here?'

In silence, the Professor took the knife and examined it with a thoughtful frown. He gave no other indication of what might have been passing through his mind.

'How the devil did that get there?' he murmured.

'It could have fallen out of Denny Fox's pocket,' said Somers. But the Professor merely shook his head two or three times.

'You can't be certain it belongs to this man — Fox is his name? — at all. The initials are fairly common — and even if it were his, it might have been put there by somebody.'

'I think you're stretching it a bit, Professor,' Faithfull interposed. 'Somers will tell you I'm not much of a one for leaping to conclusions, but I'm going to take it for granted that Denny Fox has been here this evening — '

'But how could he get past the alarms? Never before has — '

'We won't go into that just now. It looks to me as if he realized that some of the gang were coming here — maybe someone important — '

'It might even have been Lucifer in person,' Somers put in eagerly.

But the Inspector waved him aside a little impatiently.

'You see, Professor,' he said, 'I don't know what the gang had in mind, but it was something important . . . and maybe Fox broke it up.'

'And maybe they broke up Denny Fox,' put in Somers grimly.

Mallowes gave an impatient 'Tchah!' He went on:

'I do wish police and criminals would not insist on regarding my house as a devil's playground for their feuds. It seems that I am the last person to be consulted — '

His bushy eyebrows set in a ferocious scowl.

'If you'd only offer us a little more positive co-operation, Mallowes,' replied Faithfull, 'we might clear up the whole business. Your place is like jam to wasps where this radium gang is concerned.'

The Professor began to pace up and down.

'I'm just about at the end of my patience!' he snapped. 'I threatened to take action on my own behalf the last time you were here, and I've a damn good mind . . . '

But Inspector Faithfull ignored him and was continuing his search. Somers went into the little office adjoining the laboratory and drew a blank there.

As they moved back down the corridor towards the living quarters, the manservant approached.

'There's a gentleman called by appointment, sir,' he announced. 'I've put him in the study.'

The Professor nodded shortly.

'I'll be along in a minute,' he replied.

'Who is this man?' asked Faithfull at once, as soon as the servant had gone.

'I'm afraid my private business is no

concern of yours.'

'Don't be a damn fool, Professor,' the Inspector snapped. 'You may be in very great danger.'

'I keep telling you I am quite capable of looking after myself.'

Faithfull shook his head impatiently.

'This gang stops at nothing. They'll shoot you calmly in cold blood and come walking out of the study as if they're paying a friendly call. Whether you like it or not, we're staying near at hand.'

'Very well — if you insist on eavesdropping on a harmless interview about buying some new apparatus . . . '

Faithfull grunted. He was not feeling too happy so far.

'I don't intend to eavesdrop. I said I was just going to stick around. Anyhow, it seems a funny time to be discussing that sort of business.'

'This man goes abroad tomorrow, so I agreed to see him now.'

'Humph! For all you know he might be anybody — I don't suppose you've ever set eyes on him before.'

'No — but the stuff he mentioned on

the telephone sounded interesting, if the price is right.'

'All right,' he growled finally, 'go right ahead. And if he looks fishy, or if you have the slightest suspicion about him in any way, yell out.'

Mallowes nodded and went off to the study, the two detectives following him at a leisurely pace. As they passed the small cupboard containing the master switch to the alarms, the Inspector stopped and pressed the switch down.

'D'you think it's all right to let him go?' Somers whispered, indicating the retreating form of the professor. 'It looks to me as if he hasn't told us everything.'

'As far as I can see, there's no other way out of the study except by this door.' They halted about ten yards away from the door in question.

Faithfull said: 'If this really is a genuine business interview, we can hardly interfere.'

'I don't altogether trust the old bird. Looks to me as if he knows something about Denny,' went on Somers. A thought struck him, 'Good lord! You don't think the Professor's been getting tough with poor old Denny — put him on that infernal machine and — and — '

His theorizing was interrupted by the harsh clang of a bell just above their heads.

'My God! Somebody in the lab!' exclaimed Somers, setting off down the passage at a run.

As Faithfull was about to follow, the study door opened, and the Professor came hurrying out. He rushed past Faithfull, who suddenly stopped short and returned to the study door. He was just in time to intercept a middle-aged man, who had a brief-case under his arm, and appeared to be about to leave.

Inspector Faithfull looked at him for a second, then said calmly:

'Don't run away, sir. I should very much like a little talk with you — Mr. Osbert Strang.'

23

Sergeant Somers was delayed for some seconds. He discovered the laboratory in darkness and he had to fumble for the light switches. When eventually he found them, the room seemed deserted, though he noticed at once that one of the long windows was open.

He crossed over to it after a rapid survey of the room, and after a few seconds' hesitation climbed out through the window. As he was doing so, the Professor came running in.

'You stay here, Professor,' Somers said. 'Whoever it was, I think they went out this way. Tell the Inspector I've gone after 'em.'

He vanished into the darkness, which appeared particularly dense at first, and he stood still for a moment to get his bearings. He remembered his small pocket torch, but did not use it, and moved off quickly in the direction of the gates. As he did so, he heard the distant roar of a powerful car starting, and increased his pace. When he came up to his own car which was still standing at the gates, he rushed up to the policeman sitting inside and demanded breathlessly:

'Have you seen anyone come out just now?'

The constable nodded portentously and prepared to make a statement.

'Just over ten minutes back, a man went in at the gate; then five minutes later a big car drew up just along the way there. A woman got out and went up the drive, and about a minute ago she comes back walking pretty sharp, gets in the car and off they go — '

'You didn't get the car number?' Somers cut in anxiously.

The constable shook his head.

'It was a bit too far away for me to see: all I can tell you is it was one of them black American saloons.'

Somers gave a mutter of exasperation.

'There must be about three hundred thousand black American saloons on the road at this minute.'

'I can't help that, sir, can I?' replied the policeman with a note of reproach. 'I wasn't told to watch out for any other car, or to get its number.'

Realizing that this was true enough, Somers apologized.

'But you're certain it was a woman who went off in that car?'

'I'd swear to that, sir.'

'You don't remember anything special about her?'

Again the constable shook his head.

'She was wearing a fur coat — '

'Was she tall or short or fat?'

'About medium I should think — but a fur coat makes it hard to tell.'

Somers clenched his fists from sheer frustration.

'Then you remember nothing at all about her?' he tried once more.

The policeman cleared his throat.

'As far as I could see, she wasn't wearing a hat,' he said at last.

'Didn't you catch the colour of her hair, then?'

'No, sir. That street lamp is thirty yards away, and there was no other light except the side lamps of this car, and they don't amount to much. And the other car was facing the same way, so the headlights were in the other direction.'

'You wouldn't get the idea that the woman was a blonde?' the Sergeant suggested tentatively.

But the constable stuck to his guns.

'No, sir. I couldn't say any more.'

'All right,' Somers said despondently. 'Keep sharp look-out from now on. And if anybody comes out of the gate, switch on the headlights and take a good look at him.'

'Very good, sir,' replied the constable in the slightly injured tone of a man who has been reproved for doing his duty.

Somers returned slowly to the house and went back to the laboratory, where he found the Professor mooning around, opening and shutting drawers beneath some of the benches.

'Anything missing?'

Mallowes looked round quickly.

'Luckily enough, there isn't. I had forgotten to lock away some quite important papers that might have been very useful to anyone working on atomic bomb developments. Usually, I shove 'em in the safe, but as I had anticipated coming back to work tonight I just pushed 'em in a drawer.'

'Better lock 'em away now.'

'Yes, perhaps it would be a good idea.' The Professor felt for his keys and went into the office. Somers followed and stood in the doorway while the other unlocked his safe and stowed away the papers.

He asked:

'I suppose you didn't see anyone?'

'Not a sign. Apparently it was a woman who drove off in a saloon car. I suppose you've no idea who it might have been?'

'My dear sergeant,' Mallowes replied dryly, 'if I had the least idea I wouldn't be standing here now gossiping with you. Which reminds me, I ought to get back to my guest — and the Inspector.'

'Is he with your caller then?'

'I imagine so — I think he said something to him and took him back into the study — at least, that was the fleeting impression I received as I was rushing down the passage.'

'You mean the Inspector knew the man?'

'It certainly seemed like it.'

A light broke over Somers's features.

'Come on, Professor,' he said.

24

As Inspector Faithfull barred his way in the corridor, Osbert Strang pulled up short.

'I think there's some mistake,' he said.

Faithfull ushered him back into the study, closing the door after them.

'No mistake, Mr. Strang,' he replied imperturbably.

'My name is Hansell — I am here to see the Professor about some apparatus that is being made in Switzerland.'

The Inspector surveyed him silently for a few moments.

Strang was a swarthy, rather handsome type of man in the middle forties. He was getting a trifle pudgy, but looked less than his age. He clasped a brief-case in his plumpish hands as he sat on the edge of a chair.

'I suppose you've a faked identity card and passport,' Faithfull said at last. He had spent some time examining photographs of Osbert Strang during the past few days. 'Well, let's have a look at 'em.'

The other got up and walked over to the window and stood looking out for a few seconds.

'As a matter of fact, I have no need to fake any identity card or passport,' he said presently. 'When I go abroad I travel in my own name. There is no reason why I shouldn't.'

'Then why do you represent yourself to the Professor as Mr. Hansell?'

Strang shrugged.

'Over here my own name has certain unpleasant associations, as no doubt you are aware. At times, it makes things a little difficult where business is concerned. Naturally, I can't do business with a potential client if he has no faith in me.'

Faithfull nodded thoughtfully. The explanation seemed plausible enough.

'And what sort of thing were you selling the Professor?'

'Just scientific apparatus.'

'It wouldn't be anything to do with

atomic experiments?'

Strang shook his head.

'Certainly not. It's a new valve used in certain experiments for this electronic brain. The Professor will tell you himself if you ask him.'

Strang appeared to have regained considerably more assurance by this time.

He was leaning back in his chair now, with his hands thrust in his coat pockets. Faithfull said:

'And why do you call at this comparatively late hour? I should have thought yours was the type of business that would be transacted in the daytime.'

Strang smiled in a superior manner.

'I'm afraid I keep no regular business hours,' he replied. 'You see, I arrived from Switzerland only this afternoon. That's where this apparatus is made, by the way. I telephoned the Professor from the airport. He asked me to come over this evening, as soon as I'd looked in at the office.'

'Then you haven't been home?'

'I've only spent a couple of nights there in the past two months.'

'You may find one or two changes there,' the Inspector murmured, watching him shrewdly. 'Have you heard of a woman called Lydia Powers?'

Osbert Strang answered presently:

'Of course. She was my housekeeper for quite a time.'

'Why did you get rid of her?'

'I didn't. She gave me her notice.'

'She didn't give any reason?'

'I think she wanted to rejoin her mother or nurse a relative or something of the sort.'

'And you have no idea what has been happening at your house in your absence?'

Strang looked somewhat surprised.

'So far as I know, the place has been closed. A woman's been going in twice a week just to keep it aired.' He paused for a moment, then added: '*Has* anything been happening there.'

'Quite a lot.'

'You don't mean it's been burgled?'

'I don't think anything's been taken away,' said the Inspector cautiously. 'But there's been a certain amount of breaking and entering — no damage of any consequence.'

'Good God!' Strang exclaimed in apparent dismay.

He was about to make further inquiries when the Professor and Somers, came in, both looking slightly flurried.

Faithfull raised a quizzical eyebrow at the Sergeant who responded with a barely perceptible shake of the head. Mallowes looked from one to the other in some mystification.

Somers eyed Strang curiously. His face was familiar but he did not place him immediately.

'You know this gentleman, Inspector?' the Professor asked.

'I should be very glad to hear a little more about him from you, Professor,' Faithfull replied gravely. 'I understand he is known to you as Mr. Hansell?'

'But of course. You mean — you mean — ?'

'Go on. Tell us how Mr. Hansell happens to be here tonight.'

Mallowes looked at the others as if he were a trifle puzzled. 'Hasn't he told you?'

‘Yes. But I want to hear your version.’

‘It isn’t a question of a *version*,’ the other retorted. ‘It’s just the plain fact that Mr. Hansell came here to see me about some apparatus that is being manufactured in Switzerland.’

‘And you’re interested in buying this apparatus, I take it?’

‘Providing I’m allowed to import it,’ was the guarded reply.

‘Is there any reason why you shouldn’t be — apart from the usual economical ones?’

The Professor shook his head.

‘Not that I’m aware of. If it isn’t possible, I can of course fly out there and rent a lab., but it would take longer.’

During this conversation, Strang had been sitting upright in his chair, closely following the other.

‘And now, are we allowed to complete our business?’ asked the Professor at last.

Faithfull regarded him for a minute with his forehead puckered in a thoughtful frown. Then he said:

‘Very well, Professor. But I shall leave Somers just outside the door here. If you will ring for your man, I'd like him to come with me. To see if there is any sign of Denny Fox.'

'But surely — ' Mallowes began to protest; then shrugged his shoulders. 'Very well,' he agreed, pressing the bell-push.

The servant arrived, and gravely inclined his head in response to the Professor's instructions.

He accompanied the two detectives as they quitted the room and closed the door behind them. The Inspector whispered his instructions to the Sergeant, but gave no clue as to Hansell's real identity.

As they made the round of the house, Faithfull cross-questioned the manservant as to whether he had seen any other visitor who might have been Denny Fox.

The man made a polite reply to every question, but Faithfull could not help feeling that he was not telling all he knew. However, the search of the house proved quite fruitless, and eventually the Inspector went back to the study, where he found that the Professor and Strang had concluded their business, and had invited Somers inside.

'Well, Inspector?' queried Mallowes, with a nervous smile.

The Inspector scowled.

'There's something fishy about this business,' he replied. 'And I don't think you're being as helpful as you might be, Professor.'

The Professor made a gesture of protest.

'I've allowed you to come blundering here, answered all your questions to the best of my ability, and let you search the house without a warrant. In fact, you've wasted far more of my time than I can afford to spare. What else do you expect from me?'

Faithfull thrust his hands in his trouser pockets and after a pace or two across the room suddenly swung round and confronted the Professor.

'I'm convinced that Denny Fox is somewhere on these premises — alive or dead,' he snapped.

'Are you trying to tell me he's vanished into thin air?' asked the Professor with a bleak smile.

Faithfull started pacing up and down again, then paused once more.

'You remember demonstrating that cyclotron apparatus to us a little while ago?'

'Naturally.'

'I was reading only last week in the *Science Survey* that there have been some startling developments in that apparatus very recently. You'll know all about them of course.'

The other nodded.

'I think I'm fairly up to date,' he agreed. 'But don't worry, Inspector — the perfect murder hasn't arrived yet. I'm not capable of making a man's body vanish.'

'H'm,' murmured Faithfull. 'As you're the expert, I can only take your word for the time being.'

'But surely, Inspector, even supposing I could perform this experiment, is there any reason why I should wish to — er — dispose of this person whom I've never set eyes on?'

'Murders have been committed for a surprising variety of motives,' the Inspector replied enigmatically. 'I'm afraid I have no time to probe into your scientific mind now. We have to be getting back. But I should advise you to lock that cupboard outside to make sure no one tampers with your master switch.'

The Professor let out an imprecation.

'Look here, Inspector, if I'm going to be eternally pestered with these infernal thieves, I warn you I really shall take the law into my own hands!'

Faithfull remained unimpressed.

'So long as you've got any quantity of radium on the premises, I'm afraid you must expect these incidents,' he replied off-handedly. 'If you'd let me station a couple of plain-clothes men here — '

'Certainly not! I've told you before I will not have my house constantly overrun with police.'

Faithfull moved towards the door and turned with his hand on the door-handle.

'I know you scientists are liable to be unorthodox at times, Professor, but don't overdo it. We're dealing with a highly unscrupulous gang, and it doesn't help to have you throwing spanners in the machinery.'

He turned to Osbert Strang and politely inquired:

'Can we give you a lift part of the way back? That's if you don't object to travelling in a police car.'

A suspicion of a smile quirked Strang's mouth beneath his small moustache.

'Thank you, Inspector. I have travelled in police cars before today.'

He rose and shook hands with the Professor, assuring him that he would telephone him the next day as soon as he had been in touch with Switzerland.

Faithfull watched them shrewdly as they talked. Was it possible that they were putting on this exhibition for his special benefit? Were they part of this organization, and had the professor been bribed over? This old house would make an ideal headquarters for such activities as the gang were engaged upon.

Or did the professor really imagine that the man really was Mr. Hansell, the agent of a Swiss firm of scientific apparatus manufacturers? If so, Strang had gone to some trouble to elaborate his background and acquire some knowledge of his subject. That would not be too difficult of course; for he was merely a go-between, and the firm would supply all the details he required.

Yet another thought struck the Inspector. Perhaps there really was a Swiss firm that genuinely employed Strang. Since his release from prison he had been forced to go out for smaller game than in the old days. He might be looking ahead and contacting such firms as this, with a view to opening a similar business in England — getting hold of the foreign patents and all that. Faithfull was a little vague about such things, but he had heard of large fortunes being made through obtaining rights to foreign patents.

He turned all these theories over in his mind as they walked down the drive, debating as to whether he should question Osbert Strang any further. Perhaps, on the whole, it might be preferable to let him think his story was believed unquestionably, and lull him into a false confidence. For Faithfull intended to keep a very close eye on Mr. Strang during the next few days.

The constable was waiting patiently in the car and was thankful to be relieved of his vigil.

They dropped him at the nearest police call-box, and headed for the West End.

Strang, who had spoken very little since entering the car, suddenly leaned forward and said:

'Tell me, Inspector, are you concealing anything from me about my house at Sydenham?'

'That depends entirely upon how much you know yourself?'

'I've told you — to the best of my knowledge the place has been locked up and my housekeeper has been away.'

'You'll find one of our men on duty. I'll phone and tell him you're coming — though of course he'll know you. You'll also find a tunnel which leads from one of the rooms out on to the railway embankment — or did you know that already?'

'Tunnel!' echoed Strang in a slight falsetto. 'What in heaven's name is the meaning of that?'

'It has its uses. As plenty of prisoners of

war discovered. And whoever constructed the tunnel out of your house understood a bit about the job. In fact, it seems to be the work of an organization with its own staff of experts in quite a number of lines.'

'But why pick on my place?' the other demanded with an air of faint bewilderment. 'Why should anyone want to make a quick getaway from my house?'

Inspector Faithfull pursed his lips for a moment, then said:

'You probably know more about that than I do.'

'Look here, Inspector,' rasped Strang, 'if you're inferring that my business isn't on the level — '

'You have to admit,' the Inspector interposed, 'that it all appears very suspicious. For instance, I find it rather hard to believe that an elaborate tunnel of that nature could have been made without your knowledge of the fact.'

'And I tell you I know nothing about it! I'm away a good deal, and the house is closed. Somebody has obviously been using it as a sort of headquarters.

Apparently, whoever it is thinks that the fact that I've served a prison sentence will throw all the suspicion on me if there's any trouble. And it has too. I can see from the look on your face, Inspector, that you believe I superintended the tunnelling operations myself.'

'I don't believe anything that I can't definitely prove.'

At this, Strang became rather thoughtful. When he spoke again his anger had subsided.

But Faithfull was in no way deceived. He realized that Strang was one of the shrewdest types of big business men with a ready aptitude for summing up an opponent and achieving his ends by any number of subtle methods.

The Inspector was quite prepared to bide his time and say as little as possible. But that was not Osbert Strang's way. He had made his thousands by talking and listening to other people, by drawing them out and inspiring their confidence, then cashing in on the information he had gained. In his palmier days, he had been known to boast that he could make more money from a single telephone conversation than most people could earn in a year's hard work.

He continued to discuss the tunnel with the Inspector, though in a rather more objective manner, as if he were trying to fathom why any organization should victimize him in this fashion.

He even touched lightly upon the subject of his enemies, who, he declared, would be delighted to see him back in prison, and on certain financiers who feared his staging a come-back in the world of big business. He tried to draw Sergeant Somers into the conversation, but the Sergeant drove on without making any but the shortest replies to an occasional direct question. He too gave nothing away, for he sensed his superior's guarded reaction to their passenger.

However, Somers presently offered to drop the passenger at Victoria Station. It seemed unlikely that he would get a taxi to take him to Sydenham at that hour.

'I'd be very much obliged, Sergeant,' Strang replied politely. 'Of course, I'd stay in the West End if one could be certain of getting in anywhere. But it isn't too easy at such short notice.'

There was a short silence which Strang broke as they passed Hyde Park Corner.

He turned to Faithfull and demanded curiously:

'Why didn't you tell the Professor my real name?'

'Why should I? You're within the law in trading under another name.'

'Yes, that's true of course, and I appreciate your thoughtfulness, Inspector.'

'I never make unnecessary trouble. There's quite enough of the other sort.'

'I appreciate your thoughtfulness all the same — and if ever I can give you a useful tip on the stock market — '

'No, thank you. I'm not much of a gambler, apart from my weekly crossword competition.'

'Perhaps you're right, Inspector.'

The car pulled up in the station yard. He got out and wished them good night and vanished into the station. As they drove away Somers said:

'So that was Osbert Strang? Was that

the real reason why you didn't tell the Professor about him?'

'One of them,' was the enigmatical reply.

'And the others?'

'Well, for one thing,' said Faithfull slowly, 'I have a pretty shrewd idea the Professor knows already.'

25

'You mean you think that Professor Mallowes is mixed up in this affair?' Somers asked after a short silence.

'To some extent.'

'You don't think he's 'in co' with Strang or the gang?'

'That's another thing we've got to find out,' replied the Inspector, refusing to be drawn.

Presently Somers parked the car and they ran up to the office to see if there had been any further recent developments in the case.

There was nothing of any importance, and as they put out the light and prepared to make for home, Somers said:

'It all seems to have gone rather peaceful, Inspector. There hasn't been a radium robbery for four nights now. Calm before the storm, I shouldn't wonder.'

'That depends. It's more than likely that they're lying low until they find another method of getting the stuff out of the country. We've managed to block all their other outlets, and it seems they don't intend to lift the stuff until they can get rid of it almost at once. Of course, they'll be trying to make fresh arrangements during this lull.'

'Oh well,' yawned Sergeant Somers, as they came into Parliament Street, 'I think we've got 'em on the run, anyhow. I'll probably run down to the Three Sailors first thing in the morning and see if I can pick up anything there.'

'If you're hoping to find Georgia Nash, I'm afraid you're on a wild-goose chase.'

But Somers shook his head.

'I have a feeling that something goes on down there,' he maintained stubbornly.

'I don't think you're very likely to find out much at that time of morning all the same.'

The Inspector smiled to himself. He was well aware that the other's visit was solely to make sure if the girl had by some chance returned. However, there was no opportunity to pursue the matter, for Faithfull's bus came along at that moment.

When he opened his *Daily World* next morning, his eye was suddenly caught by a front page headline, and he folded the paper to read:

RADIUM GANG PLANS NEW GETAWAY
MYSTERIOUS NIGHT PLANES
Special report from Wister Hale

Although the activities of the radium gang, controlled by a master criminal known as Lucifer, have been out of the news during the past few days, the gang is busy planning new means of getting stolen radium out of the country, all ports now being under strict police supervision.

It is expected that such attempts will utilize private aeroplanes of foreign origin, which will probably land on deserted airfields no longer used by the government. Such landings would probably be made after nightfall, when the plane would pick up the radium and take off again almost immediately.

The report went on to detail recent events in the radium robberies investigations. Here again the writer showed such considerable insight concerning police activities that Faithfull muttered an imprecation which he turned into a cough when he saw a pretty girl on the opposite seat of the bus eyeing him rather curiously.

Arrived at his office, he rang up Barrington, only to be informed that the editor of the *Daily World* had not yet arrived. He rang twice that morning with similar results, and it was not until after lunch that Barrington's familiar drawl came over the wire.

'Well, Inspector, what is it this time?'

'So you've decided to drop in after all!'

'You should know by now that I'm never due in the office until after lunch,' the other chuckled. 'If I go in before then it's overtime! Anything wrong? Want some advice on our crosswords? One of the typists is doing it this week — '

'I am not interested in your crosswords expert,' retorted Faithfull severely.

'Oh,' said Barrington. 'Then I suppose it's Wister Hale. What is it this time?'

The Inspector sniffed.

'You don't seem to realize this is a case

which may well have international repercussions. Don't you think it's time you stopped this childish nonsense and gave up printing these news stories that are chiefly conjecture and only serve to confuse the issue?'

'My!' chuckled Barrington, 'we do sound grand this morning, Inspector. You're talking to the *Daily World* you know, not *The Times*. Wister Hale's still doing very well for us. Lord Tom's delighted with him, and even the advertising manager thinks he's not so bad.'

'That's all very well. But this farce has gone on long enough. If you're getting this information from inside the Yard, there'll be trouble.'

'I can assure you, that is not the case,' asserted Barrington in a more serious tone. 'And seeing it's you, I'll give you one small tip. Hale's last message — the one about the airfields — came from Taunton.'

'What the devil was he doing at Taunton?'

'Don't ask me. I'm no crime expert. I know Taunton sounds one of those harmless places — cathedral and country — but you can never tell these days. I leave you to sort it out, Sherlock.'

Faithfull grunted and rang off.

He repeated the gist of the conversation to Somers when he came in about an hour later from his trip down to Shadwell Basin.

'Taunton!' echoed Somers, pricking up his ears at the name. 'I was stationed near there for over a year during the war. Nothing ever happens in that part of the world.'

'That would provide the best of reasons for choosing such a spot.'

'But this news splash may well put a stop to them trying anything in that line. They'll think we're going to watch the airfields.'

'On the other hand, their plans may have gone forward too far, and they may decide to take a chance. After all, for a plane to land and take off again is only a question of minutes, and on a dark night it's a pretty good sporting chance, specially in one of these out of the way spots. We can't very easily police every abandoned airfield at short notice, apart from asking the local men to keep a sharp look-out. And they can't spend all their time hanging around such places.'

'But if Wister Hale is at Taunton — '

'The fact that he sent a story from Taunton does not necessarily imply that he was investigating it there. He might have been on the track of something else altogether.'

Somers nodded thoughtfully.

'I can see your angle. And that bloke is nearly always one jump ahead. I've been expecting him to trip up long before this.'

'Humph! I expect we'll have to pull him out of some nasty situation before he's much older,' the other murmured. 'Did you have any luck at the Three Sailors?'

'I had a nice glass of old and mild, one or two near-insults from the landlady when I tried to make a few inquiries, and some dirty looks from the landlord when he suspected who I was. Apart from that — nothing.'

'Your blonde friend seems to have done the vanishing trick this time all right.'

Faithfull helped himself to a generous pinch of snuff before preparing to concentrate upon the contents of yet another file.

The case was beginning to get interesting now, as the nets started to close. It looked as if the gang would be forced into the open at any moment, and they would be stung into some pretty desperate action. There was no accounting for what form this would take, and he was anxious to cover all contingencies. With the limited number of men available, this was none too easy.

As his snuff-box was almost empty, he took a small packet from his desk and very carefully refilled it. He received a fresh packet of newly ground snuff from his tobacconist in Charing Cross Road every fortnight, and was most particular as to its blend. However, he did not sample the new packet at once, but went off to see Inspector Ashton to discuss the question of Osbert Strang with him. There were several details into which he was anxious to inquire in view of the incidents of the previous evening.

He found Ashton in his office. They settled down to talk, Faithfull offering his snuff-box. Inspector Ashton took a small pinch, but did not inhale it immediately. He was busy giving the other the gist of some recent reports about Strang's activities in the world of finance.

When he did at last place forefinger and thumb to his nose, he took the lightest sniff. His reaction was startling even to Faithfull who was accustomed to seeing strong men momentarily taken aback by his own brand of snuff. Ashton gave a great shudder and recoiled as if struck by the blast of a bomb. His eyes shut tightly and he was obviously breathless with agony.

'Blow your nose — hard — quick now!' ordered Faithfull at once, placing his handkerchief to his colleague's nose. 'Come on now — blow!'

After Ashton had done his best to comply, Faithfull thrust the other's head forward to his knees. With his left hand he grabbed the telephone and asked for a doctor to be sent up right away. He ordered Ashton to keep his eyes closed, breathe in through his mouth and out down his nose to get rid of the snuff as quickly as possible.

By the time the doctor came in, he was beginning to show some signs of recovery, but his breath came with difficulty and his eyes were heavily inflamed.

'What the devil's going on here?' asked the police surgeon in a mystified tone.

'I gave him a pinch of snuff and it's knocked him straight out. Something wrong somewhere — I think I've got rid of most of it, but you'd better have a look at him to make sure.'

The doctor took a tiny examination torch from his pocket and made a rapid examination.

While he did so, Faithfull took out his snuff-box, which he had pushed into his waistcoat pocket. Very cautiously, he opened the box and carefully examined the mixture inside, rubbing a few grains gingerly between his thumb and first finger. Perhaps it was a shade lighter than his usual mixture, but it looked like snuff.

The doctor was putting drops into Ashton's eyes as he lay back in his chair.

Then he made his patient close his eyes again, and sent for a bandage to cover them.

'I don't think his sight will be affected, but it might have been a near thing,' he murmured to Faithfull. 'Better make him keep the bandage on for a few hours; then I'll look at him again. Now, let's see what's the cause of all the trouble.'

26

Faithfull gave him the snuff-box. The doctor took it over to the window, where he remained for some little time.

'I'll have to take it down to the lab,' he said at last. 'All I can tell you so far is that the stuff seems to have turned into some pretty virulent gas inside the nose. I have my suspicions as to what it is, but that isn't nearly so important as the question as to where you got it.'

'I'm going to look into that right away. Are you sure he'll be all right now?'

He nodded towards the hapless Ashton.

'I think so. I'll take him with me down to the sick bay.'

Together they helped Inspector Ashton to his feet.

'How are you feeling, old man?' Faithfull asked anxiously.

The other managed to summon up a sickly smile.

'I'll be all right presently,' he replied in

a half-whisper, with some effort. 'What in God's name had you got in that box? I've never known your snuff that strong before.'

'It's a lucky thing you dropped most of it on the floor. I happened to notice you — I was just going to offer you another pinch.'

'One pinch like that will last me a lifetime,' Ashton said, with the ghost of a chuckle. 'My eyes are still burning — '

'That'll soon pass off,' said the doctor reassuringly. 'The drops will put them right.'

Leaving Ashton in the sick bay, Faithfull went at once round to his tobacconist's just along the Charing Cross Road.

He had known Albert Pope almost since he started work at Scotland Yard, and had long since joined the select circle of customers for whom the old man blended their special mixtures of tobacco and snuff with infinite care in his little back office.

The little tobacconist looked up and smiled over the steel rims of his glasses when the inspector entered. He had a rosy complexion and silvery hair that made him look very like an advertisement for some rich blend of well-matured tobacco.

'Why, Inspector, I haven't seen you for quite a time,' he began pleasantly. 'You've been busy I suppose with this crime wave.'

Faithfull nodded a trifle curtly as he looked round quickly. The shop was empty at the time, but one couldn't very well talk there.

'Could I have a word with you in private?' he asked. Faithfull had only been in the back office once on Pope's invitation, and the little tobacconist seemed slightly surprised at his request.

'Of course, Inspector — come this way.'

He lifted the flap of the counter and went through to the back office.

He cleared some odds and ends from a chair for his visitor to sit down. But the Inspector preferred to lean against the fireplace.

For a few seconds they eyed each other curiously without speaking. The tobacconist seemed slightly embarrassed.

'No complaints about the last lot of tobacco — or snuff?' he queried a trifle nervously.

'As a matter of fact, there is. Though it's probably none of your doing, Mr. Pope. I've called about that last lot of snuff. When did you send it round?'

'Why, the day before yesterday,' replied the little man. 'My boy was away that day, so I asked the young lady to call in with it when she went to lunch.'

'The young lady?'

Faithfull had never seen a woman behind the counter in Pope's shop.

'Oh yes, Inspector — of course, it's some time since you were here. I engaged a young lady a couple of weeks back — I haven't been too well lately, and the doctor ordered me to rest more. So I advertised in the evening paper, and engaged Miss Kershaw last week. She was very obliging. Never minded running any little errands . . . and picked up the work amazingly well.'

'Then where is she today?'

The little man looked troubled.

'That's what is worrying me,' he

admitted. 'She hasn't been the last two days, and I'm afraid she must be ill or something unpleasant has happened. We hear of so many of these unfortunate incidents nowadays — '

'But surely she gave you her address.'

'Yes,' replied the tobacconist, 'she did write it down for me, but I'm afraid I have mislaid it. I'm not very business-like in that direction. Anyhow, I mustn't burden you with my little worries. What is the complaint about the snuff?'

'I'm afraid,' Faithfull said with almost a reluctant air, 'that it wasn't snuff at all.'

'Good heavens! Then what was it?'

The Inspector shook his head.

'I don't quite know. A very unpleasant sort of drug, I'm afraid.'

The tobacconist was obviously startled.

'But, Inspector, I swear it was your usual brand that I packed up and — '

'I don't doubt you,' interposed the Inspector gently. 'But I'm beginning to suspect that it was not your original packet that was delivered to me.'

The little man's eyes dilated behind the pebble lenses.

'Good heavens!' he whispered. 'But who would do a thing like that?'

'I could make several guesses. Can you describe this assistant of yours to me?'

'But — but — she seemed such a nice girl — I don't see how she could possibly — '

The tobacconist stammered in his distress.

'All the same, I shall have to ask you for a description. She may not be the culprit of course. Or at any rate she may just be the agent of the real person responsible. So if you could give me some idea of what she was like.'

'I — er — well, I'm not very good at these things,' faltered Mr. Pope. 'She was dark — about thirty, I should think — average height — usually dressed very sensibly. I'm afraid that's about all I can tell you. As soon as she comes back I'll send her right round to you at Scotland Yard.'

'No,' Faithfull said decisively. '*If* she comes back, telephone me at once without letting her know.'

The little man nodded eagerly and

promised to do this. As Faithfull moved to the door he called to him.

'I knew I wanted to see you, Inspector,' he murmured, as he began rummaging amongst a pile of papers on a desk in the corner of the room. After a couple of minutes, he produced a rather grubby envelope on which was scrawled:

Inspector Faithfull.

'I meant to send it round to you,' the other said, as he passed it over. 'Somebody left it here when I was out, so the girl said, I found it on the shelf at the back of the shop. I thought it couldn't be very important or whoever it was would have taken it to the Yard.'

Faithfull tore open the envelope and extracted a small sheet of notepaper on which was scrawled in bright green writing:

When this is read out to you, Inspector Faithfull, I hope you will realize that it is unwise to meddle with the affairs of

Lucifer.'

Faithfull slowly folded the note and

replaced it in the envelope.

He looked at the little tobacconist and said slowly:

'Somehow, Mr. Pope, I don't think your young lady will be coming back.'

27

The next morning, Sergeant Somers leaned back in his chair and propped his feet against his desk. He slit open an envelope he had found waiting in his letter basket. As he read it, he whistled softly to himself and thoughtfully stroked the back of his head. Since the recent disappearance of Georgia Nash, he had been feeling unaccountably depressed.

Inspector Faithfull, who sat at the opposite desk, was feeling just the opposite. This was possibly because his wife was back at home. He had enjoyed a well-cooked breakfast that morning and his digestive processes were working more pleasantly than they had for some considerable time.

The news that his colleague, Ashton, had completely recovered from the previous day's unpleasant experience had also cheered him up considerably.

True, he had not succeeded in discovering the identity of the tobacconist's mysterious assistant, even though Pope had found the address she gave him.

It proved to be that of a house in Notting Hill Gate, the usual house converted into small flats. Miss Kershaw was hardly known to the housekeeper. She had only been there for a few days, and now apparently disappeared.

Faithfull was now feeling almost happy as he went through the latest reports, which recorded little save matters of routine. There had been no further radium robbery.

At length Somers tossed over his letter.

'What d'you make of this? It's from an Air Force pal of mine — we were stationed at that potty little place I told you about in Somerset. He got pally with the bank manager's daughter. Now he's married her and settled down there not far from the old airfield.'

The other opened the letter and read:

Crestview,
Nettlejold Hill,
Nr. Taunton.

Dear Cop,

You remember when I was an M.P., I rather fancied my chances as a Sherlock Holmes, and reading in the World *about this radium affair impels me to take up my pen and advise you about some very queer goings-on in these parts during the last week.*

Seriously though, old man, things really have been happening up at the old airfield. I stroll that way most fine evenings, and one night last week when there was no moon, I could have sworn a plane landed there. It had no navigation lights. I thought I might have been mistaken, so said nothing at the time, but last night it happened again.

You know, of course, that the airfield hasn't been used for over eight months, so it seems to me that something fishy goes on. Nobody else seems to have spotted anything yet — as the field is quite a way from the village, and there are no houses near, as you know.

Anyhow, I'm tipping you off in case you blokes think something ought to be done about it. Anyhow, if you do follow this up, be sure to look in, and I'll promise you a drop of something extra special, if you undertake not to inquire where I got it!

All the best, rozzer,
Your old Corp,
HAL CRESTON.

Faithfull passed back the letter.

'Seems a bit of a joker,' he commented.

Somers frowned.

'He always liked a bit of fun. But he must be taking this pretty seriously. For one thing, old Creston never wrote more than a couple of letters the whole time I knew him. I remember his mother wrote him about eight times about something or other, and he wouldn't bother to answer till I stood over him and made him do it, because she'd started writing to me to find out what he was up to!'

He scanned the letter again and said:

'I think we ought to do something about it, Inspector. Remember that Wister Hale was supposed to be at Taunton. There might be a chance — I could run us down there in plenty of time for this evening. I don't suppose they'll try any tricks before it gets dark.'

Faithfull took out his snuff-box, which had been cleaned and sterilized before it was filled again before his own eyes from Mr. Pope's special canister.

The Inspector took a generous pinch, though Somers observed that he sniffed it rather more cautiously than usual.

At last, he seemed to reach a decision.

'All right, we'll go down and look round.' Somers's face lighted up at the prospect. He had not seen 'Slinger' Creston for nearly four years.

'Just the two of us?'

Faithfull nodded.

'Good. Old Slinger Creston is pretty useful in a rough house, and I dare say we could pick up a few locals.'

'The main idea is to attract as little attention as possible. So I suggest we don't arrive until dusk at the earliest.'

'Suits me. I'll give old Slinger a ring and tip him off.'

'Can you rely on him to keep his mouth shut?'

Somers grinned.

'Slinger can be as dumb as the prettiest blonde in the front row of the chorus when the occasion arises,' he solemnly assured his superior. 'This looks a sinister sort of set-up to me,' he went on. 'I'll get a permit to take the old automatic along. Just in case.'

'Please yourself,' grunted Faithfull. He very rarely carried a gun himself.

They set off for Taunton after lunch. It was a fine afternoon, and they enjoyed the run.

Somers tried to draw out Faithfull on the subject of his suspects in the case, but the Inspector seemed to prefer to brood upon his problems.

He was wondering, for instance, why Osbert Strang had paid three visits to the Professor's house since they had last seen him. These trips had been faithfully reported by the plain-clothes man whom Faithfull had detailed to shadow Strang.

Of course, he might be seeing Professor Mallowes about that apparatus. On the other hand he might be hatching up some nice scheme or other. Faithfull was reluctant to come to the conclusion that Strang had any connection with the gang. Indeed he had very little definite evidence — Strang was as wily as they make them, but in his mind he regarded him as a jury considers a hostile witness.

Strang was a slippery fish, who had had so much experience in slithering through the hands of the law that he knew every turn. What was more, his prison sentence had made him cautious, and he would not be encompassed in the net a second time without a tough fight. The stakes would have to be the highest to make it worth his while.

Radium was the biggest gamble in the civilized world of today. If the supplies of radium fell into the hands of a gang of international criminals of Strang's type, they could blackmail the world.

And now, according to the latest reports this morning, Strang had apparently gone abroad again. It might, of course, have some connection with the valves made in Switzerland, but according to the detective who had followed him to the airport he had boarded a plane for Lisbon.

Faithfull had cabled the Foreign Office Security Branch at Lisbon to be on the look-out for him, but he very much doubted if they would surprise Mr. Osbert Strang in any illegal act.

They stopped and had tea in Taunton, and it was dusk when they reached Nettlefold Hill, a village with about two hundred houses, a couple of shops and a tavern. They discovered the Creston residence without much trouble, and after introducing them to his wife, Hal Creston took them to the Tallyman's Arms for a drink.

Somers looked round the familiar bar parlour, and nodded to one or two of the locals whom he recognized again. A faint wave of nostalgia swept over him, as he gulped down his second pint. He noted that Slinger was already referring to the war years as the good old days, and concluded that he found life in his father-in-law's business rather less exciting than those nightly trips to Hamburg, which appeared considerably less terrifying in retrospect.

After a time they got a corner to themselves and chatted in low tones. For the first time since their arrival, Creston broached the subject of their visit.

'I've got into the habit of strolling as far as the airfield and back after the pub closes,' he told them. 'It's been close on eleven when I've seen the plane — or rather heard it. I didn't see more than a very faint outline one night — it's been so dark. Maybe tonight will be better. The sky's much clearer and there's quite a bit of starlight. Let's hope it keeps like it.'

He went off to the counter to get some more drinks. Somers turned to his superior and said:

'Old Slinger might be pretty useful. He's got eyes like an owl in the dark — developed them when he was navigator on night flights. Of course, he isn't so keyed up now. We shall see.'

They stayed in the bar until closing time, talking mostly of their wartime experiences. Faithfull drank his customary two pints, but the younger men were more indulgent, though they insisted that the beer was too weak to take effect. Indeed, it seemed to be true, for they strode briskly down the main street at ten-fifteen as if they were setting out on a marathon.

28

'Are we far from the airfield?' Faithfull asked. He was beginning to wonder if he was right to have left the car in the village, a decision he had taken to avoid attracting attention.

'It's about a couple of miles,' Creston informed them. 'If I'm feeling energetic I walk along one side of the common when I get there, and come back a different way.'

'You were always an energetic cove, Slinger.'

'What does your wife say about these rambles?' Faithfull asked.

'Oh, she doesn't mind. Always goes to bed at ten, and is fast asleep when I get back. But I don't do it every night,' Creston added.

'I should hope not!' Somers chuckled.

It was a starry night and by no means pitch black.

Faithfull could distinguish the shapes

of trees and cottages at a distance of about fifteen yards without much difficulty. But before they had been walking long he discovered that Creston's visual range was considerably wider. He pointed out an old windmill when they were fully forty yards away from it.

'We've walked this road a few times,' Creston cheerfully informed Faithfull. 'And run the whole way more than once when we've cut things fine.'

'I suppose there's nobody at all on the camp now?' Somers asked.

'Quite deserted. They've dismantled the huts, but the hangars are still standing. Nominally, the place is still under Government control. But we hear rumours that it will be released any day now.'

They passed the derelict windmill, with its sails creaking dismally in the chilly night wind. Faithfull turned up his coat collar. Somers felt a craving for a cigarette, but decided they could not risk showing a light in the little-used lane they were now passing through. It led only to the airfield, and would attract very few pedestrians or cars at that time of night, apart from an occasional pair of lovers.

Presently they came to the side turning which had formerly been a public road across the common, but which had been barred off when it became the entrance to the airfield. The barrier was still there, but they had no difficulty in climbing it.

'Hallo, the guard's hut has gone,' Somers commented.

They now found themselves on a heavily metalled road, which had been specially constructed for the aerodrome.

This road led to the staff quarters, then made a complete circuit of the airfield, crossing the runway at either end. Faithfull strained his eyes, but could see little, apart from a large hangar which loomed up suddenly and vanished almost as quickly as they strode on in the direction of the flarepath.

Somers looked at the luminous dial of his wrist-watch. It was ten minutes to eleven.

The wind blew more strongly across the open common and the three men began to feel the cold. They walked briskly until they came to the far end of the runway.

Somers looked at his watch again.

'Looks as if we're unlucky tonight. If you'd rather get back, Slinger, we'll hang on another hour or two.'

But Creston would have none of this. He had insisted on putting them up for the night, and likewise declared that he would share their vigil.

They continued to pace up and down. The breeze carried the distant chime of the village church clock striking midnight, and just as Somers was ruefully reflecting that he should have brought a flask along with him to help him through the night watches, they heard a distant humming. It did not seem to come from up above, and it had a strange, unusual note.

'What the devil is it?' Faithfull queried, considerably puzzled.

Creston stood with his head cocked in the direction of the sound. He seemed to be holding his breath, and after a few seconds he exclaimed suddenly:

'My God! It's inside the hangar — they've got the plane inside!'

Somers seemed a trifle doubtful, and they stood listening for several moments. Then, mingling with the hum of the engine came the metallic reverberation of the doors of the hangar banging open.

'You're right, Slinger! Come on!'

They began to run in the direction of the hangar from which the sound came. Suddenly, it grew louder with startling rapidity, and Creston, who was running a little ahead of the other two, shouted:

'Down! Get down for God's sake!'

They all flung themselves on their faces only just in time, for the plane came rushing over them with a great sweep, the swirling backwash of air from the propeller hitting them like a giant flail. The deafening roar of the engines slowly faded as the plane lifted and vanished into the night.

Creston was the first to sit up, still listening intently to the receding plane.

'Four-engined Carana,' he announced.

'Never heard of it,' mumbed Somers, slowly rising to his feet.

'Foreign job. Austria had started making 'em before they were invaded, and a few of 'em were flown to neutral countries.'

'How the devil can you tell?'

'I caught a glimpse of the shape of the wings.'

Faithfull thrust his hands deep in his overcoat pocket.

'I think we'll take a look at the hangar, anyhow,' he decided.

They found it with the doors left wide open, as if the crew of the plane had either been in a great hurry, or did not propose to return.

Inside, the silence seemed almost oppressive. It was broken only by the dismal howling of the wind, which occasionally lifted a section of corrugated sheeting with a clatter. Sergeant Somers produced his torch, and the bright beam stabbed the heavy darkness. It revealed that the hangar had been stripped very bare indeed, and was practically nothing but a shell structure. They walked to the far end, in a corner of which was a small partitioned office.

Faithfull tried the door, but it seemed to be locked.

'Sh!' hissed Somers suddenly, and they stood listening.

Abruptly Somers switched out the torch and they waited tensely in the darkness for several seconds. Then they heard a faint but unmistakable moan from inside the little office. Without further ado, Somers and Creston flung themselves at the door, which burst open at the second assault.

On snapped the torch again, revealing the office in a state of disorder, a small table and a couple of chairs having been overturned.

In a corner opposite the door, a woman lay slumped on the floor, half-propped against the wall, her hands and ankles tied. She appeared semi-conscious, and moaned as the light flashed across her eyes. Her head had dropped forward.

Somers knelt at her side.

'Good lord! Georgia Nash!'

29

Inspector Faithfull came over at once to Somers's side and helped to untie the rope around the girl's ankles.

'She's had a pretty nasty shock,' he declared, as Georgia Nash opened her eyes for a moment, then closed them again with a groan.

'Might have lain there and starved to death,' commented Creston. 'Nobody comes near this place for weeks at a time nowadays. Whoever tied her up had a pretty grim sense of humour if you ask me.'

The Sergeant placed his hand behind the girl's head to lift her up.

'Hallo,' he murmured, 'she's had a nasty bang on the back of the head.'

Faithfull pushed aside the blonde hair and examined the place. 'I don't think it's really serious. It's raised a nasty bump, though. Couldn't have been as bad as all that, or she would still be right out.'

She opened her eyes again and seemed to be making an effort to speak, but her voice faded into a sigh.

'Poor kid,' Somers said. 'She's in a pretty bad way.'

'Are you going to try to move her?' asked Creston. 'Maybe we could find a stretcher of some sort — there used to be scores of 'em about the place.'

'Wait,' Faithfull said. 'There's no hurry.'

He and Somers began rubbing the girl's hands vigorously. After a few minutes she managed to summon up a feeble smile of recognition.

'It's — it's you two again — always turn up sometime — '

'Don't try to talk yet.'

The Inspector continued chafing her hands. He examined the place at the back of her head again, and found the skin unbroken.

'Looks like a blow from a rubber cosh,' he said.

She seemed to have heard him for she gave a slight nod.

'All right,' Faithfull said. 'We'll go into all that later.'

He set one of the chairs on its legs, and they lifted her on to it. From then, she began to recover, and presently managed to stand on her feet.

'I'd rather not take her to hospital if it can be avoided,' explained Faithfull to Creston quietly. 'There might be some inquiry or publicity.'

'Of course,' nodded the other. 'We'll get her round to my place as soon as she's fit.'

Faithfull nodded gratefully.

It was after three a.m. when they got back to Creston's house half carrying the girl. Sometimes, she walked leaning on two of their shoulders; sometimes they gave her a fireman's lift; and part of the way Somers had carried her himself.

Mrs. Creston, a cheerful young woman, who had been abroad with the A.T.S. and took a considerable amount of surprising, came hurrying downstairs; she fetched some whisky and bustled off to get them some hot drinks. The colour flowed back to Georgia Nash's cheeks as she spread her hands before the large electric fire.

'You're pretty lucky to be here, young

woman,' Creston told her. 'Gosh! I haven't had such an exciting evening since the last time I was over Hamburg!'

Faithfull encouraged him to talk for a while about his wartime experiences, and also professed to take an interest in Mrs. Creston's adventures. But he was watching Georgia Nash narrowly all the time.

As a clock in the hall struck four, he turned to her and asked:

'Would you like to tell us all about it now, or will you wait till the morning?'

Mrs. Creston had disappeared by this time to put a hot-water bottle in the spare bed in readiness.

Georgia Nash said her head was throbbing less alarmingly now, thanks to their ministrations.

It had been decided that Somers and the Inspector should shake down in the large armchairs in the living-room, and drive back to London first thing in the morning, taking the girl with them if she was well enough.

'It's rather a long story,' she said a trifle nervously, in reply to the Inspector's inquiry. He said:

‘All right, you can tell us everything on the way back to London.’

Mrs. Creston returned and took the girl off to her room, leaving her husband to settle his guests for the night with blankets and rugs.

‘Sorry we haven’t got any spare beds,’ he apologized, ‘but you know what a devil it is furnishing these days. We were damned lucky to get the house!’

He turned to Somers and nodded in the direction of the stairs up which Georgia Nash had disappeared.

‘I take it you know all about the lady friend?’

Somers said:

‘We know a bit about her.’

‘Quite a smasher, eh? You blokes see all the fun.’ He paused, looking from one to the other, and added: ‘There’s only one thing puzzles me. Whose side is she on?’

‘That,’ replied Inspector Faithfull, ‘is one of the things we hope to find out tomorrow.’

30

After Creston had left them, still apologizing for his inadequate hospitality, the two Yard men chatted in a desultory fashion for a few minutes before dropping off to sleep.

'Something's got to be done to stop this using deserted airfields,' the Sergeant said.

The other yawned.

'I'll phone the A.C. first thing in the morning. Now we've established it isn't just a scare, there'll have to be a guard mounted on all the aerodromes. I dare say he'll get some help from the War Office or Air Ministry.'

The Sergeant sighed.

'It's probably too late now — the birds have flown, and they won't use that trick again.'

'More than likely,' Faithfull nodded. 'The only thing is we have to block their moves all the time as they think 'em out.

They can't go on for ever.'

'Seems a rule of thumb sort of plan to me,' Somers mumbled, settling himself into a more comfortable position.

'It's been known to work,' the Inspector grunted, 'in the great majority of cases.'

He pulled the blankets up to his chin and drained the last drop of whisky from his glass.

At breakfast time Inspector Faithfull telephoned the Assistant Commissioner at his home and gave him a brief report of the events of the night.

'Humph!' growled the A.C. after he had heard the story, 'that explains the Taunton robbery.'

'I beg your pardon, sir?'

'There was half a gramme of radium stolen from a car at a big nursing home at Taunton last night — soon after ten o'clock as far as we know. It had been rushed down there for a special case, and that confounded gang must have got wind of it. It was just being returned to London by car — two men held up the car with guns and got away with the stuff.'

There was a reproachful note in his voice, as if he thought that Faithfull might have forestalled the whole affair, as he was in that part of the country.

When he passed on the information to Somers, the Sergeant frowned.

'Now I come to think of it, a car did pass us soon after we left the pub,' he said slowly.

'Shouldn't we have seen it at the airfield?'

Somers shook his head.

'Not necessarily. They could have come out the other side of the common where they left. The road cuts straight across and comes out in another lane that winds back to the village. You know what these country roads are.'

Faithfull began to fold the blankets which were scattered over the chairs.

'I don't see how their luck can hold out much longer,' he mused.

'Seems to me a lot depends on whether we can make that girl talk.'

'She'll talk this time,' the Inspector said confidently. 'It's the least she can do after we got her out of that mess.'

At this juncture, Mrs. Creston came in to lay the breakfast, followed by her husband, hastily knotting his tie and fastening his waistcoat.

'How did you two sleep?'

'Very well,' Faithfull replied. 'That whisky of yours did the trick.'

'Wish I could say the same,' grunted Creston. 'I've been lying awake for hours, trying to figure out what those birds were really up to last night.'

'You'll see it in the papers at lunchtime — or even before that. There was a radium robbery in Taunton last night.'

Creston half choked as he was drinking his coffee.

'Good lord! So that was it! And they made a clean getaway.'

'Not quite clean — they left a sort of hostage,' Faithfull reminded him.

'You mean the girl? Good lord, yes? How is she this morning?'

Creston turned to his wife.

'She'll be down presently. I think she's practically back to normal.'

'Damn! I won't be able to see her. Your worthy parent expects me at the office at nine-fifteen sharp. To set an example to the staff, so he says. And good lord, it's turned half-past-eight now.'

He hastily gulped down two mouthfuls of toast and emptied his cup.

'Sorry to dash off like this,' he apologized, 'but we really are pretty busy. I take it there's nothing else I can do for you blokes? Stay as long as you like, of course. Joan will look after you like a mother.'

'Thanks, old man, but we've got to get straight back to Town,' Somers replied. 'It's been nice seeing you again and talking over the old times.'

'Grand seeing you too. Best bit of excitement for years. Come again as soon as you like.'

Creston gathered his hat, gloves and brief-case, and kissed his wife.

'We keep up the old country customs down here,' he explained to his guests, waved his free hand in farewell and went to get his car.

Just as the others were finishing breakfast, Georgia Nash came down and joined them. She was a little paler than usual, but seemed otherwise to be suffering no ill-effects.

Although Mrs. Creston was obviously very curious, the men did not offer to discuss the adventure of the previous evening. Her hostess passed over a generous helping to Georgia Nash, who looked up at her and said with a smile:

'The condemned woman ate a hearty breakfast!'

The two women laughed. Then the girl said:

'I'm terribly hungry, but I don't think we ought to sponge on you like this.'

'That's all right. Here in the country we manage to get our little extras, and I learned a lot about scrounging in the A.T.S.'

The conversation remained general until they were ready to go.

As Georgia Nash settled in the car, she said to her hostess:

'You must telephone me next time you're in London, and I'll put you up. If I'm still at liberty. If not, I'll leave the key of the flat with Sergeant Somers, and you can use it as your own.'

Joan Creston watched them go with a puzzled look in her clear blue eyes. Somehow, she could not imagine Georgia Nash as a desperate criminal.

For that matter, no more could Sergeant Somers, silent at the wheel, and waiting for his superior officer to begin cross-questioning the girl.

First of all, however, Faithfull paid a call at Taunton main police station. He spent ten minutes talking to an inspector who was handling the case of the radium robbery. His questions did not reveal very much, however.

It appeared that the two men who had been robbed had gone back to London, after giving a very sketchy description of their assailants, whom they had not seen clearly in the dark, and who, moreover, had been wearing masks. They had been too upset to notice the number plate of the other men's car.

Faithfull rejoined Somers and the girl, who were chatting in desultory fashion. They started for London. The Inspector sat frowning slightly without speaking for some five minutes, then turned to Georgia Nash.

'Now,' he said quietly, 'perhaps you'll start at the beginning and tell us what you know.'

31

Georgia Nash settled back in her seat, gave a tiny sigh, and rubbed her one gloved hand over the other somewhat nervously.

'It goes back quite a time — to the days when Osbert Strang was a flourishing business man,' she told them. 'At that time, I was a girl at boarding-school. My father was a fairly successful small town lawyer. He met Strang in connection with some compensation case, and somehow came under his spell. I don't know what made Strang seize upon my father, who was a kindly old soul, but he certainly mesmerized him. Persuaded him to invest money belonging to his clients in all sorts of wild schemes. He even mortgaged the deeds of our home. And then, of course, you can guess what happened.'

She accepted a cigarette from Somers, and the Inspector lit it for her. She blew out a cloud of smoke and continued.

'When Osbert Strang was sent to prison, my father lost everything, and he was in danger of being charged with embezzling his clients' money. My mother's brother saved him from that, but it just about broke up the old man. Mother too. And my brother had to leave college and take a clerk's job in a commercial office. I left school too and got a fifteen bob a week job at a dress shop. I hated it. So did all of us. We seemed to stop living and just went on existing.

As soon as I was eighteen, I determined not to be a burden on them at home and cleared off to London. I got all sorts of jobs there — some of them only lasted a week or two. But all the time I kept telling myself that I would get even with Mr. Osbert Strang one day. I'd heard all sorts of rumours about how he'd salted away quite a nice fortune — money from respectable people like my father — before the law caught up with him. One report said his wife had it in her name, but I never found out about that.'

'He would hardly have divorced her if that was the case,' Faithfull suggested.

‘I suppose not. Anyhow, I wasn’t interested in his wife. I was out to get even with Strang himself, and I was on the look-out for him, right from the day he left prison. That was one reason I took so many jobs — I felt the experience would come in useful, and I was right. I mixed with all sorts of people. Some of them who were on the shady side of the law, and I found out a lot. I had a few shocks in the process, but I thought of what Strang had done to my family and I kept on.’

‘You’re a very determined young woman.’

The Inspector eyed her admiringly. She ignored the compliment and continued:

‘So I heard rumours about this radium racket some time before the robberies started. I had been keeping track of Strang for about six months then, ever since he had left prison. It wasn’t long before I discovered he was mixed up with this gang. So I deliberately let myself get mixed up in it as well.’

‘My God, you’ve got a nerve!’ Somers declared, turning to look at her for a second.

‘The sort of life I led makes anybody tough — or finishes ’em off,’ she said bitterly. ‘It wasn’t easy to get in with that gang. They check up on everybody, and they’ve got records that would surprise you. One of the reasons they can get away with so many jobs is because they’re helped by people who’re scared of being blackmailed if they don’t obey orders. You see, they’re not regular crooks, and the police have got nothing on them to follow up.’

‘Like yourself, for instance,’ Faithfull suggested.

‘Yes. The only trouble with me was the gang hadn’t got anything on me. So I let slip to one of the boys that the police were looking for me on account of some money being missing at the office where I worked, and in next to no time he’d tipped off the gang, and I was as good as in.’

‘Playing with dynamite,’ the Inspector commented.

‘I went into it with my eyes open. They tried me out on one or two small jobs — getting information as to the whereabouts of radium in the country. They arranged for me to go as secretary to Professor Mallowes and I picked up quite a lot there.'

'You mean to tell us that the Professor is mixed up with this gang?'

She shrugged.

'That's one of the things I *can't* tell you. We were kept in watertight compartments, and the lesser lights never knew very much about the extent to which the high-ups were involved. It's some organization, I can tell you. I shouldn't think there's ever been anything quite like it before in the history of crime. All departmentalized — every member with his own little jobs — sealed orders from headquarters — just like a machine. Agents all over the place too. So you see in a set-up like that, it's the policy of the high-ups not to let the underdogs get wise to everything that goes on. We just had to do our job and keep our mouths shut.'

'But you discovered that Strang was involved?'

'Oh yes, I found out that he and

another crook are Lucifer's two right-hand men.'

'Then you know Lucifer?'

Faithfull threw in the question eagerly. Again, she disappointed him.

'That's something else I don't know. Apart from Strang, and a man named Lanfrey, I doubt if anybody knows, or ever will until the gang comes out into the open. They've got their plans laid to run the entire world. And if they corner the radium supplies, they're well on the way to it. They can put over the largest-scale piece of blackmail in history.'

Faithfull ignored this possibility. He asked:

'Do you know anything about this Mr. Lanfrey you mentioned?'

'Nothing much. He runs Lanfrey and Tellman, the big antique-dealers in Bond Street. In fact, I understand he *is* Lanfrey and Tellman.'

'Oh yes, I've seen him once or twice,' put in Somers. 'Foreign-looking bloke — wears long cloaks and carries a swordstick. I used to see him sometimes at big first nights. I noticed him because he wore a nice lot of jewellery — pretty tempting to the light-fingered boys.'

'And how do you know Lanfrey isn't Lucifer? Or that Strang isn't, for that matter?' persisted Faithfull, turning to the girl. She shook her head.

'I can't prove it,' she replied. 'It was just an understood thing amongst the people I worked with. They were always talking about Lucifer revealing himself when the time was ripe — it seemed rather uncanny sometimes. But it was also understood that Lucifer was working with us side by side. We knew very little about our colleagues or conspirators — whatever you like to call them. But any one of them might have been Lucifer. That was a pretty clever move, to throw a scare into us in case we let up at all. We never knew if the boss hadn't got his eye on us.'

'There certainly seems to have been a brain behind this set-up,' ruminated Inspector Faithfull. 'But I have a feeling it was Strang who figured it all out while he was in prison.'

'He may have done quite a lot towards it,' she replied, 'but it was well on the way to being a highly complicated organization before he ever came out of prison. Somebody else was running the show with a very firm hand.'

Faithfull nodded thoughtfully. He helped himself to a meagre pinch of snuff, which he sniffed at cautiously.

'So you were in on that dance hall job,' he murmured.

'I was sent there to keep an eye on Nicky. They had their suspicions about his squealing to the police. I tipped 'em off that he had — I happened to be just outside his office door when he telephoned you. But I never thought they'd get him for it like that. I thought they'd just stop using the place.'

'H'm,' sniffed Faithfull. 'And what did you tip 'em off about Professor Mallowes?'

'There wasn't much to that job. I just had to take a carbon copy of everything I typed and hand it in at the end of the week to headquarters. I never knew what they did with 'em. Anyhow, that job finished after a few weeks, and they seemed satisfied to leave it at that. I was sorry in one way, because I got on well with the Professor.'

Sergeant Somers put in:

'But you never managed to find out whether you were reporting his experiments or just checking on him so that Lucifer could make certain he wasn't ratting on them?'

'That's true.'

Faithfull asked:

'And what about the Three Sailors? Why did you take that job?'

She shrugged.

'Oh, that. That was all on account of Denny Fox. It didn't take me long to discover he was playing a double game. I heard him pass on a message to his pal to tell you that he'd gone to the Professor's.'

Somers asked:

'So that was why you'd disappeared that night we went down to the Three Sailors?'

She nodded.

'I'd done my work, so there was no point in my staying in that awful dump. I phoned headquarters and they dealt with Denny Fox as they thought fit. I never heard what they did with him exactly. But I haven't seen him since that day.'

Inspector Faithfull eyed her narrowly.

'You're pretty cold-blooded.'

'I'm not really. I've just had to get this way. It's the only way I can get even with Strang.'

'Humph. About this headquarters you keep mentioning Where is it?'

'At that time it was a set of very respectable offices off Broad Street — you know, by Liverpool Street Station. But the headquarters was changed — often at a day's notice — usually after a big job had been brought off.'

'And where does headquarters happen to be at the moment?'

'At a villa in Morcombe Road, Bayswater. Though it's probably been moved by now. The house is called The Laurels. About half-way up on the right.'

Faithfull made a note.

'What I want to know is how they find these places in the housing shortage?' grunted Somers.

'That's easy,' she smiled. 'Two of the gang are house agents in quite a big way.

Each of them has a guilty secret that would ruin his business if ever it became known. One is a bigamist, the other was sacked from a bank for embezzlement. So they're in the gang, whether they like it or not.'

Sergeant Somers grinned at her.

'I should imagine they're not exactly delighted. This gang of yours seems to be very cosmopolitan — drawn from all classes of society.'

'That's one of its strong points. A collection of crooks with criminal records is fairly easily rounded up, as you well know. A lot of members of this gang — the respectable type I mean — have a sneaking feeling that Lucifer might bring off this world domination coup. In that case, they'd be sitting pretty. So they go on doing as they are told.'

Faithfull asked:

'And what about last night's job? How did you come to be mixed up with that?'

'I obeyed orders and took a job at the nursing home — and kept my ears open. I passed on the news that the radium was going back to London last night, and met the two men who were doing the job. But I was amazed to find Strang was with them. This was the first time I'd seen him on a job. I thought that this was my big opportunity at last to get level with him and pay off all the old scores. I waited my chance and slipped away to a call-box to phone the police. I had just dialled when I heard the door of the box swing open — and after that I don't remember any more until I came to in the aerodrome. I remember feeling surprised to find myself alive. It's unique for the gang not to liquidate anyone who rats on them.'

'They probably planned a specially lingering death for you,' the Inspector suggested. 'They imagined you would starve to death or be eaten by rats!'

32

Georgia Nash shuddered at the other's words.

'Lucky for you we came along,' Somers said. 'There's hardly a soul goes within a mile of that hangar for weeks at a time. So it really would have been a most unpleasant death.'

'I'm well aware of that,' she replied, 'and don't think I'm not grateful. Otherwise, I wouldn't be telling you all this.'

Faithfull nodded.

'We appreciate all that, Miss Nash. Are you quite sure that's all you have to tell us?'

A tiny frown puckered the smooth forehead.

'I think so.'

'Can't you tell us anything else about this antique-dealer, Lanfrey?'

'Not very much. I've never had any actual contact with him, but I gather he's quite a sinister type. He does a lot of foreign business, I understand — speaks seven or eight languages — and I believe he looks after the gang's activities abroad, sort of liaison officer or whatever you call it. You see, Inspector, you have to accustom yourself to the fact that this organization is run very much on the lines of a large international trading corporation, in spite of the fact that its activities are undercover.'

'I can't quite see how Lanfrey fits in,' admitted Somers, as he accelerated to pass a lorry.

The girl explained:

'He's the eccentric type. He has a reputation for it, and can get away with all sorts of unusual proceedings without arousing very much suspicion. What's more, it is quite normal for him to have any number of foreign visitors in the ordinary course of business at his galleries. You must see that there are considerable possibilities.'

The Inspector mused:

'And I suppose he travels a good deal in the ordinary course of business too.

The customs people would be familiar with him. Been passing him through for years I dare say. H'm, it sounds an interesting set-up, though it would probably be a devil of a job to prove anything against him. However, we're on our guard.'

The Sergeant asked:

'And what about Strang? Do we pull him in now?'

Inspector Faithfull shrugged.

'He's probably five hundred miles away at this minute. And we've nothing actually proved.'

'But I've told you he's in it up to his eyes,' protested the girl.

'It's your word against his,' he reminded her. 'And a clever counsel would soon ferret out that you have a personal spite against him.'

Somers said slowly:

'Not much use just being on our guard, if we don't go out and get results.'

'We'll be getting results before the week's out,' the Inspector assured him. 'In the meantime, Miss Nash, you've got to watch your step very carefully. Is there anywhere you can hide out for a couple of weeks?'

'Why?'

'Your ex-colleagues left you for dead, remember, and if they discover you're very much alive, they're liable to try to make amends for their first blunder.'

'I can look after myself.'

'Oh no, you can't,' Somers snapped, and there was a hint of possessiveness in his tone. 'You do as the Inspector says — we've quite enough trouble on our hands without having to get you out of any more tight corners,'

'Well, well,' the girl murmured, and her husky voice could not repress an amused tone, 'I'm sorry to have been such a burden.'

'You've been very helpful,' Faithfull told her. 'But if everything you've told us is accurate — '

'It's true — of course it's true — '

'Then you really are in some danger, you know. I'm quite aware that you're capable of looking after yourself in the normal way of things. But you should know that the Lucifer gang is by no means the usual gang of crooks. It really would simplify matters if you were safely out of the way.'

'It's just a question of whether you put yourself safely out of the way, or whether the gang does the job,' Somers commented dryly.

'Well,' she hesitated, 'I have an aunt at Clapham Common.'

'That'll do fine,' said Faithfull quickly. 'We'll phone her as soon as we get to London.'

'But she hasn't seen me for ten years.'

'Now's her chance to make up for lost time,' the Sergeant grinned.

'And she's frightfully fussy. I know I'll hate it there.'

'It'll only be for a couple of weeks at the outside, maybe less,' Inspector Faithfull reminded her. 'If you get fed up, you can come and see the wife and me over at Mitcham — it isn't far.'

'In fact, you're in for a riotous two weeks,' the Sergeant said.

She met his eye and could not resist his infectious grin.

'So that's settled.'

Faithfull was scanning the few notes he had taken. 'Oh, just one more thing. Those two men who did the job with Strang last night. Did you know them?'

'No. They were new to me. Probably that was why Strang came himself to keep an eye on them.'

'Can you describe them?'

'I didn't really take very much notice of them. I only saw them for a few minutes. There was a tall, cadaverous individual, dark hair turning grey — he'd be in the forties. Strang called him Slim. The other man was about average height, sandy, fairly thickset — oh yes, he had a cast over his left eye.'

'Anything distinctive about their dress?'

'The tall man wore a double-breasted mackintosh — rather a loud tie. The other wore a check cap — he drove the car — had large gauntlet gloves. I can't remember anything else.'

'Their voices?' the Sergeant suggested.

'Nothing outstanding about them. Though I did think once or twice the tall man had some trace of American accent. Then I thought I was mistaken, or maybe it was just a slight twang he had.'

The Inspector looked questioningly at Somers, who shook his head to signify that neither description was familiar to him.

Faithfull frowned. He said:

'Maybe they had been in the States some time.'

The car had reached the outer suburbs now, and they waited while the girl telephoned her aunt at Clapham Common.

'Keep your eye on her,' Faithfull advised Somers — the latter had a more uninterrupted view. 'We don't want any more accidents in telephone boxes.'

'But who could possibly — ?'

'We might have been followed all the way from Taunton.'

'Not very likely, I should think.'

All the same, Sergeant Somers concentrated on the telephone box. He did not speak for two or three minutes. Then he said softly:

'You think she's in danger?'

'It all depends whether they discover she is alive. If they've written her off the books, then she's fairly safe — if she keeps out of the way. On the other hand, if they should happen to go back to that airfield and find she's gone — '

'I should have thought they'd have been too busy with other things to go ferreting round after a girl.'

'There seem to be a devil of a lot of 'em,' the other reminded him. 'They could easily spare someone for a job like that.'

'Yes, I suppose it is rather important to them that she doesn't talk; though I must say this gang seems to be shut off in watertight compartments, so that if one section goes phut it makes no great difference. Look out — here she comes.'

When Georgia Nash returned to the car she was smiling.

'The old dear had quite a shock,' she told them. 'However, she's putting a hot-water bottle in the spare bed.'

'Then that's all right,' said Faithfull in some relief. 'And I shall expect you to telephone us every morning to say you're alive and kicking. If we don't hear from you before midday, we'll be over at

Clapham Common by lunchtime.'

'That would certainly throw Aunt into a panic. She has quite enough to do to make the rations go round as it is.' She yawned and stretched. 'It's nice to see old London again,' she went on. 'Taunton was beginning to get me down. Even Clapham couldn't be more depressing at this time of year.'

'Can we trust you to go straight there?' Faithfull asked her, as they began to approach the West End. 'You can get a tube, or there are plenty of buses.'

'All right, Inspector,' she smiled, a trifle amused at his fatherly manner. 'I know my way around. But I ought to pick up a few things at my flat first.'

'Might be a bit risky,' he told her.

Inspector Faithfull frowned as he considered this.

'But I wouldn't be more than five minutes,' she protested.

'I don't like it. Somebody might see you and pass the word around.'

'Nobody in the building — '

He interrupted her.

'You never know.'

'But Inspector! You can't expect me to go to stay at my aunt's without even a pair of pyjamas. She'll be offering to lend me one of her woolly nighties, and I couldn't bear that.'

There was a ghost of a chuckle from Sergeant Somers.

They were now rapidly nearing the West End, and at length Faithfull relented.

'Very well, Miss Nash. But you're to take Somers with you — and turn up your coat collar to hide your face as much as possible.'

He asked the Sergeant to drop him in Piccadilly, and went on back to Scotland Yard from there. When Sergeant Somers came into the office half an hour later, the Inspector looked up from the little batch of memos that had accumulated.

'Everything all right?' he asked.

Somers wore a slightly puzzled expression.

'Oh yes, there was no trouble,' he answered.

'You went right up to the flat with her?'

'Yes. I went inside and waited while she packed a case.'

Faithfull sighed, as if that were a weight off his mind.

'That's something settled anyway. Where was this flat of hers?'

'That's just what's worrying me,' Somers confessed. 'Her flat's in Soho — in fact it's just two floors above the flat where Val Harris lived — and where Lem Knight was murdered.'

Faithfull's hand went to his waistcoat pocket and he slowly extracted the inevitable snuff-box.

'Interesting,' he mused. 'Very interesting indeed.'

'Inspector,' said Somers anxiously. 'You don't think she had anything to do with that murder?'

The other took a pinch of snuff before replying.

'I think,' he said deliberately, 'that Miss Georgia Nash hasn't told us quite everything.'

33

With the help of Sergeant Somers, Faithfull spent the greater part of the following day making some discreet inquiries concerning Mr. Lucas Lanfrey. They found it none too easy.

It seemed that Lanfrey had been established for over twenty years, and had built his shop into one of the largest antique businesses in London. Unlike most of his competitors, Lanfrey did not specialize in one particular art. His galleries, which were the most extensive in Bond Street, contained rooms devoted to pictures, china, pewter, miniatures, etchings, plaques and medallions. In fact his boast was that he catered for all tastes and all pockets. A large proportion of his customers lived in the respectable dormitory suburbs and he was content with modest profits to ensure a large turnover.

Lanfrey did not pretend to be expert in every department under his roof, but he employed men who knew their job and paid them well. His own speciality was Sung porcelain, but this collection was private and not for sale. It was reputed to be worth a fabulous amount. However, anything of Oriental origin attracted him; this perhaps being due to the fact that his grandmother was Javanese, as Faithfull discovered on investigation at the Aliens Branch.

Lanfrey's was a mixed ancestry. His mother had been a highly temperamental Spanish actress, who achieved a certain notoriety by stabbing one of her lovers and escaping to England. His father had been a fairly well-known portrait artist in his day, but he had inherited a small fortune and promptly stopped painting. Lucas Lanfrey had been sent down from Oxford in the early years of the century and had spent the next ten years travelling the world, spending a considerable time in China and Japan. He was extraordinarily secretive about those years, according to other antiquarians with whom Faithfull discussed him.

In fact, there were many gaps in

Lanfrey's history which might have had some considerable significance in this particular case.

But the Inspector's most intensive inquiries failed to associate the antique-dealer with any member of the underworld. There had never been the remotest suspicion, for instance, that he might have been a receiver of stolen property. True, he had figured in a couple of actions for slander, but these had been settled out of court, being the result of quarrels with well-known public men whose political opinions he resented. Lanfrey was certainly a character, but there was nothing to prove that he was a criminal type.

Apart from the fact that he had been registered as a shareholder in Plastic Utilities (Mayfair) Limited, he appeared to have no connection with Osbert Strang. The fact that this was yet another of Strang's ill-fated enterprises might have antagonized Lanfrey towards him, unless the antique-dealer had 'got out' in time.

Faithfull passed on all this information

to Somers, in case it might suggest some fresh avenue of exploration to him. But the Sergeant was equally puzzled. After running through the papers for the second time, he looked up with a frown.

'I suppose she couldn't have made a mistake,' he murmured tentatively.

'Miss Nash doesn't strike me as the sort of person who would make that type of mistake,' the Inspector replied decisively.

'This doesn't seem to throw much light on the activities of Lanfrey,' Somers nodded to the batch of reports. 'What do you propose to do about it?'

The other rose slowly and took his hat and mackintosh from the cupboard in the corner.

'I think I'll take a stroll round to his place in Old Bond Street. I hear they welcome people looking round, with no obligation to purchase. If they should have a nice snuff-box, I might go up to a pound.'

He drifted out in that apparently aimless manner which had deceived more than one criminal.

Somers grinned to himself, then lifted his telephone receiver, started dialling Georgia Nash's number, hesitated, then replaced the receiver.

After all, it was only half an hour since she had telephoned to say she was all right.

Meanwhile Inspector Faithfull strolled leisurely down Bond Street, enjoying the wintry sunshine and crisp, frosty air. He paused now and then to look in jeweller's windows which displayed a particularly attractive array of precious stones likely to tempt the smash-and-grab boys, and appraised the chances of a gang making a clean getaway. It would be none too easy in this narrow thoroughfare, he decided, unless an escape could be made very quickly down one of the side turnings.

Lanfrey's shop occupied a prominent site on the corner of one of these streets that branched off Old Bond Street. The most critical observer could not deny that it made the most of its generous window space. What appealed most to the shopper of limited means was the fact that all the goods carried a neat price ticket.

Faithfull inspected each window carefully, then stood for a few moments on the corner before going in through the main entrance. He wandered through a room devoted to needlework pictures most artistically displayed, into another devoted to Worcester porcelain. He drifted through a third room which contained a wide variety of miniatures, and eventually climbed the stairs.

He found what he sought in a small alcove on the third floor, where over a hundred snuff-boxes were set out in a neat glass case.

The prices varied from five shillings for a box resembling that which he possessed himself to five hundred pounds for an exquisite little affair in old gold beautifully chased and set with tiny rubies.

Faithfull picked up a more reasonably priced article made of pinchbeck, and was critically examining the workmanship when he became conscious of another man standing at his side.

'Are you interested in snuff-boxes, sir?' asked a silky voice.

He turned and recognized Lucas

Lanfrey from the photos he had managed to secure of him at a well-known photographers of celebrities.

'I, too, am a victim of what is so erroneously described as the pernicious habit,' continued the smooth tones. 'And I always maintain that a large proportion of the pleasure is derived from handling an artistic snuff-box.'

He had a pedantic manner of speech that was quite distinctive.

'Yes,' said Faithfull slowly. 'I'm inclined to agree with you that there might be something in that.'

Lanfrey inserted a thumb and forefinger in his waistcoat pocket and produced an exquisite specimen in dull gold with a very small miniature let into the lid. Flicking the lid open, he extended it to the Inspector. Faithfull took a small pinch, waited until the other had helped himself before sniffing it cautiously. He had to admit that it was an excellent brand, even if it were not entirely to his taste.

Meanwhile, he took a quiet estimate of his vis-à-vis.

Lucas Lanfrey was a man in the early fifties, but might have been taken for less, on account of his pink complexion and general well-preserved air. Cosmopolitan to his finger-tips, thought Faithfull. Dangerous customer. The type who can pull strings in all sorts of unexpected places.

He noted the perfectly fitting suit and that the antique-dealer wore two obviously expensive gold and platinum rings on either hand. The only trace of the Orient in him was in his eyes which slanted just the merest fraction more than the average.

Lanfrey was speaking again.

'If you care to come to my private room,' he said, 'I can show you some interesting little boxes of Oriental origin. I suspect they were used at one time for opium, but they're very attractive all the same.'

'I should be most interested.'

Lanfrey led the way along the corridor to a door marked 'Private' which he opened to reveal a fair-sized room furnished as a sitting-room in colourful

Oriental style. In one corner was a small inlaid table on which were over twenty small boxes. Several were black lacquer inlaid with mother of pearl, and the workmanship was impeccable. Others appeared to be made entirely of mother of pearl, and two or three were silver and gold, two of amber and one of a vivid green substance which the Inspector thought might be jade. They were of varied shapes, not usually found in Europe.

The antique-dealer picked them up and fingered them appreciatively, giving his visitor a brief description of the attractive features of each.

After a time, Faithfull's eye wandered round the room and came to rest on a large upright cabinet, something like a single wardrobe in shape. It was painted black, with large golden dragons embossed on the double doors which opened down the centre. And propped against the cabinet was a narrow-bladed sword with what appeared to be a golden handle inlaid with precious stones.

'That's an unusual piece,' he said

during a pause in the conversation, nodding in the direction of the cabinet.

Mr. Lanfrey turned and looked in the direction indicated, then nodded with some satisfaction.

'Yes, I'm particularly proud of that,' he replied, moving over towards it.

'What is it exactly?'

'It took me quite a little time to discover that when I first saw the piece,' Lanfrey told him. 'Eventually, I discovered it was a magician's cabinet of Indian origin. It's probably about a hundred and fifty years old. As you are doubtless aware, magic is one of the most popular forms of entertainment in India, and there's no doubt that in those days the travelling magician was the only diversion provided for millions of unfortunate people.'

'But what would a magician do with this cabinet?'

'That rather puzzled me too at first. Until I noticed the slots in the sides of the cabinet — just large enough to permit the sword to pass through.'

He picked up the sword as he spoke,

and walking round the side, inserted it in one of the slots.

'Now do you see?'

'You mean the magician locked somebody in the cabinet, then poked the sword through the slots?'

Inspector Faithfull vaguely recalled an illusionist act on those lines which he had seen at a music-hall some years back.

'Exactly. You notice that there are quite a number of those slots — it would seem to be impossible for the man inside to escape.'

'You mean he couldn't avoid the point of the sword? I wouldn't be so sure of that. Some of those Indians are pretty slim, and uncanny contortionists — and providing they knew the order in which the thrusts were made, well, I don't suppose anyone was ever killed inside the cabinet anyhow.'

'I find that somewhat difficult to believe.'

Lanfrey pressed a gold knob at the side and the double doors suddenly sprang open.

He said: 'Take a look for yourself, my

dear sir, and see how difficult it would be.'

Somewhat cautiously, Faithfull poked his head inside and noted the innumerable slots through which daylight showed.

'You will see that there are even slots in the top of the cabinet,' continued Lanfrey, pointing in that direction.

As Faithfull turned his head upwards, he felt a sudden jolt in the small of his back, stumbled forward and hit his forehead against the back of the cabinet.

'Here — what the devil — ' he gasped, but his words were cut off by the loud slam of the cabinet doors behind him, which were obviously controlled by a powerful spring under pressure from the outside knob.

He was trapped.

34

The detective hammered on the doors.

'Let me out! Lanfrey! Let me out!'

There was a tiny pause, then the silky voice said:

'So you recognized me, Inspector Faithfull?'

'What's this mean? What's your game?'

Faithfull thumped the doors, and discovered that the cabinet was made of metal nearly half an inch thick.

'I'm afraid that noise isn't going to help you very much, Inspector. This room is remote from all the others, as no doubt you noticed. And the cabinet muffles your shouts quite appreciably. You'd better relax and listen to what I have to say to you. Can you hear me plainly?'

'I can hear,' Faithfull grunted after a brief pause.

'Good.' The suave tones hesitated for a moment, then went on: 'You see, Inspector, I too recognized you. I have been expecting you for some days — don't ask me why. I had a feeling that your relentless routine would lead you in this direction. You see, I am quite an admirer of your methods. I have a far greater respect for them than many of my colleagues have showed. That is why I made my plans for this visit. And you must admit that they have worked admirably so far.'

'What the devil are you getting at?' the Inspector snapped irritably. He was beginning to feel cramped.

'I have a proposition to make to you, Inspector, and you would be well advised to give it your serious consideration. In fact, you are hardly in a position to turn it down.' The silky voice suddenly developed a sinister intonation. 'It is because I admire your methods, that I am offering you this opportunity. My colleagues, if they were here, would doubtless have no hesitation in liquidating you on the spot, as they have done with other people who have interfered with their plans in the past.'

'I wish you'd come to the point,' Faithfull growled.

'Certainly. I can put this little proposition very briefly. I simply require your undertaking to abandon your present activities and leave the country. I can find you suitable employment in several other countries — you have a choice of Brazil, Switzerland, Norway or Australia — you see we cast a wide net. Your new job would be considerably more remunerative than your existing one, though a trifle more unorthodox shall we say?'

Faithfull snorted with scorn.

'You can say what you damn well like!'

He started feeling round the cabinet with his hands in the hope that it would bring to light some hidden spring or another means of exit. Something told him that it would be advisable to play for time.

'You see, Inspector, I consider you our most dangerous opponent. So, for that matter, does Lucifer. You have fooled many of the others with your outward stolidness and apparent lack of imagination. But I know you're a force to be reckoned with, and I made my preparations. Now, if you are prepared to be reasonable and enjoy the benefits of a milder climate for say a year or so, you will find yourself in a very pleasant position when Lucifer is in supreme power.'

'I should have a better chance of judging that if I knew who Lucifer was!'

There was the sound of a tiny chuckle from the other side of the door of the cabinet.

'Oh no, Inspector, that doesn't really enter into the immediate problem. You are hardly in a position to make terms, you know.'

'You don't have to remind me,' the Inspector replied in a grim voice.

'So I hope you're going to see reason,' continued the silky tones. 'I'm afraid I can't give you more than two minutes to make up your mind. It's a clear-cut issue, and you are a man of action.'

'Two minutes — it's not reasonable — '

'I am taking no chances,' came the curt reply. 'It's on my own responsibility that you are getting a chance at all. I'm doing this because I think you would be a useful man to us.'

'I am sorry,' the Inspector snapped back, 'but the answer will have to be 'no'. Now, what do you propose to do about it?'

There was a brief pause, then Lanfrey spoke:

'It's quite simple. It will be another performance of the old illusion of stabbing the man in the cabinet. Only this time it won't be an illusion. The other assistants who entered the cabinet may have been very slim; they may have been contortionists. You, I think, are neither.'

'You mean you'll stab me in cold blood?'

'But of course. It will be a nice clean death.'

'You won't get away with it as easily as that, Lanfrey. You don't think I came here without leaving word.'

'I don't doubt that, Inspector. But I have managed to dispose of an occasional body very successfully in the past. I shall count ten. So you still have an opportunity to change your mind.'

He began counting in a steady monotone.

Faithfull clenched his fists as the relentless voice went on.

'Seven . . . eight . . . '

There was a metallic sound as the sword tapped lightly against the side of the cabinet.

'Nine!'

The door of the room was suddenly opened and a rough, hoarse voice cried:

'Drop that sword — drop it!'

'What — ' hissed Lanfrey. 'You!'

The sword clattered to the floor.

'That's better. Now put your hands up!'

The next thing Faithfull heard was two revolver shots that sounded almost as one. What was obviously Lanfrey's body thudded to the floor near the cabinet. Then there was silence save for a moaning sigh from near the door of the room.

The Scotland Yard man began thumping the doors of the cabinet and shouting at the top of his voice. After what seemed an interminable interval, there was a sound of running footsteps, and a gasp of surprise from someone who had just entered the room.

The Inspector shouted again, and presently a man's voice said:

'Who are you there?'

'Never mind that. Get me out!'

'What's happened?'

'Let me out — I'm Inspector Faithfull from Scotland Yard. Press that button thing at the side of the door.'

'Yes, yes! Very well!'

The owner of the nervous voice seemed more nervous than ever. But in a couple of seconds the doors snapped open again.

Faithfull blinked in the stronger light, came out of the cabinet, and straightened himself. He took a quick glance at the newcomer, ascertained that he was harmless, then looked down at Lanfrey, who had been shot cleanly through the heart. A small silver-plated pistol lay near him. Having made sure the man was dead, the detective went over to the other inert figure that lay by the door.

'Denny Fox! I thought I recognized the voice.'

He knelt beside the unconscious man and found that a bullet had penetrated his head. He tried to lift him a little, and as he did so, Fox seemed to recover consciousness for a minute.

'That swine was quick on the draw,' he whispered in a weak voice. He struggled for breath, then spoke disjointedly.

'Little black notebook — in one of his pockets . . . '

He relapsed into unconsciousness again.

'Get an ambulance — quickly!' Faithfull told the young man who had released him, and the other hurried off to obey.

Faithfull turned to the unconscious man again. He feared the wound was a fatal one. A brief examination showed that the bullet was lodged in the head.

With the ambulance came Sergeant Somers, wide-eyed in his amazement at the spectacle that greeted him.

'Good Lord, Inspector! What on earth's been happening?' he asked.

Faithfull pocketed the little black notebook he had been studying.

'There's been trouble,' he said briefly.

Somers stooped and looked at Denny Fox.

‘What the devil’s he doing here?’

The other slowly shook his head.

‘That’s something we have to find out,’ he replied. ‘I’m afraid the poor chap won’t live to tell us.’

35

The Assistant Commissioner leaned against the oaken mantelpiece in his room, and gazed down at Inspector Faithfull.

'Things seem to have been looking up,' he mused.

'Yes, sir.'

'This is really the most amazing case I've come across for years,' continued the A.C. 'If you had come to me in the first place with this report about Lanfrey, I should have laughed at you. Why, I've bought stuff off him myself.'

He walked over to the window and stared out across the river.

'That was why I didn't come to you, sir.'

The other swung round with an interrogatory air.

'There are so many apparently respectable people involved in this case,' Faithfull hastened to explain, 'that we can't afford to accept any personal assurances for their integrity. Not even if we've known 'em for years.'

The A.C. nodded understandingly.

'I quite appreciate that now. That notebook you got from Lanfrey certainly opened my eyes. I've had suspicious reports on several of the people mentioned from the other men working on the case, but dammit they seemed so far-fetched. It appeared quite fantastic to suspect them.'

'You have to bear in mind that many of them are being blackmailed,' pointed out the Inspector imperturbably. 'And in that case, the more important people are the easiest victims. They have so much to lose if they are mixed up in a scandal. When you come to think of it, they haven't very much alternative but to do as Lucifer tells them.'

The A.C. rubbed his chin with his hand.

'You don't think Lucifer is amongst those names in the notebook?'

'I should be inclined to doubt it.'

'Well, anyhow, you had a narrow shave,

Faithfull. I'm rather surprised you pushed your head into a trap like that. I thought you were a bit more cautious.'

The Inspector said mildly:

'Comes a time, sir, when we have to take chances.'

'Quite so. Lucky thing for you that Fox turned up just then. What on earth was he doing there, anyhow? Haven't you any ideas about that?'

'I'd prefer to keep them to myself until I can check up with a certain individual who might confirm them,'

'I see. Well, I hope that affair last night will be the last of these radium robberies.'

'I sincerely hope so, sir,' replied Inspector Faithfull in a non-committal tone.

'Anyhow, I've got all the people in this notebook under strict observation, and we have a military guard on all airfields, so I think we really have blocked every exit this time. They can't possibly get the stuff out of the country.'

'It's worth taking a pretty big risk for half a million pounds,' Faithfull murmured.

'You think they'll have a go, eh?'

The Inspector nodded.

'Yes, sir, with another change of tactics.'

'All right, we'll see. We've got to keep on our toes, and produce some pretty big results before very long.'

'Very good, sir. Might I have that notebook back again for a little while?'

'Yes, I think so. I've had all the names duplicated and circulated round everybody concerned with the case.'

Faithfull took the notebook, and pushed it into his waistcoat pocket and went back to his own room. Here he caught Sergeant Somers rather guiltily replacing the telephone receiver, and guessed that he had been talking to Georgia Nash.

'Is the A.C. putting your name forward for a medal?' asked the Sergeant with a grin. Faithfull shook his head.

'He has too many other worries,' he said.

Sitting at his desk, and taking out the black notebook, he proceeded to study it.

The long list of names and addresses

was written in neat, almost microscopic calligraphy. Slowly he turned the pages, examining them closely. The last four pages of the book were blank save for one name which had been scribbled in pencil rather more hastily, as if Lanfrey had taken it down over the telephone.

It read:

Miguel Castana,
16 Florida Court,
Half Moon Street, W. 1.

Somers came and peered over Faithfull's shoulder, slowly deciphering the name.

'Couldn't have anything much more foreign than that!' he declared thoughtfully. 'Have you made any inquiries about him?'

The other nodded.

'The Aliens people are pretty emphatic that he is a perfectly respectable scientist from Rio de Janeiro, and that he has been coming here for years to buy scientific apparatus for a large clinic he controls there. His references are apparently the highest possible.'

'I dare say. But there are some fairly big bugs mixed up in the case.'

'That's true enough,' Faithfull admitted, 'but I have a hunch that Castana is an exception. You see his name is scribbled in pencil.'

'Does that signify anything special?'

'That's what I propose to find out. I'm going along to see him now.'

Somers seemed a trifle surprised.

'You're taking a few chances lately, Inspector,' he commented dryly. 'Want me to come along — just in case?'

Faithfull considered the idea for a minute.

'Perhaps it would be as well,' he decided. 'I'm not exactly anxious to run into any more little episodes like the Bond Street affair.'

He turned to get his well-worn mackintosh.

'You keeping an eye on the Nash girl?' he demanded abruptly as they went out.

'Of course. She phones us every day.'

'And how often do you phone her?'

Somers reddened.

'You said yourself she was in a pretty

dangerous position,' he protested.

'Humph! Well, as long as you don't go taking her round London's gay spots.'

'What — on a sergeant's pay!'

Faithfull's solemn features relaxed for a moment.

'All right,' he smiled. 'We won't go into that now.'

They went out and managed to find a taxi in Whitehall.

Florida Court proved to be a block of expensive luxury flats which were apparently let on a short-term basis at prohibitive rentals.

Number sixteen was on the first floor, and the detectives made their way up the stairs, which were covered with a thick carpet. The staircase and corridors had an air of discreet opulence which could not fail to impress.

At the top of the first flight, Inspector Faithfull paused for a moment and said:

'I think it would be as well if I went in alone. We don't want to scare this bird.'

Somers was none too pleased, but made no comment.

'You take a look round the place while

you're waiting,' the other continued. 'Give me twenty minutes, and if you don't see me then, come and ring the bell.'

'O.K.'

The flat they sought was to the left of the landing, and Somers walked on slowly up the stairs as the Inspector rang the bell. Presently, a maid answered the door, and he asked to see Mr. Castana, saying he was there on urgent business, but refusing to give his name. She showed him into a large lounge, with long french windows which opened on to an iron platform which was part of the fire escape. Faithfull rapidly absorbed the details of the room, including a large television receiver in one corner. Presently, the door opened softly and he turned to see a short, plump man, with olive skin and dark hair, standing in the doorway.

'Mr. Miguel Castana?'

The man nodded.

'I am Miguel Castana.'

The voice was of a cultured type, softly spoken, with barely a trace of accent.

'What can I do for you?'

'I have called with reference to Mr. Lanfrey, the Bond Street antique-dealer.'

'Lanfrey?' The smooth forehead wrinkled the merest fraction. 'I do not think I know him.'

Faithfull took a photo from his pocket and passed it over.

The other pursed his lips.

'So! That is Mr. Lanfrey! I know him as Mr. Brown.'

Faithfull nodded.

'I rather suspected as much,' he said evenly.

36

Inspector Faithfull went on:

'He has contacted you about some radium, I take it?'

Castana took a pace forward.

'Please — may I ask who you are — and what this is to do with you?'

The Inspector quickly made his identity known.

The plump olive features showed no sign of surprise.

'You are trying to tell me that this Mr. Lanfrey is in some way connected with the radium robberies we read so much about lately?'

'Exactly.'

The other went over to a highly polished walnut bureau in one corner and unlocked it, taking out a sheaf of papers.

'You will wish to see my credentials, naturally, Inspector,' he said suavely.

Faithfull took the papers which certainly had an impressive heading and an official appearance. They were letters of introduction to various well-known scientists and research laboratories' personnel. There was also a passport and visas which were quite in order, and had apparently been used for a number of years.

The Inspector scanned the papers carefully.

'Do you mind telling me what you are over here for, Mr. Castana?' he asked presently.

'But of course. I am here on behalf of my clinic to buy supplies of certain rare drugs and also some of the excellent apparatus that is being made in England today.'

'I see. And have you a commission to purchase radium?'

'Not exactly. But I am always in the market for radium, if the price is right.'

'Have you bought much radium in the past?'

'Not very much. Just over a gramme to be exact. I can refer you to the source of supply if you wish.'

Faithfull shook his head.

'I won't go into that now. I am more

interested in what Mr. Lanfrey had to say to you.'

Castana lighted a Turkish cigarette from a box on the table.

'I'm afraid I can't help you very much, Inspector,' he replied. 'All I know is that this Mr. Lanfrey called on me two days ago and offered me half a gramme of radium at a very reasonable price.'

'You didn't ask him where he got it?'

Castana replied with some hesitation:

'Er — no — we had not met before, and it hardly seemed polite.'

'You didn't suspect that it was stolen radium?'

'At that time I had only been in this country about twenty-four hours, and I had not heard very much about the robberies. Afterwards, it did occur to me that the radium might be stolen, but I knew that I could always refer to the police if necessary — the English police are so reliable.'

Castana showed his large, gold-filled teeth in a flashing smile.

'And what was Mr. Lanfrey's proposal?'

Castana shrugged.

'He was to telephone me and arrange when the radium could be delivered, and I was to pay for it with a draft on the Bank of South America, payable to 'bearer'.'

'H'm . . . And you've heard no more?'

'No.'

Obviously impressed by the Inspector's serious expression, Castana continued a trifle anxiously:

'You appreciate, Inspector, that I wish to have nothing to do with any illegal trafficking in radium. On the other hand, I am only too willing to help the police.'

'Right,' said Faithfull briskly, 'you can help us quite a lot, I think, Mr. Castana.'

He pulled out his wallet from an inner pocket and took out a slip of paper.

'I would like you to telephone these people, and invite them here tomorrow afternoon, say at three-thirty. Tell them you are flying back to South America at midnight, and that you are interested to take some radium back with you.'

Slightly bewildered, Castana accepted the slip and thoughtfully scanned the list.

'Are you sure it will be all right?' he queried somewhat anxiously.

'There will be nothing to worry about if you do exactly as I will tell you. Don't tell them anything more than I've just told you, and above all, don't give the impression that you're throwing a party. Each of them must think that he or she is the only person who will be there.'

Castana nodded, taking a mental note of his instructions.

Faithfull walked slowly across to a distant corner and stood looking at the television receiver.

'That's a very fine set,' he remarked absently.

'Yes.'

'It works, I suppose.'

'Oh yes — you would like to see?'

'No, no, don't bother now. I take it that you draw the curtains when you use the set?'

'That is so. The room should be as dark as possible of course.'

The Inspector nodded thoughtfully.

'That's interesting. Very interesting. It might be an idea to arrange a little television demonstration tomorrow afternoon. Quite an idea.'

He moved towards the door.

'Thanks for your co-operation, Mr. Castana,' he said. 'You'll telephone those people right away? And I'll be here about three tomorrow.'

The other seemed a trifle dubious, as he let Inspector Faithfull out of the flat.

The Inspector turned at the door and said:

'If, by any chance, some of those people on the list don't seem to be interested in radium tell them there'll be a television demonstration that they mustn't miss on any account.'

'Very well, Inspector.'

Castana hesitated with his hand on the door-knob, then said:

'I understand these people connected with the radium robberies are rather desperate characters, and I — er — well I dislike unpleasantness.'

'I'll handle that, Mr. Castana,' Faithfull assured him. 'Just get those people in that room and leave the rest to me.'

37

That same afternoon, Somers came into the office and found the Inspector reading the evening paper.

'Look here,' he burst out impulsively, 'what's going on with Val Harris?'

Faithfull looked up slowly, laid down the paper and said:

'I arranged with the people at the nursing home for Miss Harris to be released on parole for a couple of days. She's much better, and she had one or two little things to do in Town.'

'But dammit all — ' Somers began to protest, when the other interrupted:

'How did you find out, anyhow?'

Somers looked embarrassed.

'As a matter of fact, Georgia Nash told me,' he admitted.

'And how the devil did she know?'

'I — er — well — she asked me if she could get some papers from her flat — she said they were rather important, and she didn't like leaving them there.'

'You mean you let her go back?'

'Oh, I went with her — never let her out of my sight,' added the Sergeant hastily.

'Well, I can believe that much at any rate,' Faithfull said, drily. 'But I wish you'd told me. Did you see the Harris girl yourself?'

Somers shook his head.

'It was Miss Nash who caught a glimpse of her just leaving the building.'

'And did she see her?'

'I don't think so. She had her back half-turned to us. Miss Nash recognized her because of an astrakhan coat she was wearing.'

'H'm. Oh well, I suppose there's nothing we can do about it now. But for goodness' sake do tell me next time before you go moving people around. I like 'em to be where I can put my hands on 'em.'

The rebuked Sergeant fell into a moody silence and rifled furiously through the letters in his file.

Faithfull returned to his evening paper.

Owing to the hectic events of the previous week, he had forgotten to send in his crossword competition entries, an occurrence which he was determined should not happen again.

He had already confided to his wife that he felt in his bones that he was due for a prize this time, anyway. Martha Faithfull had not been in the least impressed. She never overlooked an opportunity to pour scorn upon her husband's efforts in this direction. 'You never were any good at winning prizes,' she was wont to remark. To which her husband always made the retort that he had won a certain Martha Giles!

Somers finished his letters and went on to examine a file which was in his tray. The thought that Georgia Nash had promised to accompany him to the Star Cinema at Clapham slowly restored his good humour.

At length, Faithfull folded his paper and began to detail his plan of campaign for the following day.

'Half a dozen men should be ample,' he decided. 'There are really only two ways out of those flats — through the hall or down the fire-escape. Of course, there are three ways out of the hall, but we can station our men there as soon as all the guests have arrived, and they're bound to see anyone coming down by the stairs or the lift.'

'Better warn 'em to keep well out of sight — mustn't give anyone the slightest suspicion of what's going on,' Somers commented.

Faithfull nodded his agreement.

'We'll get there early and fix that,' he said.

'And the list of names? Are they actually people connected with the case?'

'They've all had some connection with it — one or two are lesser lights in the gang — '

'H'm,' Somers mused. 'They might start a rough house.'

'I don't think so. The way I hope to arrange things, we should have them just where we want them.'

'Oh well,' sighed the Sergeant, 'it's high time we had a big show-down.'

Faithfull shook his head reprovingly.

‘You ought to have learned enough about my methods now, to know that I never force a big show-down until I hold practically all the cards.’

The other grinned.

‘What about Bond Street?’ he demanded.

‘That was forced on me. I merely went there to take a look round.’

Somers queried:

‘By the way, have you found out any more about Denny Fox and what brought him there?’

‘I’ve got one or two ideas, but I’m still waiting to contact the parties concerned.’

‘You’re acting damned mysterious just lately,’ grumbled Somers.

The Inspector smiled enigmatically.

‘All in good time,’ he replied.

38

The next morning, Inspector Faithfull was summoned to the Assistant Commissioner's office almost as soon as he arrived.

The A.C., who was sitting at his desk, looked up as Faithfull walked in.

'I've just had the Home Secretary on the telephone,' he announced. 'He's playing hell over the radium job. Says it ought to have been cleared up weeks ago, and he's getting diplomatic notes about it from one or two of the embassies. He's worried it's going to blaze up into a bad scare.'

The other absorbed this information without venturing any comment. The A.C. toyed with his paper-knife and frowned at a letter on his desk.

'Well?' he said presently. 'I gathered the last time I saw you, that you hoped to clean up this gang any day.'

'I don't think I put it as strongly as

that, sir. But I am hoping to see some definite results today, as it happens.'

This somewhat surprised the Assistant Commissioner.

'You mean — Lucifer?' he queried abruptly.

'I hope so, sir. It's a shot in the dark. But I think it might be effective for that reason.'

'What are you driving at?'

'I expect to have some news for you, about four o'clock this afternoon.'

'The devil you do!' grunted the A.C. 'Well, don't go in for any more funny business like that affair in Bond Street. I mean to say — no unnecessary risks.'

'You can rely on me for that, sir. The Bond Street business was unplanned. This is different.'

The Assistant Commissioner scrawled a design on his blotter, his eyebrows narrowed in thought.

If this were any ordinary routine job, he wouldn't have hesitated to trust Faithfull, but it had reached serious proportions, and he was debating whether he should handle it himself. On the other hand, old

Faithfull had apparently brought matters to a head on his own initiative, and in the circumstances he seemed to be the best man to tackle the job.

'All right, Inspector,' he said at last. 'But take plenty of men with you. A couple of hundred if you want them.'

'I don't think that will be necessary, sir,' replied the Inspector with a vestige of a smile. 'I've already made the arrangements.'

'Then for God's sake don't hesitate to ring up if there looks the faintest chance of anything going wrong.'

'What's come over the old man,' Faithfull asked himself. He wasn't usually as jittery as this. However, he merely inclined his head to signify his acceptance of the order.

'As soon as you've got Lucifer, I'll pass the word to round up the rest of the people in that notebook,' the A.C. continued. 'But we want to lie low until we have got him, or he'll hop out of the country at the first chance.'

'I quite agree, sir. I think I'll have some news by four o'clock.'

And Inspector Faithfull went out.

He negatived Somers's suggestion that they should use police cars that afternoon, and the men arrived in two taxis, which dropped them in Piccadilly soon after two-thirty.

Faithfull went and made friends with the caretaker of the flats, and presently the men began to arrive singly and were conducted down to the basement.

Somers had been stationed outside to keep an eye open for anyone who looked suspicious, and he was to stay there until all the visitors had arrived.

Soon after three, Faithfull went up to see Castana. He found him a trifle nervous, his podgy hands working nervously as he mopped his forehead with a silk handkerchief. He told the Inspector that all the people he had telephoned had declared their intention of being present.

'Now relax, Mr. Castana. As far as you are concerned, this is just a friendly little party. If it starts to get tough, you simply fade right out of the picture and leave everything to me. Now, let's draw the curtains, shall we?'

There were heavy green velvet curtains, and they left the room completely dark.

Acting on the Inspector's instructions, Castana switched on the set to make sure it was working.

There was the merest glow from the screen which was insufficient to offer illumination by which anyone could be recognized.

'Don't switch it on until all the people have arrived,' Faithfull said. 'That's very important. On no account must the set be switched on until everybody is seated.'

Castana nodded.

'I will take out the plug over by the wall there. Just as a precaution.'

He did so.

'Now, just one more thing,' continued the Inspector slowly. 'All these guests of yours are under the impression that they are to be the only visitor at this particular time. You will have to apologize — say that you have a small party to see a special television demonstration that will only take ten minutes. Ask them to join the party while they are waiting. Is that clear?'

Castana carefully recapitulated his instructions until Faithfull was satisfied that he understood them perfectly. Then he placed two rows of four chairs each some ten feet away from the television set, allowing ample room so that anyone could pass comfortably between the rows, even if people were seated.

By this time it was twenty past three.

Faithfull gave a last look round the room, then turned to Castana.

'You can have a small whisky if you like,' he suggested.

Castana shook his head.

'Not yet,' he replied. 'Afterwards, perhaps.'

Faithfull nodded approvingly. 'All right, I shall be in the kitchen. You gave your maid the afternoon off?'

'Oh yes.'

'Good. Well now, the main thing is to set everybody at ease when you show them into the lounge. It'll be pretty dark, of course, so you must go in with them, keep talking all the time, apologize for keeping them waiting, and so on.'

'And if two of them should arrive together?'

'You can cover that up all right, when you explain about the television demonstration.'

'Yes, yes of course. I see.'

The front door buzzer sounded.

Faithfull at once disappeared in the direction of the kitchen. He left the door open a couple of inches, and could hear Castana's voluble explanations to the first guest.

This seemed to proceed satisfactorily, for it was barely two minutes before the buzzer sounded again, and the second guest disappeared into the lounge.

Some ten minutes later, six people were sitting silently in the lounge, and such had been Castana's never ceasing flow of voluble conversation that they had not recognized each other. Still chattering gaily, he stooped and switched on the television set, making a trifling adjustment to get the picture more clearly in focus.

The silent audience watched a musical clown playing tricks with various instruments for some minutes, then the door opened quietly and the shadowy figure of

Inspector Faithfull entered the room. He turned down the volume of the loud-speaker, and addressed himself to his audience.

His voice sounded rather more assured than he really felt, for he was certain that if Lucifer were among the people in the room, he had only gone in because he was well armed and confident that he could handle any emergency.

However, the Inspector stood near the set and began to speak slowly:

'I think most of you know me — and maybe you guess why I am here.'

A shadowy figure in the second row made an involuntary movement, and Faithfull added quickly:

'I shouldn't advise anyone to try and get out of here before I have finished. This room and the whole building are most effectively surrounded.'

He paused for a few seconds, then proceeded in a deliberate tone.

'We are going to try out a little experiment. I have reason to believe that one of you has a quantity of stolen radium on his person, and this will be revealed quite simply with the help of the television set. I am going to ask each one of you to walk across the room, and the movement of the radium will affect the television waves, cause a flash on the screen. Quite an elementary device, really. However, if the person with the radium would like to save any unpleasantness and own up here and now?'

He paused invitingly, but there was no response.

On the screen of the television set, an acrobatic dancer was twisting and kicking in silent abandon. Faithfull had now turned off the sound completely. For a few seconds, nothing was heard in the room but the penetrative humming of the set. The Inspector found himself speculating as to whether Somers and his men were in position by this time.

'Well,' he challenged, 'who comes first?'

'I will.'

The rasping voice was indubitably that of Professor Mallowes.

'You're getting quite a scientist in your old age, Inspector Faithfull,' he chuckled as he moved towards the set and passed it without any effect on the screen. 'Does that satisfy you?'

'Thank you, Professor. Who comes next?'

The next person was a woman from the front row of chairs, but the screen still showed no reaction. One after another, they filed past, but each time without result, until the last person, a woman, was about to resume her seat.

Then there was a sudden explosion of light on the screen.

Faithfull at once flashed his pencil torch on the woman, who was now clutching a handbag, which she had just picked up.

The Inspector clicked on the electric light, then turned to Georgia Nash, who stood blinking in the unaccustomed glare.

39

Georgia Nash was staring at the neat black bag she was holding.

'This isn't mine,' she said. 'I must have picked up the wrong one.'

The Inspector was beside her. He snapped:

'Can you prove that?'

'Why, of course. Look — this is mine.'

She picked up a dark green bag, on which were the initials 'G.N.' in gilt letters.

Suddenly, the woman next to her snatched the black bag Georgia Nash still held in her left hand. She backed towards the door, snatching open the bag as she did so.

'Don't move! Don't move — any of you!'

She had produced a neat little automatic pistol from the bag.

All the others looked questioningly at Inspector Faithfull who stood motionless.

'I'm afraid you are only complicating matters,' he said quietly.

'We shall see about that. You'll never get me alive,' the woman retorted, her face drained and tense.

Osbert Strang, who had been sitting at the near end of the second row, made an involuntary movement.

'Lydia!'

'The window, Osbert,' she snapped at him. 'I'll keep them covered. Draw the curtains.'

He obeyed. A man, who was obviously a detective, was standing on the iron platform outside. Escape in that direction was barred. Lydia Powers thrust her handbag underneath an arm. With her other hand she began slowly to turn the knob of the door.

To Strang she said:

'This way — you'll take the gun and keep them covered long enough for me to — '

Strang was moving over to the door quickly now. Inspector Faithfull still made no attempt to interfere.

Lydia Powers opened the door, and still facing the little group, moved back a pace and was immediately seized from behind in the strong arms of Sergeant Somers. He grabbed the revolver at once and wrenched it from her grasp.

She struggled furiously, and Strang rushed to her aid. Faithfull and another man, however, who had appeared on the scene restrained him. There was a wild look in his eyes and he shouted:

'Lydia! For God's sake — don't — '

Still struggling furiously, she gasped:

'They'll never take me alive.'

She clenched her teeth until the muscles in her face tautened. For a moment, she seemed to choke, then her whole body went limp and she would have fallen to the floor if Somers had not maintained his hold.

Osbert Strang tried to fight his way to her side, calling to her all the time.

Somers looked puzzled.

'She's fainted,' he said.

'No — she had a cyanide capsule at the back of her teeth,' Osbert Strang moaned.

Faithfull strode over and picked up the inert woman's wrist.

'You're right,' he said grimly. 'I'm afraid your ex-wife is beyond our help.'

40

Ten minutes later, Inspector Faithfull returned to the lounge, having telephoned a brief report to the Assistant Commissioner. As he opened the door, the animated conversation which had been in progress suddenly died away.

'Any trouble with Strang?' he asked Somers, who shook his head.

'No, no, he went quietly enough. I think the woman's death took the spirit out of him. He seemed quite attached to her.'

Georgia Nash said:

'I always thought it was rather queer their getting a divorce.'

The Inspector nodded.

'That was one of the most ingenious parts of their plan to throw us off the scent. Nobody would suspect that a man and woman who had just been divorced would be starting a most highly complicated criminal organization. I must say it deceived me for quite a while.'

'What I can't understand is why she staged that affair in the house at Sydenham,' Somers muttered.

Faithfull nodded thoughtfully.

'A clever move. If you remember at that time, the gang's outlets were being closed up rather quickly; it was essential to distract our attention into other channels. So she proposed to give me just enough information about their dupes to switch us into that direction. Incidentally, it would disarm any possible suspicions about herself at the same time. I have an idea that her men rushed in a bit too soon, and she was not able to tell me as much as she had planned, but it was a neat trick all the same. It enabled Strang to complain that the gang was victimizing him because he was an ex-gaolbird. Yes, Lydia Powers was a very clever woman. She took a First in Economics at Oxford, then went over to Science and did some research for a couple of years with our friend here.'

'The best assistant I ever had,' said Professor Mallowes promptly. 'She had an amazing brain which seemed to absorb everything. At times it made me positively envious.'

'Why did she leave you, Professor?' Georgia Nash asked curiously.

'To marry Osbert Strang. In fact, she went at a day's notice. I never even knew she was engaged. She really was a most extraordinary person. It was quite a blow to me — I was just nicely launched on my first atomic experiments, and I was never able to replace her effectively. I thought when her husband was mixed up in that scandal she might come back. But I never heard from her.'

'It was the scandal that seemed to give her mind that twist in the wrong direction,' Faithfull said. 'She got obsessed with the idea that Strang had been given a raw deal, and she planned to be revenged on society. Of course, lots of other people have had the same idea, but they never planned it as thoroughly and with such fiendish cunning. After getting her divorce, to distract any possible attention from her purpose, she used the money Strang had salted away to buy information of every description that would place people in her power. Unfortunately, in this civilization of ours, money can accomplish a lot of things. It certainly did the trick for her. She used to visit her husband in prison occasionally, presumably to report progress. I don't doubt they had some sort of code — and it would take a very clever prison warder to get the least inkling of what those two were up to, if they set their brains to work on a problem.'

Somers observed somewhat reproachfully:

'I can't think why you never told us about her before, Professor.'

'Why should I? I have had dozens of assistants in my time — and there was nothing noticeably criminal about her behaviour while she was with me. In fact, I found her an extremely reliable person, as I told you before. I'm rather surprised to hear some of the things you've been saying about her, Inspector. I hope you are sure of your facts.'

'Aye, I'm sure enough,' Inspector Faithfull replied. 'I've been checking them over for some weeks now. It hasn't been easy, and she's thrown me off the trail more than once. That affair at Sydenham distracted me for a while, until I found she had a job as an air hostess. That was about the time that Wister Hale drew our attention to the fact that air hostesses were being used to smuggle out the radium, so I began to put two and two together, particularly as Miss Powers gave up her job as soon as we started the check-up. She had taken it under another name, but I had her photo identified by two of the pilots.'

'But that did not prove that she was the mysterious Lucifer,' said the Professor.

'Of course not. There were dozens of people who might have been Lucifer, and the odds were heavily against him or her having a criminal record.'

Faithfull helped himself to a larger pinch of snuff than usual and sniffed it deliberately. Then he turned to Somers:

'You remember the affair of the snuff-box?'

'You mean that stuff that nearly blinded poor old Ashton?'

'Yes. I got my old friend Mr. Pope to

identify Miss Powers's picture as well — she had been acting as his assistant for a few days. It was then I began to feel that suspicion was pointing rather strongly in her direction, and I felt the time had come to set the trap for which we have to thank Mr. Castana for his assistance.'

Castana smiled deprecatingly. He patted his still damp forehead with his silk handkerchief.

'I think perhaps a small whisky now — eh, Inspector?' he suggested.

'That is very generous of you, Mr. Castana. We have put you to a great deal of trouble.'

'Not at all.'

Castana went over and opened a cocktail cabinet. 'You have taught me how advisable it is to take every precaution in purchasing radium, Inspector. I am very grateful for the lesson.'

Faithfull noticed Val Harris's eyes light longingly on the whisky decanter, and said:

'I had you invited here to teach you a lesson, too, Miss Harris. I hope you'll see where the sort of thing you have been dabbling in is liable to end.'

She did not reply at once. Then she said very quietly:

'Last time you came to see me at the home, Inspector, I told you about that man — the one I saw leaving the flat the day Lem Knight was murdered.'

'Yes?'

'It was the dark man — the one you call Strang. I'd never set eyes on him before, but I'd know him again any time.'

'All right,' Inspector Faithfull nodded approvingly. 'Now you can run along. I told them you'd be back at tea-time today.'

She eyed the decanter wistfully.

'Couldn't I just have a small one?' she asked.

'Very well — plenty of soda with it, Mr. Castana.'

She accepted the drink gratefully.

41

Castana busied himself playing host, and after Val Harris had gone they sat over their drinks and discussed the events of the afternoon.

The conversation veered to the question of the motive for murdering Lem Knight, who had apparently been one of the key men of the organization.

The Inspector admitted:

'I've never been quite sure about the reason for his death. All I know is that he had been in touch with several of the gang's victims, and had either been trying a little blackmail on his own account, or else he had been getting together with them with some idea of overthrowing the gang — at a nice profit to himself. Whichever it was, the news got around to Lucifer, who decided that Knight must be liquidated.'

Georgia Nash looked hard at the Inspector.

'There really is something a little uncanny about you, Inspector,' she murmured.

'Why do you say that?' asked Somers.

'Because the Inspector's right down to the last detail. You see, it was I who passed on the information to Lucifer. Knight had been trying his little blackmailing tricks on me. I got quite a good credit mark for that bit of work.'

Castana looked from one to the other in some bewilderment with each new disclosure. Then he shrugged his shoulders and poured out some more drinks.

'Before you go, Professor,' said Faithfull presently, 'I'd like to hear exactly what happened that night Denny Fox paid you a visit.'

Professor Mallowes smiled wryly.

'You're a very inquisitive person, Inspector,' he replied with a twinkle.

'I have a weakness for clearing up details.'

The Professor emptied his glass and carefully set it down.

'You can't say I didn't warn you, that I

was liable to take matters into my own hands.'

Somers grinned.

'You certainly did!'

There was a note of satisfaction in Professor Mallowes's tone as he continued:

'You were right in your conjecture that Fox paid me a visit on the evening in question. He arrived about ten minutes before you did. He warned me that Strang would be paying me a visit — which I was aware of, naturally, though I knew him as Hansell. But he said the idea was to keep me talking in the study while a certain person, who he suspected might actually be Lucifer, rifled my safe in search of the records of my latest experiments.'

Sergeant Somers whistled softly in surprise.

'However,' proceeded the Professor, 'Fox was anxious that Strang shouldn't know he was there — so you appreciate that I had no alternative but to conceal his presence when you were questioning me about him, because Strang was present.'

Inspector Faithfull put in:

'And where was Fox?'

'As a matter of fact, he was hiding under the dust sheet that covered one of my pieces of apparatus.'

'Well I'm damned!' muttered Faithfull.

Sergeant Somers laughed outright.

With a tiny self-satisfied smile, the Professor went on:

'After you'd gone that night, I had a long talk with him, and I decided it was about time I took a hand in things, for my own protection. We concluded that we could be useful to each other, and we certainly made some progress. For instance, we found out about Mr. Lanfrey, and we managed to get a room opposite his establishment so that we could observe his movements rather more closely. Fox was watching that day when he saw you go in, I should imagine. What made him decide to follow you, I suppose we shall never know.'

'Lucky for me he did,' the Inspector grunted. 'I have that to thank you for, indirectly at any rate, Professor.'

'Yes,' the other replied blandly. 'I think

you have. However, I was only too pleased to be of some service. This organization had done quite enough damage, and incidentally, I flatter myself that in another couple of days I would have laid my hands on Lucifer myself.'

'Is that so?' Faithfull growled in a sceptical tone.

Somers and Georgia Nash exchanged a smile.

'I can't understand why Denny Fox didn't tip us off,' continued Faithfull. 'After all, he was in our pay.'

'Ah, he knew that it might upset his chances if he was premature. It suited him to work with me, because I could help him to keep under cover.' The Professor rubbed his hands gently. 'Anyhow, I'm glad it's all cleared up now. Possibly, I shall be able to proceed with my experimenting without any further interruption.'

The Inspector said:

'We still have to round up some of the lesser lights. But I don't anticipate much difficulty there. I don't think you'll have any further trouble.'

'I sincerely hope not. If I do, however, I warn you, Inspector — '

'You'll take the law into your own hands — I know.'

'Anyhow,' said the Professor, draining his glass, 'I have been glad of this opportunity to renew my acquaintance with my former secretary — though I can't think what the devil she's doing here.'

They all regarded Faithfull curiously.

At length he said:

'Miss Nash is here because I thought she might like to get her last story on the Lucifer case.'

'What do you mean?' Somers demanded in astonishment.

'I told you at the time Miss Nash confessed her connections with the Lucifer gang that she hadn't admitted quite everything,' Faithfull reminded him. 'She didn't tell us that one of her many jobs was that of a newspaper reporter. When she became involved with the Lucifer organization, she thought she might as well cash in on her newspaper experience and do a little crime reporting on the side.'

'Good Lord!' exclaimed Somers. 'You mean she was — '

'Wister Hale.'

Georgia Nash smiled.

It was an attractive smile that showed her flawless white teeth to great advantage.

'That was very clever of you, Inspector,' she said softly. Then she turned to Sergeant Somers.

'Don't look so startled, darling. Wister Hale is retiring at the end of the week.'

'I should jolly well hope so!' was the Sergeant's retort. 'You clever women scare me.' He scratched his head. 'Why, I never had the least idea — how the devil did you discover all this, Inspector?'

Inspector Faithfull took out his snuff-box, changed his mind and slipped it back into his pocket. He replied airily:

'It was just a question of routine.'

* * *

It was Saturday evening.

The Sergeant and Georgia Nash had been to tea with Mr. and Mrs. Faithfull, and had now gone to the pictures.

The Inspector sat with his slippered feet on the kerb while his wife cleared away the tea things.

Mrs. Faithfull stood at the door with her laden tray and asked:

'Think there's anything between those two?'

'Eh?'

She repeated the question. He shook his head impatiently.

'It's no business of mine.'

'Well, he is a nice young fellow,' she persisted. 'And she seems a decent sort of girl.'

'H'm,' Faithfull conceded. 'I dare say she'd make a better wife than some of those actresses he's been running after.'

'They seem properly suited to one another,' his wife continued. 'I know one thing — she'd make a lovely bride — I hope they'll ask us to the wedding. We'll have to think of a nice present.'

Her husband grunted, but made no other comment.

'I dare say he'll soon get promotion

too,' she went on. 'He looks a smart young fellow.'

'A bit headstrong,' old Faithfull growled. Then reluctantly: 'Oh well, he's young yet. He'll settle down.'

And he waggled his toes comfortably in his carpet slippers.

THE END

We do hope that you have enjoyed reading this large print book.

Did you know that all of our titles are available for purchase?

We publish a wide range of high quality large print books including:
Romances, Mysteries, Classics
General Fiction
Non Fiction and Westerns

Special interest titles available in large print are:
The Little Oxford Dictionary
Music Book, Song Book
Hymn Book, Service Book

Also available from us courtesy of Oxford University Press:
Young Readers' Dictionary
(large print edition)
Young Readers' Thesaurus
(large print edition)

For further information or a free brochure, please contact us at: